By Casey Vagg

First Edition. Edited by Proof Me Write Editing Services
Australia

Printed by IngramSpark

First Printing, 2020

ISBN: 978-0-646-81825-2

This book started as a notion in my mind and ended up becoming my baby. But it could never have reached the lengths it has without the help of a few amazing people.

To my dad, Gary, my mum, Jill, and both of my sisters, SJ and Jandi, I would like to say thank you for not only reading my book and loving it, but for giving me your editorial critiques that helped me to polish this book into everything I had dreamed it could be. Gypsy became a part of our family, and all of you cared about her as much as I did, and I love you all for that. I would like to thank Shannon for introducing me to your talented wife, Bec, of Proof Me Write. Thank you Bec for reading and editing **Gypsy***, and also for all of the support and encouragement you have given me. You have been fantastic, and I appreciate you greatly.*

To my friends, Zara, Mat, Dallas, and Sam, for listening to me go on and on about the progress of **Gypsy** *and always being so supportive and enthusiastic. I adore you all.*

And to Shan. Mate, what can I say? You have been incredible. From helping create my cover, to all of the advice and fiddly bits like formatting. Your friendship, knowledge and benevolence have been an absolute blessing, and I will be forever in your debt. And lastly to my favourite three boys in the whole entire world. Tyler and Phoenix, I could never have written this book if it wasn't for your understanding in my absence, and your hilarity in my presence. You boys will always be my sunshine. And to Jason. You have been my number one fan through all of my crazy dreams. You have sacrificed for me, supported me and cheered me on through this whole book. Thank you for always believing in me. I love you.

Gypsy

CHAPTER 1

The glow of the morning sun was whispering its full moon dreams upon Gypsy's shoulders as she sat and pondered the meaning of this day. With her back against Olly - her favourite willow tree - and her thoughts in the clouds, her eyes shuttered with images of what today would bring. Gypsy needed Olly for times like this; times of crisis and times of need, but also times of joy. The wildflowers surrounded the river like monks offering their blessing to the passing ripples, every colour more magnificent than the last.

Olly's branches hung over the water and tickled the noses of cheeky fish as they swam by, while the leaves would fall like snow and bring with them a sweet song of morning and untouched dew. Gypsy found herself slightly uncomforted by the sun as it glared in her eyes and interrupted her serenity beneath this tree, but as she had a lot on her mind, she was not going to let this miniscule detail affect her current mood – the life changing mood. The *what if?* mood. The *is this the start of a whole new life?* mood. The *what the hell was I thinking?* mood.

She watched and giggled as fisherman came by in their quiet little boat with lines thrown in to capture the unsuspecting fish, but little did they know, those fish were too busy dancing with Olly's branches and playing hide and seek with the turtles below.

"Don't worry guys, I got you." Gypsy winked at the water. "You won't find any fish around here!" She shouted to the fisherman, "Too many crocs!" Their heads flicked like slingshots to each other, a concerning look of death upon their naive faces. The motor built up speed and the boat whooshed off into the distance without so much as a *'Thank you'*.

Dumbasses. She chuckled to herself.

Gypsy sat there for hours under that tree and thought about all kinds of things. Like, why she wasn't in France eating cheese, drinking wine and making random friends and memories that would last forever. She mourned for a bigger life and would question where she truly came from while silently whinging about her lack of identity. But it was the curiosity inside this mischievous girl that led her to today, and the events that would inevitably unfold from her decisions.

"Haz, I'm home!" Gypsy called as she walked into the house her parents had bought for her. The house was an old weatherboard home that was thirsty for a touch of paint. The back of the house was surrounded by jasmine, filling her backyard with the sweet aroma of its flowers. The bees quite enjoyed the jasmine as they buzzed around it most days collecting the ingredients they needed for their golden honey. Gypsy used to fear the stingy little bastards, but once she discovered the importance of bees, her stingy worries subsided, and she welcomed them with peace. But jasmine bushes and bumblebees aside, Gypsy still had an itch in the back of her butt that told her she needed a change of scenery. She loved her house, but she had an ache – and a butt itch – that warned her if she didn't get out and move on, her brain may just spontaneously explode. And she didn't feel it would be appropriate to leave that kind of mess for Haz to have to clean up. He can barely clean the bathroom.

The smell from the jasmine had flooded the kitchen and the kettle had just finished its morning whistle. Gypsy's heart could already feel the sweet, sweet joy that the coffee would bring once she had her first sip.

"Where have you been?" Haz yelled out. Haz is Gypsy's roommate but comes across more like an incompetent moron who needs 24/7 care. But Gypsy still loved the goofball.

Haz had recently gone through a terrible breakup which had made him resemble something along the lines of a dried-up mushroom in the corner of the kitchen floor. His girlfriend had left him for the mailman and told him he had the 'man parts of a lizard'.

"Her exact words." He had said at the time. But as Gypsy tried her hardest to hold back the giggles reflecting on the whole lizard accusation, she could see how deeply cut Haz was. *Suck it in Gyps,* she breathed. The insult cut him to the core of his man parts and bruised his ego so bad that he said he stood and watched it float away like a helium balloon, awaiting the burst from the hot sun... never to return.

"Goodbye, ego." He waved his hands to the air recollecting her harsh words. But as the months went by, Gypsy continued to try her best to help him through, and Haz continued to be a mushroom. Until one day when he insisted the problem was the mailbox.

"We MUST get rid of that fucking mailbox!" He screeched.

"What? Why?" Gypsy asked, confused.

"Mailmen are evil, scum sucking creatures from hell." He seethed.

Gypsy acknowledged his concerns and obliged without delay. It only meant going into town to the PO box to fetch the mail. She didn't mind the walk, but how do you spell 'inconvenience'?

Gypsy walked back from Olly this morning via the PO Box, and it didn't hurt one bit.

"Where have you been?" He asked again, a little too much eyebrow raising for her liking.

"Down at Olly. Time ran away from me. Are you ready to go?"

"Almost, just got to grab my boots." He scurried off to his room like a squirrel chasing a nut.

Gypsy watched him run off, and something inside her knew; he was almost healed.

Into Gypsy's car they climbed, and pumped the tunes a little too loud, but the wind was in her hair, and the air was fresh. It was a beautiful day. Past the bottle shop they go, past the local playground and past the basketball courts. By the time they drove past the supermarket they were screaming the words louder than the speakers and having their own dance party that was sure to have inspired some laughter from the people they passed. Gypsy would consider this type of rambunctious exercise a perfect gym workout. *Oh, yes abs, I feel you there, under my shirt like a washboard.*

"Ok, we're here." She puffed as they pulled into the drama school. "I love gorilla week." Gypsy laughed as Haz exited the car in half costume.

"Actually, *I* love gorilla week." Haz said, pretending to claw her with his gorilla hands.

"Have fun!"

Haz flung a hand in the air as his goodbye gesture and waddled off to meet the rest of the drama students in the hall.

Gypsy sat in the car for a few moments longer and imagined what she was about to do; where it may lead. She has always carried a sense of loneliness within and questioned her place in this sometimes-twisty world. But she hoped today might give her some reassurance of a future where she can belong and breathe a peaceful quiet into her soul. A quiet that would encourage her to see the world in a different light.

On her way to the medical clinic for an appointment, Gypsy somehow found herself sitting in a pub. She wasn't too sure how she got there, but she figured the map must have given her the wrong directions. Not one to argue, she sat down and ordered a beer. Her appointment wasn't until 10am anyway, so she had half an hour.

The elderly lady that handed her the cold beer had the audacity to eyeball Gypsy like she was doing something wrong.

"What?" Gypsy said.

"Oh, nothing. Just wondering why a lovely young lady like yourself is drinking a beer this early in the morning."

"Lady, it's like 9:30." Gypsy said, clearly confused at the old bat's concern.

"Forget I said anything."

"Oh, I'll forget alright." Gypsy called out. "Few more beers will do the trick!"

What is wrong with me?

Gypsy was never this rude. Her nerves were all over the place. She knew that when she walked into the doctor's office, he would smell the beer on her instantly, but she didn't care. She needed courage right now like she needed air.

An old man sat at the end of the bar, and Gypsy wondered if this was her husband, cheering her on from the sidelines while she made the money. His eyes were glued to the coffee cup, almost mesmerised with its existence.

"She's always like that, you know." He spoke.

"Like what?"

"You know, a little..." His hand wiggled side to side, "judgey."

Gypsy looked back to her beer. "Hmm. I don't usually drink this early." She lied.

"I don't usually drink coffee." The old man chuckled.

"So, why today?"

"Today? Well, dear," The old man paused. "Today is the anniversary of my wife's death." A little smile ran its warmth across his wrinkled face. He looked like it was all he had left; a smile to hide the pain.

"I'm so sorry." Gypsy frowned sympathetically.

"How long?"

"Oh, going on eight years now." Another smile.

"So, why the coffee?"

"Well, dear, when you get to my age, you tend to have a lot of children, a lot of grandchildren, and a lot of friends. You want to know the annoying part?" He said, like he was cluing her in on an age-old secret.

"Sure." Gypsy was intrigued.

"When they love you, they don't leave you alone. Hence the coffee."

"OK…?"

"You see," he said sucking his lips, "instead of the young ones leaving me to reminisce about my wife, maybe put on an old record and flip through some photo books, they like to crowd my house with noise, jump all over my furniture, bring much too much cake and bother themselves with looking after me."

"Sounds like a good family." Gypsy said.

"Bah!" He shook his head. "I only like the little pip squeaks. The older ones just bicker and argue over who gets my spoon collection when I'm dead." He threw his arm, accidentally knocking over his coffee cup. Nothing poured out which made Gypsy wonder how long he had been sitting at the end of the sticky bar.

"I'm sure they are only doing what they think is best. I would love to have a big family that loved me that much." Gypsy said, almost regurgitating a feeling of sadness. It swelled a little in her throat and threatened her tear ducts.

"Shit!" Gypsy jumped up, sculling the rest of her beer. "I have to go. Good luck with your family today, and I'm sorry about your wife."

"What's the hurry, love?"

"Going to find my own family." Gypsy said as she grabbed her bag.

"Oh," The old man's eye's widened, "you must be thrilled."

Thrilled, nervous, shitting myself. "Spewing fucking rainbows, Mate."

"OK, then. Good luck." He waved behind his weary head. Gypsy ran out of the pub with a belly full of beer and a heart full of hope.

Please be good news, she prayed.

"Hi, my name's Gypsy, I have an appointment with Dr. Inker." Gypsy smiled.

"Sure, Hun, have a seat over to the left there and he will be with you soon." The receptionist pointed her tuck-shop arm to the left without looking up from her solitaire game. Dr. Inker wasn't a 'drinker' though Gypsy had heard stories of his stoner days. He knew Gypsy's father through work and even though her parents would be able to help her in an instant if she would just ask, she decided this was something she wanted to keep to herself. Dr. Inker is bound by the medical code of ethics to keep her visits to himself, so this made her feel a little more relaxed.

"Thank you." She smiled back and dragged her thumping heart towards the other three sad broken bodies. Gypsy liked this game; Guess the sickness. She has no idea what the others have, or had, or are going through but she can never help but wonder. *This man across from me with his arm in plaster and in a sling with a hand full of what I am assuming is pain killers is really hard, but I'm going to guess he has a broken arm. I know! I have a gift. So smart. OK... harder one. Woman across from me with a pram and a child at her feet. Is it her or the child? The child is coughing and spreading it's disgusting phlegmy germs all over the chairs and toys, but the mother has a bloody nose and is rubbing her belly. Hmmm...? I'll come back to her.*

It was then that she noticed the guy in the corner, early thirties, reasonable attire, Thor-like sculpted body. He was staring at the wall; blue with clouds and green mountains, a sun setting in the background. Probably wishing he was there and not here, she figured. *A dreamer.* He had sandy blond hair and eyes that were so intensely stuck on every shape and curve of the mural on the wall that she could only imagine the deep thoughts that were swimming around in his beautiful head. She found a little smile start to form in the corner of her mouth and just as she realized it had crept up on her, the dreamer shuffled in his chair and looked straight across the room to Gypsy's gawking eyes. *Oh shit.* Her own eyes darted instantly downward as if the floor screamed her name. "GYPSY!"

Humiliation overtook Gypsy's whole being and she could feel her face blushing beetroot red. *Ahh, shit.* Gypsy couldn't remember the last time she had a visit from her old friend 'Embarrassment'. Then she remembered the see-through shirt incident at work, which she still hasn't discussed with anyone except Marcy. Let's just say it involved a very uncomfortable situation with her boss and his wife and, well, she doesn't work there anymore. Gypsy decided it was time to lift her head, but as she started the upward journey, she heard her name being called.

"Gypsy?"

Embarrassment, is that you? She thought, shocked.

"Gypsy?" The doctor called again.

"Oh yes, that's me." She nearly wanted to lunge at him for the escape. As she walked away to her fate with the doctor, her eyes flicked to the side to grasp a quick glance at the sandy haired guy, and as her heart thumped just a little harder, she noticed his intense eyes, noticing her. A smile swept across one side of his gorgeous face and Gypsy felt herself blush once more. She started to ponder what such a Godly creature would be at the doctor's for, but only managed to come up with a blocked colon, or ball warts. *Ugh.* She cringed at the thought.

"In here." The good doctor gestured, and Gypsy's thoughts toggled from curiosity, to fear.

Gypsy walked into the old doctor's office that was glittered with diploma's, awards, and the rest. "Listen, Gypsy," Dr. Inker started. His hair was white with age and blown all over the place like he had spent the morning flying a kite.

For Christ sake, man, comb your hair.

He looked at her with a very serious expression which only made Gypsy crave a vodka. A good strong vodka that would peel the skin from her lips…

"What's up, Doc?" She replied. She was never any good under nervous situations. Gypsy figured that if she had a carrot and a funny cartoon voice he would have laughed.

"Gypsy." He started, and Gypsy held her breath. "You've had a reply to your letter. You have been waiting some time for this," Gypsy's face washed white. "and I know it is quite scary delving into the unknown, but I just want to make sure you are prepared." With one raised eyebrow he continued on, while Gypsy patiently sat and listened to the pros and cons that would accompany the letter, sealed in a plain white envelope. He explained that as it is addressed to her, he has not read it before handing it over, so he can't give her any idea as to the outcome – it was Gypsy's unknown, Gypsy's leap of faith, Gypsy's life.

Breath in, breath out...

Gypsy walked out of the room in a sort of daze. Imaginings of a happy reunion came flooding to her mind, while her fight and flight mode shoved them aside, replacing them with fearful 'what if's'. She held the plain white envelope so tight it curled in her sweaty palm and creased the unknown words.

As she rounded the corner, her companion in flirtatious crime was still sitting there – though she wasn't really surprised considering doctors' offices and their time management skills. She gave him a smirk and went to pay the bill.

After paying a ridiculous amount of cash for ten minutes of the Doc's time, she asked for a piece of paper and a pen. She had decided that since this was a life changing day, she might as well have some balls and add some adventure to it, so she quickly wrote down her phone number.

"What do you think about cartoon boobs?" Gypsy looked sideways at the receptionist.

"I'm sorry, what?"

"Should I draw some boobs on this?"

"Boobs? Honey, what on earth are you talking about?" All of a sudden, the receptionist's game of solitaire wasn't as exciting as the crazy lady standing in front of her.

The pounding in Gypsy's chest reminded her that she still harboured some form of insecurity and may not be completely care-free.

"Ok, no boobs then." Gypsy said as she handed the pen back to the receptionist, whom Gypsy thought resembled a slightly cranky wombat.

"Thank you." The wombat said. "Enjoy your day."

"You too." Gypsy smiled. She took a deep breath and turned toward the guy who she was secretly hoping did *not* have ball warts. Little beads of sweat continued forming in the palm of her hand as she walked closer to the guy with the sandy hair. Gypsy had grabbed his attention and he shuffled in his chair, sitting up a bit straighter and rubbing his hands down his thighs. It was at that moment Gypsy knew she wasn't the only nervous one.

"Hi." Gypsy said.

"Hi." He smiled his pearly white teeth her way. Gypsy's mouth became instantly dry and she wondered what the fuck she was doing. She searched her brain trying to muster up some form of wording - English preferably - but all she could find was "Um… For you." She said with an awkward wink, then threw the bit of paper on his lap. She could almost feel the contents of her stomach start to defy gravity and return upwards to where it had begun the journey of digestion. Without another word she did a 180 spin and walked away, out the doors and into the street.

"You are such a chicken…a fucking chicken." She mumbled to herself.

"Sorry, dear?" A voice from the heavens spoke. But Gypsy turned to see the noise came only from a little old lady.

"Oh, sorry, I was thinking out loud, I guess…" Gypsy said. She could smell the strong scent of whisky coming from this lady, her two lonely teeth chattering against each other as if they were about to fight. Gypsy stood in mute silence at the pure nonsense that had just unveiled.

Oh god. She thought.

Now comes the fear of rejection. It swirled around her belly like a tornado of fears, pushing unwanted thoughts into her already anxious mind. Gripping the white envelope Gypsy managed to bring herself back to reality with pure curiosity. All of a sudden, the past few minutes of humiliation were now put onto the back burner as a new tornado grew within her gut.

On her way to pick up Haz, she could feel her stomach rumbling over the sounds of the radio. She hoped it was only hunger, not a shit fuelled gurgle caused by a double shot of anxiety.

"Haz, mate, how was class? Are you rocking at being a monkey yet, or what?"

"Yeh, good, but I'm fuckin starving." He rubbed his belly with his gorilla glove still on.

"Me too... same old, same old? Or do you want something different?" Gypsy didn't want same old same old but thought she'd let him have the choice tonight. These long days really take a toll on him. Gypsy figured she may as well have children; Haz has pretty much got her prepared for them. She always wanted a big family, but the thought of having children still scared her. She could barely look after herself and Haz, let alone a smaller version of herself crawling around in shitty nappies and throwing food all over the house. Plus, she had much bigger plans for her life.

She would love to travel the world and taste the flavours of different cultures and sit in unknown places while eating unknown food.

When she was young her Mum was a high-flying businesswoman and her Dad was a physician. She can't remember a time when they took her anywhere. Apart from Sundays – their fun days – they would go down to the beach for half of the day, but it was all very scheduled, and she would always pretend not to notice her Dad looking at his watch every time he blinked. Gypsy's mum had an actual roster for dinner in the house; it was beef and steamed vegetables Monday-Wednesday, chicken and steamed vegetables Thursday-Friday, pasta on Saturday and fish with salad on Sunday. There was no point trying to get her to display any sort of adventure or God forbid be spontaneous, because she would scoff and say, "Don't be so silly, you can't have pasta on beef night, that's ludicrous!," then would put her hand to her forehead as if she were about to pass out. Gypsy offered to make dinner one Friday night, but instead of being grateful, her mum just yelled at her to "Make sure it's chicken!" Just for once she would have loved tacos, or pizza... why not throw in some Chinese food? Hell, she would have been happy with eggs on toast just to mix it up a bit.

So, now she gets to choose…most of the time.

"Frank's Bar, obviously." Haz declared like there was no other choice. His mouth dripped with anticipation and his order was clear, "Burger, chips and a thickshake." He nodded. It was done. All Gypsy really wanted was a salad; a nice fresh crispy lettuce-filled salad.

"My arteries hate you, ya know." She laughed and shook her head, while Haz gave her his puppy dog eyes.

"Whatever." *No point arguing.* "Buckle up." They drove to Frank's so that Gypsy could eat a burger, feel like crap, and then worry about her fat arse. It had been a while since she had done it, but at one stage Frank's become so popular in their regular diet that Gypsy had learned to throw up after gorging; it made her feel less whale-like. "I really need to ask Frank to put some salads on his menu…" Gypsy sighed as they pulled up to the parking lot.

"Franky! What's going on man?" Haz walked in and sat up at the bar. His mouth actually started drooling down his face as he read the menu.

"Got any new ones, Frank?" Haz asked, looking hopeful and excited, his eyes reflecting the menu in technicolour.

"Not since Bundy was in town, Haz. But I think Shirl has put sweet potato chips on the menu. Hold on." Frank did a 180 swing, "SHIRL!" Frank yelled down the hallway. "SHIRL! YA GOT MORE OF THO- "

"Fuck! What?!" Shirl screamed at him from the cooker. Her voice sounded like she had lost a fight with a sandpaper sandwich.

"Oh, Shirl!" Frank laughed, "I thought you were out the back." He put his hand on his beating heart and turned to Haz with a frightened smile.

"Well next time you want to deafen someone, fuck off somewhere else and do it." She said.

Gypsy loved Shirl and Frank, but they really got her thinking – *is this what 50 years of marriage does to a person?* - she cringed.

"Sorry." He rolled his eyes. "Haz wants to tr-"

"I know what he wants to try, you wanker, I was right behind you." She snarled and threw some slices of sweet potato in the fryer.

Such a beautiful couple.

Suddenly, Gypsy felt a hand that wasn't hers over her mouth and an arm that wasn't hers around her chest.

She tried to scream but couldn't get it out! *Oh my god, this is it*, she thought, *I am going to be kidnapped and cut into three thousand pieces because no one I know can afford any ransom! People will go to my funeral and say things about how I was a wonderful person, with beautiful hair and an excellent CD collection, but really could have tried harder to defend myself... bastards. I hate my funeral already.* She squirmed and kicked with all her might, legs and arms flailing around like she was trying to swim in a thunderstorm, then…*Contact*! She slammed the heel of her foot right into the kidnapper's junk.

"Bitch!" A familiar voice screamed in pain... it was Marcy. Curled up on the floor cupping her lady parts in agony. Her face was a picture of suffering.

"Marcy!" Gypsy's best friend and companion in all things mischief… If it weren't for her, Gypsy would probably have a much healthier relationship with alcohol.

"You know if you keep pulling that face the wind will change, and you will never get a man to tame your wild side." Gypsy chuckled, putting her hand out to help Marcy up. "So, what's cracking, Honey? Apart from the bruised vagina."

They hugged, and Marcy slapped Gyps on the arse, giving it a little squeeze. "You're such a perve." Gypsy laughed.

"And I love it." Marcy winked. "Although, my vagina is burning like a bitch now," She winced. "I'm on my way down to Nicki's house. She's got herself a new membership to this thing called Wines of the Month, or some such thing, and I'm going to help her drink it." She smiled a cheeky smile and looked at Haz, who was provocatively eating her with his eyes.

Excitement filled Gypsy's face "Dude, I'm in. Frank, I saw a man sleeping in the alley behind the shop, please give him my burger and chips." Frank nodded as he turned away back to his cooking, giving sideways glances to his beloved Shirl.

Gypsy threw the keys to Haz, "See ya later on tonight, you take my car."

"Can I come?" He called behind them, but they were already on their way.

Gypsy and Marcy skipped out giggling, and singing:

"One hundred bottles of wine on the wall, one hundred bottles of wine…"

They laughed and sung all the way to Nicki's house. And as the natural happiness took over Gypsy's body in the sweetness of the High Tide air, she remembered her letter snuggled peacefully in the console of her car. *It can wait another day.* She smiled a grateful smile and thought: *Yep. Just one more day.*

Brad

CHAPTER 2

It was 10pm at the moment, and without any delay, it will soon be 10:01.

Brad stared at the grandpa clock and watched the hands go around, ticking like a time bomb in his mind. They were slower than usual but still faster than he wished.

BANG, BANG, BANG. The front door shook with violence.

His heart skipped a few beats then started up again. He decided now was not the time to answer the door. Never was the time to answer the door. When all of a sudden, the front door rattled in the night, fell to the ground, and in they came. "Brad!" A male voice screamed out "Where you at, boy?"

Shit. Brad jolted inwardly. The sweat already beading on his forehead. He had been avoiding this like the plague, but he knew this day would come.

He decided there was no point trying to hide, it would only make things worse. Plus, something inside him already knew that they were coming, and he should have been prepared. So, he sat on his couch in the loungeroom, across from the grandpa clock, next to his half empty bottle of vodka and waited for them to find him. Oh, how he dreamed of owning a shotgun right now. He gritted his teeth as he heard their stomping and their voices get closer to him. *Game face, Brad.*

"Well, well, well. Bradley Mains. Thought you could hide forever?" Thomas McGill said as he casually strolled into Brad's loungeroom, smacking his bat on his open palm.

"Sorry, boys, wrong house." Brad said, not moving from his seated position on the couch.

"Don't play with me, you know exactly why I'm here." Thomas spoke through his gritted teeth. He had no patience for bullshit.

"I know why you're here." Brad called out. "And I tell you now…he fucking deserved it!" Brad had waited for this moment long enough. He was officially sweating vodka and was not in the mood to be messed with either. Or maybe he was just pretending to be tough and was trying to convince himself of his invincibility. He could smell the testosterone in the air that seemed to ooze out of Thomas' and David's pores. Or was it his pores that oozed?

Thomas projected an evil laugh and stared at the photos on Brad's mantlepiece, knocking one to the floor

"Oh, Bradley, Bradley, Bradley… there you are, pumpkin." His smile grew wider as his teeth came up for air, spanning the room where Brad sat patiently. "Did you really think we would forget about you, and the mess you made of our brother?"

Brad scoffed. Although he was ready for a fight, he still had the sweat on his forehead. This man was a big strong looking man, with muscles the size of basketballs, and a rounded red face. He had definitely drunk a lot of alcohol in his time too, by the looks of his stomach and skin; bloated and red. Brad had heard stories about Thomas, scary stories, and this man was not to be messed with. Although, one story that did not seem to fit his current situation was the one about this man working on the weekends as an elegant showgirl. Brad stared a long hard stare and tried to imagine him in his finest sparkling gown and beautiful wig, with foot long eyelashes and gold painted lips.

Now, usually Brad had no problems with how people dressed, but when they are standing in front of him threatening brutal damage while he imagined them in drag and singing show tunes, all of a sudden, he didn't seem quite as scary. Suddenly Brad wasn't sweating... he was laughing. Not a little chuckle, like when someone says a joke that's not funny, but you want to be polite, but a full bellied laugh, one that comes from within, and takes over your whole body like an unseen force.

Brad held his stomach with one hand and had the other over his eyes, tears of laughter sneaking out from underneath his hands, and making their way down his cheek.

"What the fuck are you laughing at!?" Thomas screamed. His brother, David, took a step towards Brad and tried to pull off a threatening face, pointing his knife Brad's way.

"You call that a knife?" Brad said, with an eyebrow raised as his laughter turned to an evil smirk. Then out of nowhere, the smirk was gone. Brad jumped up with a look of death in his eyes, produced a knife from under his shirt, and in an instant sliced David across the throat, causing a splatter of blood, and a deathly silence. Turning to Thomas, who had his bat ready to swing, Brad dove at him pulling him straight to the ground.

With the knife under his chin, and a beating heart that thumped into the stillness of the house, Brad breathed heavily "It's a pity, you know. If your brother and that bitch had just given me the bracelet, none of this would have happened."

Skye

CHAPTER 3

Skye's Monday started like any other….

"Skye, soup's on!" The words were yelled through the bedroom door. Her eyes opened to an incredible amount of sun beaming in the window above her bed, bathing her in a golden tint. She laid and watched the tiny particles of dust dance in the stream of light and imagined them to be star dust. Skye looked around her room in admiration at the way the light shone through the led-light wind-chimes that hung over her window; colours of the rainbow danced over the walls, bringing them to life. The hardwood floors reflected the glowing sun on the shiny surface and warmed up the room just slightly so it would comfort your soul in the brisk morning air.

"Well," Skye said, "another day, another what the hell to wear?"

Cameron walked into the room, disrupting her peaceful serenity.

"Good morning sleeping beauty." He took a painful glance at the pile of clothes in the corner of the room "Geez, Skye, I know they seem really scary, but there's this thing in the laundry called a washing machine. And if you go into the hall cupboard you will find an almost extinct creature called the *Iron,* it even comes with its own *ironing board."* He said this wiggling his fingers like he was a ghost. Cam is Skye's boyfriend, and the love of her life.

"Ha-de-ha, Smart-ass." Skye's hands rested firmly on her hips "You know I hate washing. Can you do a load for me today? I'll make it up to you tonight..." She said seductively, as they both looked at the messy bed, covered in clothes. Cam didn't bite, "Ok, fine, I'll bring home pizza for dinner." She knew Cam could never say no to pizza. Cam's Great Uncle Nicky left him his pizza shop when he died, and Cam had to give it up to his cousin Melinda because he knew he wasn't a businessman and he didn't want to send the business down the drain. He couldn't do that to Uncle Nicky. Melinda, however, drove the business down to the ground within 3 months. It turned out she had no idea how to run a business either and was now sipping iced red wine on the coast of Greece. Her trip being paid for by the very small amount she had received from the sale of Uncle Nicky's shop, and Cam ended up with nothing.

"Throw in some BBQ Ribs, and you've got yourself a deal, Toots."

"OK, deal." Skye winked.

"Alright, now that that is sorted... your porridge is ready and going cold, so hurry up. You've got twenty minutes to make like a hockey game..."

Skye looked at him quizzically

"...And *puck off.'"* He added.

"You're an idiot." Skye's giggle escaped into the morning air.

Cam recently lost his job at the local supermarket for getting drunk at work. It wasn't just the fact that he was drunk, but after finishing his hip flask he decided to collect all of the trollies in the car park and found himself rolling the entire train of trollies into an unsuspecting BMW. The damage of course was pretty bad. He was fired on the spot. So, now Cam looks after Skye, as she is the sole bread winner, bacon bringer, egg flipper, in the relationship. He swears he's looking for a job, but unless it's under the cushions on the couch, he'll never find one.

Throwing on some old jeans, her favourite vintage t-shirt and a hoody, Skye walked out of her room, only to find herself tripping over a big box of... of... *what was that?* She squinted her eyes and mouthed while reading: **1000 hard bristle toothbrushes.**

"Manny!" She screeched, crawling to her feet "Can you take this shite into your room?! I nearly just killed myself" His door creaked open; Manny's head poked out followed by a puff of smoke.
"What's up Dude?" Manny squinted his stoned eyes, barely reflecting her annoyance. "It's like, super early to be yelling."
"Um, Manny, you got a pretzel stuck to your cheek..." Skye tilted her head to the side like a curious farm animal and watched Manny proceed to peel the pretzel from his cheek and eat it, crunching the words "That's where you

got to." Looking over Manny's shoulder and into his room, Skye noticed the state of it and concluded that somewhere in there must be the long-lost city of Atlantis.

"Well, Manny, you got to move this crap out of the hallway, I almost broke my fucking foot."

"Ok, ok, Dude, chill. I'll move them soon. I'm in the middle of a killer compression session in my cupboard with a chick called Angel… you want to join?" She looked at him and nearly laughed, then noticed – he was serious.
He stood there with a wide-open smile as if waiting to find out if he had won a prize, but as enthused as he was in his invitation and as much as Skye would love a good laugh right now, she simply didn't have time to waste.

"No thanks Mann, it's almost 8:30, and I got to go to work. Rain check?"

"Sure Skye." He shut the door forgetting of course the box of toothbrushes and its army of followers. Manny and Skye had been friends forever, and she loved him dearly, but sometimes, he was just a bit of a pain in the arse.

Skye spun around and walked into the kitchen just as Cameron threw her porridge in the microwave to heat it up. "Sorry I took so long. Did you notice the amount of crap Manny has laying in the hallway?"
Cam looked from the microwave to Skye "Yeh, he ran out of a few things and had to stock up."

Manny had his own 'shop' on the internet. He buys things cheap in bulk and sells them at a higher price to make a profit. "He's a genius, really." Cam said.

"Who on earth would buy a toothbrush from the internet?"

"Meh," Cam said, "People do. I mean, look at you, you have to get up and go to work today, but not Manny." Cam laughed and gestured down the hallway, "He gets to sit in his room stoned all day and make money from his computer. You got to give the guy two thumbs up."

Skye agreed with a shrug. "What happened to you last night? Did you sleep on the couch again?" They both looked at the microwave that had just pierced the air with its ding.

Cam grabbed the porridge and shoved it in Skye's hands. "It's hot," he said, "and, yes I did, sorry babe, it's those bloody late-night movies. Speaking of which, can I borrow your credit card?" Cam grabbed a scrunched-up piece of paper out of his pocket, revealing a phone number. All that ran through Skye's mind was *here we go again*. Late night movies come hand in hand with late night infomercials. And Cam was a sucker for infomercials.

"Here we go again. 'Severe Impulse Shopper Syndrome'." Accused Skye.

"But, but…" He begged.

"No way!" Skye snapped, shaking her head.

Cam looked confused. Obviously, the many arguments they have had in the past about his infomercial shopping has made no impact on him. "Why?"

"How are you going to pay me back?"

"Well…"

A decade of silence went by.

"I… am going job hunting today, actually no, I'm going busking." He announced very proudly.

"Really? Coz I don't know if I should believe you, Cam.

It's always, *I'm gunna do this, I'm gunna do that,* and you know what? It never happens!" Skye shook her head. Cam played guitar and liked to think he was the next Hendrix. He was *not* the next Hendrix. Skye has watched him busk before, but the way he looked at other woman that watched him gave her the creeps, and although he assures her that she's being ridiculous, she just doesn't need to be imagining horrible things like him showing some random chick his G chord, while the random chick shows him her G spot!

Cam looked a little defeated "Hey man, you know I'm trying here. I really am. Plus, they are having a sausage sizzle with a raffle and all kinds of stuff down at the park today; there will be lots of people." He came and sat down with her at the little round kitchen table, "Should make a fair bit." Cam folded his hands in his lap and stared at them, inspecting his fingers.

"Well, you cough up the cash and I'll hand over the card."

He looked up at her impatiently and disappointed "Ok." He said and dropped his gaze again.

8:40am, *shit! I gotta go.* Skye jumped up and kissed Cam on the cheek. She grabbed her bag and yelled goodbye to Manny as she made her way over the boxes and out the front door into the sunny town of Kanville.

Skye walked outside of her little town house and down the street past Old Clickety Clack's house, who, as per usual, was sitting on her front veranda smoking a cigar and stroking a toy cat, her long grey hair floating around in the breeze.

"Clickety clack, clickety clack." She shouted out to Skye as she passed Clickety Clack's gate.

"Good morning ma'am." The words came out of her mouth through a sideward smile.

"Click! Clack!" She replied. No one knew the truth as to why those were the only words she would come out with. She used to keep to herself, but the clicking and the clacking started about a year ago. Everyone has their own story behind it. Skye's mind imagined horses clopping down a cobblestone street, like maybe she was run over by one, she guessed.

Walking past the corner fruit shop Skye found herself an apple from the top row. Shining in the morning light. Firm and juicy. Calling her name.

"80 cents." The fruiterer said. Skye handed over $1 feeling pretty chuffed with her self-control and new healthy lifestyle. 80 cents was nothing compared to the price of a coffee and a bacon muffin. Or for that matter the price of her health. But *hot-dang,* what she wouldn't give for a bacon muffin.

Once she reached the green gates of the High Tide Tip, Skye could already smell the disgusting air of this filthy place. With one foot in front of the other, she walked up to the main office that displayed a piece of wood branded 'home sweet home' above the door and let out a sigh. *My life has resorted to this,* she thought. It was 9:02 and nobody was around. *Coffee time.* Skye sat staring at the boiling kettle that looked about 50 years old and watched the steam rise to the ceiling. Her inner voice tried to

33

persuade her that management didn't get the kettle from outside in one of the rubbish piles. But somehow, she wasn't convinced.

In her head swam daydreams and a faint feeling, most likely from the smell of rubbish. The smell had her so deep in thought that she didn't notice the car. BEEP, BEEP.

"Sorry Sir, good morning, just drive onto the weigh bridge, please." The scowl on his face told Skye that this man was having an *excellent* day.

"How much?"

"$17.20"

"What? $17.20? How the fuck do you justify that?! I pay a Tip Charge in my rates, along with nearly $400 a year for my bins. I don't see why I should have to pay to get rid of this pile of crap! This is outrageous." He shook his head angrily, "I am a person of this community, and I pay my rates and taxes as much as the next bloke. I only make $17.00 an hour!"

"Sir, I don't make the rules, I just work here." Skye was thankful for her little office and the window that separated them as she eyed him and his humungous beard that made him look like a brushtail possum latched onto his face and died. He huffed, paid and drove his wagon off into the mounds of societies past.

This was a constant battle between her and the bringers of the rubbish. No-one believed it was right to have to pay to remove rubbish, and she didn't believe it was right that she got paid so little to put up with those people.

After work, on the way home Skye dropped into Ted's Pizzeria & Bar and was welcomed by a sea of smiles and hellos. Ted used to work in advertising until he decided it wasn't for him, and his passion laid in pizza. He and Cam get on great.

"Ted! How's the wife, dog, kids and all that jazz?"

"Great, great, Skye. How are you?" He eyed her up and down. "Been working today I see."

"Yes, unfortunately. Ahh well, if I didn't work, I couldn't come in here and give you all my money now, could I?" She laughed and slapped him on the shoulder; a sign of affection.

"Haha! That is true Skye, that is true." He clapped his hands together. "Now, what can I get my favourite girl on this lovely night?"

"I'll grab 2 large specials, garlic bread and 2 bottles of cola, thanks Ted." *I'm forgetting something.* "Oh, and ribs!" She laughed. *I swear if my head wasn't screwed on…*

Skye took her number, a seat next to a family of 4, and waited for the pizza to be cooked. Quietly she sat and looked around at the posters on the wall of France, Italy, Greece and other various places around the world. Skye has never been out of the state, and would probably sell her left foot, right hand, and all the shoes she owned to go travelling. "One day." She sighed.

As a young girl, Skye always watched the planes in the sky and dreamed of being able to fly anywhere she wanted. She would have dreams about going to America and Europe and Iceland… Her Dad liked to tell her, *'Work hard, get a good job and you will be able to afford to do anything you want'*, yet here she was, sitting in this pizza shop, with $68 and 20 cents in her pocket to last the rest of the week, she works at the local waste depot, her boyfriend is a couch potato and the only other friend she has is a total stoner who never even leaves the house. *Ahh life, what a grand place to be.*

A smell appeared from nowhere and disrupted Skye's daydream. Pizza. "Earth to Skye." Ted was waving the food in front of her, wafting the delicious smell of mozzarella, tomato and bacon straight up her nose.

"I'm sorry Ted, I was in a daze." She was busy shaking off the images of her childhood and dreams that never became real.

"Enjoy your pizza, and here's a little something for you and the boys." He handed her 3 ice-creams. "Tell them I said 'Hi' won't you."

"Oh, Ted you're a beautiful man. Will do, thank you."

Skye walked along Spring Street and watched the passing traffic roll by in a blur of yellow and red. The sun was setting over the ocean and the smell of jasmine hung in the air like a promise of tomorrow. Kanville was such a peaceful town. Everyone was like family and she never felt unsafe.

Skye walked into the house, throwing her jacket and keys by the door.

"Hi guys. Pizza's here." She called out as she put the pizza on the bench and went to have a shower. Manny and Cam scurried into the kitchen like wild animals.

"Awesome Dude, thanks!" Manny said as he whizzed by her in a flurry of colour.

"No worries just save me some." Closing the bathroom

door Skye felt a strange sense of peace overcome her. As the herd of wild animals were out in the kitchen going to town on a Ted's Special pizza, she took a moment to breath. The smell of soaps and shampoos, the incense by the bath and the candles surrounding it. Skye started to zone out just before noticing her lipstick laying on the floor in the corner.

"How'd you get there little buddy?" She asked, picking it up.

Hold On. Skye's heart stopped and sank to the bottom of her belly.

"This isn't mine." Her face instantly screwed up as if trying to comprehend what she was looking at. Here she stood, completely perplexed while cold blood rushed to every inch of her body. For starters it was pink. *Who the fuck wears pink?* Then she remembered the howling coming from Manny's room last night. *OK, Skye, just breath, no heart attack necessary.*

"Manny." She shook her head and let loose the air in her lungs.

Skye decided to open up the lipstick and used it to write on the bathroom mirror: WAS ANGEL WORTH IT?

Then snorted and left it on the sink for Manny to find. There was probably no need to be such a smartarse, but none of his one night stands ever seemed to be worth it.

That night Skye had a dream. She dreamed she was falling out of a moving car. Cam was behind the wheel and he was laughing at her as she was screaming for help, and as her hand slipped from the door handle, she looked up to notice that there was someone else in the passenger seat of the car. Skye struggled to see the person as they were only a shadow, but she could hear this person laughing at her, and just as they slammed close the door, knocking her to the moving ground, she woke up. With sweaty palms and a racing heart, Skye looked to her left to find Cam snoring happily beside her, unaware of the hurtful act he had just committed in her dream.

"You awake?" Skye shoved her elbow into Cam's cheek, but he only grunted. He rolled away from Skye, who suddenly found herself with a strange urge for baked beans. Her tummy actually rumbled the words; *Baked Beans.* She was awake anyway, so figured *what the hell?*

"Hey Skye" Manny smiled, as she made her way into the kitchen, scratching sleep from her squinted eyes.

"Hey Mann, what are you doing up? It's three in the morning." Skye took a seat beside him around the tiny kitchen table they had picked up from a garage sale the year before. She casually snatched the beer from his hands and yawned before swigging it down.

"Couldn't sleep Dude. Plus… there's a chick in my bed that snores like… like a wild goat… running from a heard of wild boars… running from..."

"Bummer." She cut him off. She didn't really care.

"Tell me about it! But anyway, what are *you* doing up this hour of the morning?" He said this pointing his finger at her, like the punisher to the victim.

"Couldn't sleep. Had a bad dream, but at least I wasn't floating around uncontrollably like I usually am."

Skye said, rubbing her belly at the thought of the

queasiness those dreams cause her.

Manny reached over and grabbed the beer back out of Skye's hands, swigging it down in agreement.

"Oh, before I forget, I found one of Angel's lipsticks on the bathroom floor last night too, I just put it on the sink if she is looking for it." Manny's eyes glazed over a little before responding.

"Yeah, I saw the mirror." Manny chuckled. But Skye sensed a slight confusion in his response.

There's something he's not telling me.

Skye brushed off the strange moment and decided she wasn't hungry after all.

"Night, Mann, I'm going back to bed."

"Cool, Mate. Sleep well." Manny blew her a friendly kiss and shook his beer, examining the remains of the bottle. "You owe me a beer." He called out.

"Whatever, Dude." Skye waved and walked away into the darkness of the early morning.

"Skye! Skye!" Cam ran into the bedroom with a bucket of water like a maniac. It was still dark outside, but she could see the flickering of light coming through her curtains.

Skye jumped up as quick as she could without her bed falling through.

"Fuck, I'm up! Don't throw that shit at me!" Her eyes were as wide as possible as they screamed at him with their own silence.

"Skye, get up, Old Click Clack's house is on fire!" Cam ran from the room like it was his own pants on fire.

Suddenly Skye's heart was pumping faster as she jumped up and ran for the hose in the back yard, but Manny was already on it. Running back past the kitchen window she flicked her head to the side and noticed one of Manny's one-night stands sitting gracefully at the kitchen table smoking a cigarette and not giving a damn about the craziness going on around her. She had scruffy hair and mascara weeping down her face. *Is that Angel? Or a different one?*

"Shit, you go for some strange creatures of the night, Manny." Skye mumbled to herself, shaking her head. She ran into the kitchen and approached the smoking devil.

"Are you going to help?" Skye asked in a huff.

"Listen," She said, filling the kitchen with smoke and tempting the smoke alarm, "I don't give a flying fuck about your little fire, if I don't get my morning cigarette in peace, then you DON'T want to mess with me."

Ok, so this chick's fucking crazy.

Skye was already back out the door as this chick was rambling on about mood swings and smashing people.

"Has anyone called 000 yet?!"

"They're on their way." Cam yelled back.

"Click, clack, clickety clack…" Skye ran around the side of the house to find Old Click Clack sitting on her front doorstep with a toy cat, a box of cigars and a brown photo album, screaming into the concrete. Her hair was singed over one whole side of her head, and she had both her eyebrows missing.

"Click clack!" She shouted at Skye as she ran past her and over the fence to the old woman's house. The house was on fire only on the side that was closest to their house, almost jumping from Click Clack's living room over to Skye's. In her failed attempt at finding a hose, Skye started filling buckets with water and throwing them over the flames.

"Where the hell is the bloody fire brigade?" She screamed at Cam as he flew by.

"On their way, apparently!" He ran up the side of the house and threw a bucket of water over the monster that was creeping closer to Skye's house and gulping up the left-hand side of Old Click Clack's.

After a wild 20 minutes of throwing water, blazing flames, and Manny deciding it was time to die, the fire truck finally arrived. The flames were put out and things calmed down in Skye's little house of horrors. Click Clack had been checked over by the ambos and was told she was lucky only her hair had caught fire – her face was fine, and there was no sign of smoke inhalation. She was given the all clear but was told to rest and could not return to her home until the police had done their investigation into the fire. Manny's pick up was still sitting in the kitchen smoking and drinking a can of scotch she found in the fridge.

"She's stunning." Skye said sarcastically to Manny as she walked past him and out the back door. "Hey, Cam…" But he was on the phone and only threw his hand up in the air at her as a gesture of requested silence.

"I think someone needs to go out the front and talk to Old Click Clack." Skye asserted. But Manny and his girl just looked up at her like she was talking Japanese, passed a glare at each other and headed for the bedroom.

"Cam," She said, walking back outside, "Do you want to go talk to Click Clack?"

"I'm on the phone." Cam looked at her frustrated and walked away to the far corner of the backyard.

"Right." The smell of smoke and smouldering possessions filled the air and clouded the neighbourhood. The glow of the flames that had consumed the morning was still present in Skye's mind, filling her with a lingering dread. People had returned to their homes after the eventful morning and found solace in the fact that it was not their house that burned. Skye felt the pressure of the horrible mess made by the fire as she knew she would end up being the one to help Click Clack sort it out. Though it wasn't as bad as it seemed in the early hours of the morning, the smoke was slowly settling and revealed a house that will need some major repair. Click Clack was still sitting there with her cat, photo album and cigars while Skye put her hands on her hips and did the pose of a superhero, gearing up for her time to swoop in and save the day...

"Hi." Skye said, getting closer to the terrified woman on her front porch.

"Click… Clack…. Click…" She started pouring her eyes out, crying uncontrollably. But Skye's protective nature was busy fighting her gag reflexes. The woman smelled horrible. She could feel her cape flying in the wind behind her, and imagined its gloriousness, but the woman smelt like she hadn't showered in a year. *Should I hug her?* She pondered. She wanted to show this poor woman some comfort, but at the same time, did not want to gag once she entered the woman's atmosphere.

Taking a deep breath, Skye sat down beside her.

Goodbye sweet air - hello Click Clack.

"Hi… I'm not sure we have officially met yet. My name is Skye, and the two guys that helped save your house are Cameron and Manny." Skye noticed she wasn't wearing a wedding ring, but she had a white line where it seems one used to be, like the sun tattooed around this ring to make sure she never forgot. Skye jumped up and walked inside to get a blanket and pillow from the hallway closet placing them on the couch in the loungeroom, taking a few more sweet breaths of air in anticipation before walking back out to sit with Click Clack.

"You are welcome to stay at our house if you want. There's no spare bedroom, but there is a couch which I think you will find most comfortable." *'I think you will find most comfortable'? Who am I?* Skye thought to herself.

"They call me "Lady Skye." She mumbled in a posh accent, mocking her own speech and confusing the old woman beside her. Skye was horrible in bad situations. She always found a way to make a joke to avoid things getting too real. "I will get you a towel so that you can have a shower if you want?" *Please say yes, please say yes…*

Click Clack only grunted with a nod.

Oh, thank fuck.

As Skye got up to walk back into the house, she heard, "Skye." Looking around, she didn't know where it came from, then the ridiculous penny dropped, and she realised it came from Click Clack. *Oh my god!* She thought as this was the first time Skye had ever heard the old duck speak an actual word other than 'Click' or 'Clack'....

"Excuse me?" She said, not sure if she was hearing things.

"Click clack, click clack." She replied, and the hope that she had in having a conversation with this woman faded away, only to be suffocated by the smoke that remained.

The next morning as Skye got ready for work, she couldn't find any clean clothes. So, rampaging through clothes she hadn't worn in years, she found her old favourite pair of cargo pants – *why did I stop wearing these?* – She threw them on and decided to skip breakfast today.

"Cam, can you look after Click Clack? I've got to go; I will see you tonight."

"Sure thing." He replied over his shoulder, his eyes not budging from the telly, he waved one hand in the air.

Skye ran out the door and made her way up the road to start her journey to work. She dropped in and got a newspaper from the newsagency, and a bottle of water. She started to notice that everyone was looking at her a little funny… some even laughed. On the way out she looked at her reflection in the window. She checked her hair, her shirt, if there was any food on her face. *No.* She was starting to feel a little self-conscious now. *What's their problem?* She made her way to work and it seemed that all day she was getting the same reaction, but nobody said anything. After an hour of copping the giggles, and questioning one of the guys, who assured her she looked fine, she decided she didn't give a shit anymore. Not one single shit was to be given today. *Fuck 'em.*

All Skye wanted was to go home, have a shower and put her feet up with a nice cold beer. Friday was her night to relax and watch a movie with a beer. It was her only chill out night, as it had become a regular thing on a Saturday for Cam and Manny to invite over their friends, listen to music too loud, drink too much and cause the inevitable – the piss-eth on the floor-eth. In other words, someone would always end up pissing on the bathroom floor. Safe to say, Sunday was Skye's cleaning day. But tonight, was Friday, and this Friday was her turn to buy the beers. Considering she can't carry a slab of beer on a 20-minute walk, she rang a taxi.

Man, I need a car…

"Hi' She said to the taxi man… '*Steve*' his name tag said.

Steve nodded to Skye, "Evening Miss, where to?"

"To the drive through bottle shop, then to Spring Street, please."

"Sure thing Miss." Steve said. He had a big head of dreads which he flicked to the side. "I've got a mate that lives down there. Nice area. He's got the blue house on the corner, big dog that's always barking..." He went on without moving the car anywhere. "You know it?"

Yeh Mate, don't really care… just want a beer. "Nah, I don't, sorry."

"Doesn't matter," he said, "Good bloke though."

And off they drove into the Kanville night to spend the last of Skye's money.

They pulled up to Skye's driveway, beer in hands and her aching body dreaming of the couch.

"Thanks, Mate, keep the change." She said to Steve, who she was sure would be grateful for the extra 10 cents.

Cam was sitting on the front porch surrounded by all the pot plants. He had told her years ago that she needed to stop buying them because she tended to forget they need water. He was right.

"Hey," She said walking up the path towards the house, "I've got the beer. Did you get the movies?" Cam stood up with saucepan eyes and a hand over his mouth.

"Shit, sorry Dude, I was busy trying to keep Click Clack entertained all day… man, that is one weird woman." Cam grabbed a beer out of the box and followed her into the kitchen. They sat at the little round kitchen table and let the beer run through their veins like liquid gold.

"Well, we could do something else with the little energy I've got. Let's play Snakes n Ladders Skull." Skye said.

"Dude, that's a little dangerous." Cam laughed.

"Only for me." Skye laughed. "I'm the one that always seems to have a full drink when I get a ladder or a snake. You know, I sometimes wonder if you boys have actually rigged the dice." She said, jumping up to put the beers in the fridge.

"Skye, what's with your pants?" Cam started laughing uncontrollably.

"What?" Skye looked down searching her cargos.

"Dude, you have a massive rip in the back of your pants! Hahaha can't you feel the breeze on your arse?" At this point he was slapping his knee and had tears rolling down his face. "And you wore these all day?"

"Well fuck me." Skye laughed "*That's* why everyone was looking at me funny today. Now I remember why I stopped wearing these pants. How hard is it to let someone know? How hard is it to say, 'hey man, you've got a rip in your pants and I can see your arse?'" Skye shook her head in disbelief that not one person had the guts or decency to let her know.

"All day." She emphasised. "All fucking day." Her head still shaking, she took a sip of her beer. "Ok, embarrassment and ripped pants aside… what's for food? I've worked all day Dude, and I'm starved!'

"Fuck off, Skye." He looked at her all ticked off. His mood had done a 180 in a matter of seconds. *Great.*

Skye tilted her head to the side like a puppy not understanding what his problem was and confused at his switch in emotion.

"You're not the only one with a life, Skye. I do shit with my days too, and I'm not your fucking slave." He snarled and looked back towards the cupboard where the game was.

"What the hell, Cam?" Skye rolled her eyes.

Fuckin change your tampon, Mate. She wanted to say but didn't have the balls.

"Whatever. I'm having noodles. And you can get screwed and make your own."

"Hmm." He said, ignoring the last 20 seconds. Skye's mind wandered… *I don't even know what his bloody problem is. He's seemed so moody lately, and it didn't seem to matter how happy I tried to be towards him, he just seemed distant, almost like he hated me for having the nerve to exist in the first place. Then the next second, we were best mates and lovers. Lots of joyful sex and joyful laughing. We got on like a house on fire. Some would say a joyful house on fire. But lately... lately there was no joy. Only houses on fire.*

"Ooh, beer." Manny trotted into the room and dived for the beer like a sports star. Opening his stubby he came and patted Skye on the shoulder. "What up, Skye? You know, that Click Clack is definitely something else." He looked at her sideways and sat down on the kitchen chair.

"Yeh?" *So is Cam,* she thought angrily. "Well, where is she anyway?" Skye bent her neck towards the loungeroom in a humble search for Click Clack.

"She's in the loungeroom staring out the window. I offered her food today, but she just screamed 'Clack!' at me and went back to staring again." Manny laughed a little at the memory.

Curiosity overtook Skye as she put her beer down and got up to walk into the loungeroom.

"Skye, your pants!" Manny pointed.

"Yeah, yeah I know."

Click Clack was sitting on the couch motionless. She looked like a sad sculpture who was in the present but whose mind was in the past. Skye didn't really want to disturb her, but she had always believed in being a good host, and can't just let her sit there all day and not eat... Besides, she's taken over Cam's couch, and quite frankly, Skye was in no mood to have Cam sleep in her bed tonight. *Arsehole.* She thought. Pushing her hatred for men named

Cam aside, she wandered toward the old lady who's mind had been captured by the intriguing window.

"Hi." Skye smiled and gestured towards the kitchen "Can I make you something to eat? I'm about to make some noodles. It's nothing flash or anything, but it is food." Skye's eyes ping-ponged back and forth from Click Clack to the window. This lady was spiking her curiosity more and more.

Skye thought it might be best to leave her in peace, but as she turned to walk out of the room, the tiniest of squeaks came from the mouth of the broken lady, and Skye heard a very quiet "Yes please." *Oh my gosh, she spoke again!*

"Sorry, did you say yes?"

"Noodles." The word was whispered, but clear.

Stunned, and with a strange sense of accomplishment, Skye replied, "Noodles it is then." And walked back out to the kitchen with a face of pride.

"Guys, I am a fucking magician." She beamed. "Click Clack spoke to me again."

"Bullshit." Cam said dismissing her words, which he seems to be getting very good at lately.

"Are you sure you're not just trippin' out, man?" Manny said.

"No, Manny, I'm not a stoner like you," She laughed, "And I know what I heard… I asked her if she wanted noodles and she said, 'Yes please, noodles.' They both just looked at her and laughed, brushing off her ridiculous lies. "It's not the first time; she said my name yesterday after the fire, too." Still nothing. "Whatever, dudes. I know what I heard."

They spent the rest of the night playing card games, while Click Clack slept a disturbed sleep in the loungeroom. And once bedtime came, Skye slept peacefully beside a forgiven Cam.

By the time Skye woke in the early hours of the morning, she could feel the vice already squeezing her head. She tried to replay the events of the night before but could only come up with putting a spoon in the microwave and going on and on about the Tip. Then suddenly it hit her like the vice had finally crushed her skull… *Oh, the poor woman…* She started laughing, remembering waking Click Clack up to make her sing: "If you're happy and you know it clap your hands… Click Clack! If your happy and you know it, clap your hands, Click Clack!" The vice was now in pieces on her floor, snapped from the crushing reality of Skye's drunken immaturity.

What is that ringing? She hunted down that horrid sound and found it coming from under Cam's pillow. Instinctively picking it up, Skye saw it was a private number.

"Hello…" Nothing. "Hello?" She repeated, but still nothing.

Skye sat on her front step in a meditative pose, surrounded by all her beloved plants – some lush, some not so much – the colours radiating in the dull overcast morning. The wind-chimes play and dance with the fresh breeze as raindrops casually fall on their metal parts causing them to make tiny tinkling sounds. The rain from last night brings a slight mugginess to the warm earth and heats the air. Skye contemplated the roots beneath the dried soil and figured now was as good a time as any to water her plants. As she stood up, and stretched toward the sky, she was interrupted by a voice:

"Hello?"

Skye spun her head to see a lady standing on the front path with a bright yellow umbrella.

"Uh… Hello?"

"Hi, my name is Sandra, I am a family friend of the lady that lives next door, one of the other neighbours said they think she might be staying here with you?"

"Oh, ok, are you here to take her? She is in my loungeroom. Terrible thing that happened, isn't it?" Skye shook her head in gloomy disbelief. "Not sure how it happened… maybe the stove was left on or something?"

"Oh, it's horrible." She agreed, "We don't know what caused the fire, but you're right, it could have been that…" She trailed off. "Anyway, I am here to collect her. We have some contractors coming to help fix up the house. Most of it's not too bad, but it will still take a bit to make it liveable again. I am going to take her home with me for a while until they fix some things up."

Sandra, you are a legend…

"Awesome, thank you." Skye said, smiling back. "We weren't sure if she had family, or what to do, I guess. I am not really equipped to have her here… Not enough beds, you know? And we kind of thought we would help tidy up a bit, but if you have contractors…"

"Yeah, it's fine, they are getting paid, they can do the

job, but thank you, I appreciate it, I really do."

"Did you want a cup of coffee or tea or something?" Skye gestured towards the house "Maybe just get out of the rain for a minute?"

"No, thank you, I'm ok, I would just like to pick her up and get going. Traffic's terrible." She said.

"Right this way." Skye ushered Sandra and her yellow umbrella into the house.

When they reached the loungeroom where Click Clack was sitting, Sandra went straight over to her and put her arms around her.

"Are you Ok?" She said looking into Click Clack's eyes, then back to Skye. "Why isn't she talking? Why aren't you talking? What's the matter?"

"She doesn't say much" Skye chimed in. "She only ever says click or clack to us. Why is that?"

Sandra looked at Skye like she was nuts, like *she* was the crazy one.

"That's ridiculous, she's obviously in shock. That makes no sense at all." Standing up she helped Click Clack up to her feet and turned back to a confused Skye. "Look, she's obviously been through something pretty traumatic with her house nearly burning down and all, so I think it's best if we just go." Her attitude a little more disturbed than a minute ago.

"Traffic. Yes." Skye said.

"Yeah." She nodded. "Thank you again. Once the men have fixed up the house, I will be bringing her back, I am very busy myself, and can't look after her for too long. But, once she's back could you… could you keep an eye on her for me?" Skye couldn't tell if Sandra was here because she cared, or because she felt obligated too, but at least she was here.

"Here's my number. Please call me if anything happens again." She handed Skye her number scribbled on a torn off piece of paper and walked Old Click Clack out of the house. It wasn't until the car had left down the road stirring up the rain on the tarmac that it hit her; *Why didn't I ask Sandra for Click Clack's name?*

Gypsy

CHAPTER 4

Gypsy woke up in Marcy's bedroom with the worst hangover she has had since the day she was born. This is not to say Gypsy was hungover the day she was born, but considering she never met her birth mother, anything is possible.

Her thoughts swum around in her head like little glimpses of the night before, bashing into each other, creating a chaotic mess of mini stories. Were they real? Or was it just her dream pretending to take on the form of a night just passed? Her body tingled and she could feel the anxiety start creeping toward her throat, her belly and her soul.

All across the world there are normal people waking up fresh and going out for breakfast with their friends, ordering lattes and cappuccinos while some hipster waiter brings them their smashed avocado on gluten free toast with a side of heirloom tomatoes and smoked salmon, accompanied by a cute little ceramic bowl filled with crème fraiche. Funky jazz music plays on the speakers of the uptown café and the smell of the coffee fills the noses of all those fresh morning joggers that pass by the smashed avocado eating citizens while they gasbag about their fresh little lives. Gypsy on the other hand, well, she is drowning in a sea of self-loathing and fury. Her air is not fresh, she doesn't have coffee beans up her nose and she certainly wasn't going for a jog. No, she's in a world of pain and regret. The wine has turned rotten in her veins and is slowly making its way out of all her pores. Her morning air is filled with the smell of a brewery and sweaty nightmares. Her brain feels so yuck, she could almost swear she will never drink again. *Never, ever, ever.*

"Ok." Gypsy coughed with a forced enthusiasm. "Beer…where the hell's the beer?" Gypsy arose from her horizontal position like a zombie. She searched the kitchen high and low, but nothing even resembling a beer was to be found. *Argh.* She stood in the kitchen with her tingly fingers pinching at the skin of her throat in an attempt to open her airways.

"Beer, sweet beer, where for art thou anxiety killing beer?" Her eyes rolled back in her head and found flickering lights among the darkness of her eyelids. "Time to wake the girl."

"Marcy!! I need beer!" She squealed with all the strength she had, hoping for an answer, but the only response was a groan from the loungeroom floor. She walked in to check that it was Marcy and not a stray dog looking for scraps of food in the loungeroom, but it was in fact Marcy, laying spread eagle on her belly, face to the floor, and what seems to be spaghetti all through her long hair. *What an angel.*

She looks as though she had tried to get undressed at some stage but had failed miserably; she had one leg of her pants off and one sleeve of her t-shirt off. God only knows how they even made it home last night. Gypsy was gifted a memory of the early hours of the morning. She had climbed up to the roof of the house with Marcy in an attempt to await the sunrise. It was then that she decided to thank her lucky stars she was still alive.

"Marceeeeeeeey…" Gypsy dragged out the word, draining the energy from her soul and shaking Marcy with her incompetent hand... "Marcy, where's the beer? I need it before they take me away in a body bag."

One eye opened on Marcy's close-to-comatose face and a glimmer of light sprung into Gypsy's heart.... But it was a short-lived light as Marcy started snoring again, and the glimmer all but stuck its middle finger up at Gypsy's hopefulness.

"Well, I'm giving up." She stopped fighting her will to live and just dropped down beside Marcy on the floor. *Ahh sleep, will you marry me?* Gypsy drifted off into the back of her mind, the place where dreams were made, and hangovers were cured.

"Oh, my, god! what is that horrible sound?" Gypsy rolled over to find the sound coming from her bag; a three-dollar messenger bag from the Op Shop to match her grungy style. Gypsy reached for her mobile phone... it was a private number.

"Not today, buddy." She ignored the call and threw the

phone across the room, just missing a $200 glass sculpture of Charlie Chaplin. Her heart stopped as her head flicked to the left to make sure Marcy hadn't seen that... *still sound asleep.*

"Fuck." She wiped her brow. "Night, night Marc. Night, night Charlie."

RING RING.... *Oh, damn you technology! I really am going to smash that phone, yep, I'm going to smash it and stomp it and burn it...* "GO AWAY!" Gypsy punched the air, like that was going to help. Although she wanted it more than her tight throat wanted beer, she simply was too awake now to sleep. She sighed and kicked Marcy in the leg.

"Marcy, you awake?" She kicked her again. Still nothing. Deciding water was the next best thing, she took a deep breath, clapped her hands, and struggled like hell to get off the floor. Gypsy looked like some kind of turtle that was stuck on its back fighting with every inch of power it had left to just... roll... over. She had gone surf fishing with a mate years ago and she was taken to this certain spot where they had to carry the swags, chairs and esky down a very steep sand dune. The sand dune was brilliant to get down, because you could just roll, but the next morning, once the beauty of the sunrise had disappeared and the warmth of the campfire had burned out, it was time to carry everything back up the dune.

"This is fucking horrendous." Gypsy had cried at the time. The more she tried to get up the dune the more she slipped back down. Each time she grasped for handfuls of sand to pull herself up or stuck her feet in to climb, all the

sand would flow back down dragging her with it like an avalanche. Her attempts were futile. And Gypsy screamed the whole way up that fucking sand hill of death. By the time they got back to the car, her mate had realised that Gypsy had left her chair back at the beach. But even as her frustration subsided, she still shook her head and said –

"Fuck the Chair." Leaving it there for the next adventurer ready to take on the dune of death. Gypsy couldn't help but reminisce about that sand dune as she attempted to arise from the floor.

Like a true champ, Gypsy mustered up every bit of strength, from every inch of her body, and with great triumph, heaved herself halfway up - thanks to the couch and some nifty moves that she obviously learned in some kind of ninja school.

Ok Gypsy, you're halfway there.

A crazy rush of adrenalin and power overcame her, and she rose upwards like a rocket ship heading towards the moon. She reflected her pride as she did a little star jump of victory and with a huge smile on her face, took a bow.

"I'm up!" Gypsy beamed.

"What the fuck are you doing?" Marcy muffled with her face squished on the pillow.

"I," Gypsy said with great pride "got up off the floor." She put one hand on her hip and tipped her invisible hat.

"That's lovely. You do realise you are a wanker, don't you?"

"Yes, yes I do. And I'm ok with that." She smirked.

"Well, since you have achieved the apparently impossible, can you get me a beer, please?"

Gypsy nearly jumped on her with excitement "What?! Yes! Do you have any? Anywhere? I tried to ask you earlier, but-..."

"Beer, Gyps... not story, just beer..." She said with slight frustration. "Box in the laundry. It'll be warm, but I don't care, just be quick, this bitch needs a hair of the dog before the hangover kills me." She looked down to her half-dressed body "Be gone with you demon! Hey, is that how I'm dressed?"

"Hey, do you think now might be a good time to check out that rehab clinic?" Gypsy laughed.

"Beer, woman!" Marcy screamed as she threw her pillow at Gypsy's head.

After a warm beer, a few litres of water and a very long cold shower, Gypsy felt slightly alive. She put on her clothes from yesterday, which only made her feel dirty again. She considered borrowing some clothes off Marcy, but she knew it would only bruise her ego as Marcy's stick figure clothes would have sharp edges and were not designed for muffin tops. Kind of like when you squeeze the last bit of toothpaste out of the tube and the toothpaste oozes from the top. Staring into the fogged-up mirror with bloodshot eyes Gypsy saw a person she could not recognise. These eyes, these wrinkles, the fight against gravity. A tear started falling down her cheek. Gypsy's perplexed mind assumed she must have killed all of her good brain cells last night. Gypsy doesn't cry. Not even if there was a little puppy dog stuck in a drain. No.

She watched as it trickled down her face and took up

residence on her chattering jaw line. It's need for existence was the only thing that kept it clinging on and stopped it from falling. So powerful was its grip that even as she shook her head side to side it only smiled at her and held on tighter.

Gypsy stared into the mirror at this little drop of emotion, for what felt like a century. Questions plagued her mind - *Where has my life gone? What have I been doing these last 32 years? And where the hell am I going?* And then suddenly, like the pain of losing a friend, the teardrop fell and splattered on the floor to be lost in the millions of drops of water left behind from the shower. Like an unknown face in the crowd, it was gone. Gypsy was hit with a painful sadness, she wanted to find that tear and save it, but knew it was impossible. All she could do now was to hope it would be happy among all the other drops of water and wish it well in its travels.

Gypsy had a hunger in her belly that wouldn't subside, and she figured Frank's is the only way to fix it. So, after gathering up Marcy, they started the half hour walk down to Frank's. Hangovers and fresh feelings of regret in their bags, weighing them down and making it even harder to walk. Gypsy always feels a slight sense of regret when she is hungover, but she never knew why. This universe is a funny place, and to the stars in the night sky, we are just little speckles of dust floating around on the surface of this lonely planet, not one of us more important than the other. But to all the little humans on this earth, we all have separate lives and stories and memories and circumstances, all individual feelings and fears and loves. Not one of them the same. The number of things going on in one person's life is but a mere drop in the ocean of the human race. If one life is so complex on its own, then imagine if you could feel everything that every single other person feels as well. *We may just explode.*

"How are you feeling?" Gypsy asked Marcy.

"Pretty shite, not sure I'm going to make it all the way to Frank's."

"We'll be right. We'll get some bacon and egg rolls, and then go sit at Thumper's in the beer garden for the rest of the day. Nothing cures a wine hangover like more wine." Gypsy knew she had a letter to attend to today, and wondered if maybe she was avoiding the reality of it all until she felt a little more human.

Marcy started looking a bit queasy, her green face and lop-sided walk was one indication, but as she started throwing up over someone's front fence, Gypsy got the strange feeling that maybe Marcy wasn't kidding about feeling shite.

"Are you alright?" Gypsy laughed. She couldn't help it.

After a minute the silence was broken. "Oh. My. God." It was more gurgled than actual words.

"Ahh, there's nothing classier than a broad in a pretty blouse and high heeled shoes throwing up in someone's garden." Gypsy smiled, looking around at the beautiful day.

"So, how's it going with that fella you've been seeing?"

"What fella?" Gypsy sat up from the grass in the beer garden at Thumper's and stared at Marcy quizzically. The sounds of an acoustic guitar and a man singing about his heart beating for some lady's breasts played in the background, and all around were people enjoying the music and their Saturday Sippers beneath the shady trees.

"The guy you were telling me about last night! I still can't believe you have started seeing someone and just failed to mention it to me the second it happened. I am starting to think you are keeping secrets from me, missy."

"That? Oh, that was no one. Just some guy I met at the doctor's office." Gypsy said. "He may have ball warts anyway." Although she joked, she felt hopeful, but she didn't want to put too much pressure on the vibe just yet as it was still early days. "I don't really know him; I gave him my number and he rang me yesterday while we were at Nicki's. We agreed to meet up on Wednesday for a coffee in Kanville." She waved her hand at Marcy like it was nothing.

Marcy sat up and pulled back her sunnies "Kanville? Why so far away? … Anyway, you wouldn't shut up about him all night. You rang him at like 5 O'clock this morning! And yes, before you give me that *'why didn't you stop me'* face, I fucking *tried* to stop you…" Gypsy looked at her shocked, "Come on Gyps, you know what you're like. Like…"

"Yes, I know what I am like, and I am a stubborn cow! But Dude!" Gypsy shook her head.

"I wouldn't stress if I were you, you literally rang, didn't say a word, and then you passed out. Thankfully, I was there to hang up the phone for you so he couldn't hear you snoring." She laughed.

"Thanks Marc. So, hold up; we went to sleep at 5 AM? No wonder I feel like crap." Gypsy laid back on the grass and covered her eyes from the tormenting glare of the sun and continued to hear the heartache of the solo performer and his guitar.

Brad

CHAPTER 5

Brad sat on the hardwood floor of his loungeroom, with his back against the couch, staring at the mess. He could just pack up and go? Leave town and never look back. But that would look suss when the McGill brothers are considered missing persons, and Brad has a well-known connection to Jeffery McGill – the third brother. Jeffery has been shacking up with Brad's ex for the past whatever years. He is a druggo and a thief. And as much as Brad didn't want anything to do with the pair of them, he had received a letter that had hit him hard. It was then that he decided he had to steel the bracelet back. But when Jeffery and his scabby face got in the way, threatening to '*bash the shit*' out of Brad, every inch of Brad's body spiked with anger, and unfortunately, poor druggo Jeffery ended up in a coma and is probably never going to wake up. Brad was never charged with the assault and he knew this was because his ex – Carly – wanted to get him back her own way.

But here lays another one of Brad's problems: Brad is

monotonous. Brad is so monotonous that people would notice if he suddenly disappeared. Mrs Cray down at the corner store would notice when he didn't turn up to get his morning paper for so many days, the mailman would notice when his mail box started filling up, his clients would notice when his shed was shut for too long, and his neighbours would notice when he didn't mow his lawn on Saturday morning, go for his afternoon walk, or feed the stray cat around the back of the alley where all the bins pile up.

"Where's Brad?" they would question. And as each neighbour, shop owner, workmate and cat got together and pieced together the puzzle that is Bradley Mains, they would soon conclude, that Brad was gone.

Of course, once this happened, the newspapers and the headlines on the 5pm news would all start talking about the McGill brothers who had gone missing. Now, lucky for them, they were dead! Brad thought this idea was a little twisted, but true nonetheless. They *won't get caught for trying to kill him.* They *don't have to go on the run. Even if* they *were found guilty,* they *were dead.*

Brad, however, was not. Brad could still get caught. All he could think of was going to jail.

Would he be able to get off lightly since they came into his house and threatened to kill him? Could he plead self-defence?

But if he stayed, then maybe he would not stick out like a sore thumb on the detective's suspect list. They always fucked it up in the movies. Could he get it right?

Sure, he could hand himself in, but what if there is some

crazy chance that he might just get away with killing the two scumbags…

Before he knew it, he had cleaned up all of the blood while contemplating his future. The two men's bodies were lying next to him on a blue tarp. Good ol' Thomas and his precious bat was staring straight at him with a lifeless eye. The blood had dried on David's throat and the white writing on his black t-shirt had turned red.

It seemed like a lifetime that Brad had sat staring at Thomas's lifeless eye. They were looking into each other's souls, yet the dead man's soul had left the building long ago.

OK, its quick-thinking time. Brad wrapped the men up in the tarp and waited till dark. That's when he will drag the bodies out and put them in the boot of his car. That's when he will get rid of the evidence. And that is when he will choose to pretend none of this ever happened.

Skye

CHAPTER 6

Today, Skye's dad is going to see her.

It's his birthday, and he is taking her out to lunch. "*He* is taking *me* out to lunch. Now, considering it is his birthday, shouldn't *I* be taking *him* out for lunch?" She had questioned Manny. Since Skye was little her dad had always been an amazing and supportive father. He wasn't one of those absent dads you hear about that leave their kids in cars while they play the pokies – Skye was his world. *"It's you and me against the world, kiddo."* He would always say.

Skye grew up in High Tide but moved to Kanville after her mum died when she was 5. "Now, she was a lady worth knowing." Skye would tell people. Her mum was like this shining light that would walk into a room and slap a smile on your face, without you even meaning to do it. It was infectious. It seemed like she wore the sun around her neck and her hair was made of music. She would twirl over to Skye just begging her to dance, in her favourite yellow dress. There were days Skye remembered running with her out of the house and into the rain, but not just average rain, the big fat rain that washes away the heat of a sunny day. The smell of the rain in the air would fill her lungs with that sweet freshness and the grass would glow and sparkle like glitter was thrown over it in the storm. Skye's mum would insist they dance and dance they did. Their arms would be up towards the sky with their fingers outstretched to catch every last raindrop as they spun around and around. The look of pure happiness on her mum's face as she would flood Skye's soul with a feeling she only knew as normal, is an image she could never erase from her mind.

She died when Skye was 5. It has been 20 years since the car accident that took away her light, her happy, her Mum, and that image still remains her most precious possession.

Skye's parents got married on a beach at the edge of town when they were 22, and Skye was born not long after. *'She was the love of my life'* her dad would say as he reminisced and told stories about how they met. Skye would tell funny stories from what she could remember, and they would laugh and cry all at once. The stories would bring her to life and make her presence felt as if she were sitting right there with Skye.

It took Skye's dad a very long time to come to terms with her death and an even longer time to get rid of her many possessions. It wasn't until recently that he decided he would pass the boxes to Skye to keep and dispose of as she saw fit.

Last night Skye sucked down some red wine and

rummaged through the boxes in search of the dress. Like travelling through time, the contents of the boxes contained memories she thought she had long forgotten: a vinyl record that brought back the sounds of a sunny Sunday and the smell of chicken and veggies roasting in the oven; the image of her mum sipping red wine and dancing with her dad in the kitchen. The windows of the house were open, and neighbours would wave from their back fence as they threw a barbeque for friends and neighbours. All the kids in the street would ride their tricycles up and down the street while the older kids played basketball at the local hoop on the corner.

There was a brush; gold and silver, still with a couple of stray dark blonde hairs stuck in the bristles.

A notebook filled with poems and drawings, and a black and white photo of her parents sitting on a park bench in front of a corner store.

Ahh, there it is. As the tears she did not realise were running down her face were slowly drying up, she pulled out the yellow dress. Skye handwashed this dress that still, after 20 years, smelled of her mum. It was for this reason only that hot water was all she needed in the hopes the smell would somehow be stuck in a time warp inside this dress and its remains would forever hold the spirit of her mum's past and the memories of her light.

So now here she sat on the edge of her bed, the following morning, staring at her reflection and waiting for the doorbell to ring.

"Hey Skye, I think your dad just pulled up out the front." Manny stood by the door and eyed the look on

Skye's face. "Nice dress, Dude."

"Thanks Mann." She smiled, a steady yet anxious smile that he would not understand. Then the doorbell rang.

"Dad!" Skye smiled and wrapped her arms around him as he stood outstretched at the front door, a little tear welling up in his eye at the sight of the yellow dress. "I know, I hope you don't mind." She said, reading his thoughts "I thought it would be nice?" Anxiety crept up her throat.

"No, no... not at all. It's just... you look so much like your mother." He smiled as the tear escaped and rolled down his cheek like an accidental vulnerability. "You look beautiful, Honey. I'm glad you wore the dress." He must have sensed the anxiety. They hugged tightly and left down the front steps of the white weatherboard house.

"So, how's it going with Cam? I heard he lost his job as the trolley guy?" Skye's dad said this with an air of disappointment in his voice. It was no secret that he hated Cam. *'He's no good for you'* He would say regularly. But eventually he had to give in as he could see how much Skye loved him, and as her father, wasn't he supposed to be supportive? Skye saw the shift in attitude a little while ago and thanked him for it.

"Yeah, he did. Got drunk at work apparently." She knew if it was anyone else her dad would laugh about this, *but fuck it,* she thought. "I know, I know what you're thinking, he's a loser and I am better off without him? You know what? I agree some days. But the crazy thing is, I love that loser, you know? He's *MY* loser."

"Honey, you know I am always here for you, and I will support you in anything, but I honestly just don't know what you are doing with this guy. He's only going to drag you down."

Ok, so the attitude's back…

Skye's tummy rumbled above the noise of the chatter.

"Dad, lets order." She smiled "Anyway, Cam left the house a couple of hours ago to go job hunting, so he is trying."

"I only want what's best for you, Skye." He said, reaching for her hand across the table.

"I know, Dad."

Skye and her dad sat at a table in the sun outside the café and ordered every piece of cake on the menu. They talked about what he has been up to – not much – and how things are going with work.

"How is the business going, Dad? Is Bradley Mains Furniture Co. bringing in the dough?"

"Always, Honey." He smiled. "Although, I do need an apprentice if you want to come work for your old man?" He winked.

Skye just laughed. "No thanks Dad, I think I'll stick with the tip."

In the midst of her giggling, Skye raised her head and noticed something that made all of the blood drain from each limb of her body. Suddenly she was cold, oh so cold.

That fucking asshole.

It was Cam, sitting at a table inside the same bloody café with another woman. She looked older than Skye but not by much. He was touching her hand and she threw back her head laughing and giggling with him as they sipped what looked like cocktails! *Cocktails! It's fucking lunchtime on a Wednesday!* she thought with fury. There was only one thing that sat in the front of Skye's mind now, she *had* to know who this bitch was, this bitch, who is sitting with *her* man, holding *her* man's hand and laughing with *her* man's laugh. She had brown hair and a confidence about the way she flailed her arms around like an idiot while she laughed and gave Cam those 'I wanna fuck you right here, right now' eyes. And that's not the worst of it, because he was laughing back, he was flailing his arms, and he was giving her the eyes. The fury within Skye was starting to take over. She almost wanted to… *I think I'm going to…hold it in Skye…don't murder people in front of your dad.*

If Skye could have asked the universe for one thing right now, it would be that Cam would throw this woman on to the table and kiss her frantically. This would surely give Skye right to go over there and stab the bitch in the face with a fork. She watched as the woman flicked her hair and pouted her lips like a fish.

"What's the matter Skye?" Brad looked at her curiously, braking the insanity that was crawling around through her insides scraping at her throat and clawing at her chest. Skye's blood was no longer cold, it was fucking boiling.

"Nothing, nothing." She said flippantly looking away and focusing her energy back onto Brad.

This was her fight. She wasn't dragging her dad into it. But the look on her face left Brad unconvinced.

"You sure?" He said shifting in his seat to look behind himself.

"Dad, it's cool, it's ok, I swear." Skye almost yelled, bringing him back. She didn't want him to see; she didn't know what he was capable of.

"Ok." He said cautiously. He knew something was wrong but knew better than to push it.

"Look…how about we go and see a movie or something? We could go bowling, or go down to the pub and have a nice stiff drink? Come on, Dad, it's your birthday, let's go celebrate. Anyway, I can't look at another piece of cake or I might end up painting this walkway with the colours of black forest cheesecake and mint cream sponge."

Brad laughed and nodded "To the pub it is."

Fucking excellent choice, Dad.

As Skye stood up, she took one last look behind Brad's shoulder and into the cafe where Cam was now kissing the bitch.

He hadn't noticed Skye sitting out there in plain sight.

Good, Skye thought as her mind wandered and her imagination ran a little wild. She didn't want this argument in front of her dad. She knew he will most likely bash the living shit out of Cam. If she was truly honest with herself, she would actually be scared for the safety of Cam. Brad is built like a brick shithouse and she wouldn't put it past him to throw a few good punches in her honour, but she just didn't know when they would stop.

I fucking hate that scumbag right now, but I don't really want to see him dead on the floor of this lovely establishment with half his brain in the salad buffet and an eyeball in someone's soup. Imagine the mess?

"Skye? Are you coming or what?"

She paused, looked back at her dad and turned away from her deceitful dick of a boyfriend. "Yeah, let's go."

After Skye and Brad had cleared the pub of all its whisky and played enough games of pool to be considered champions of the town, Brad recklessly drove her home. They hugged goodbye and she stumbled into the house with her heels in her hand and her heart proving its strength in her chest. *Thump. Thump. Thump.*

Skye managed to get through a pretty proper drinking session without spilling the beans about what she had witnessed today, and figured she deserved a medal. A big shiny one. A big shiny, sharp medal she could use to stab Cam in the face. *Yes, perfect.*

When Skye got inside her white house, she could hear the noise of Manny and Cam playing Xbox in the lounge and could smell something cooking in the kitchen. Roast chicken. Skye's favourite.

"That you, Skye?" Cam yelled from the living room, but Skye didn't have the need to reply to him. She still hadn't decided if she wanted to make this a civil conversation or if she wanted to go absolutely off tits and see where the wind blows her. Skye wants answers, but she knew that if she goes 'crazy' and expresses the evil inside of her right now, then he will only lie, act like a victim, and run from the house leaving her with nothing but unanswered questions and a face full of tears.

I WANT TO SCREAM!!

Skye was feeling the full effects of whisky and pain, mixed together in her belly, causing an upset that didn't even feel human anymore. So, she figured this may not be the best time to converse about the imminent death of her relationship.

Skye walked out to the loungeroom and let her eyes be entranced by the floor, so they did not reveal the horror inside. "When's dinner?"

Manny kept frantically pressing buttons on his remote.

"Should be about ready."

"Good." She mumbled and walked back to the kitchen to grab some water when suddenly Cam appeared.

"How was your dad?"

Just the sound of his cheating voice made her furious. She looked at him with squinted eyes.

No. I am keeping it together. I am waiting until I am sober.

"S'all right." She stammered.

"Shit Babe, had a few too many?" Cam laughed and walked over to her with open arms.

Oh hell no. Not if you were on fire, fucker.

"Nope." Skye pushed him away and walked over to check on the roast. The smell of the chicken, the veggies… Skye thought of her mum.

"What?" He looked confused. "Fuck, sorry for giving a shit."

"Got a job?" She snapped.

"Aah, yeah, well there are some hopefuls. I handed my resume into a couple of different places and one did say they would call me back over the next week or two." He was scratching his cheek. He always scratched his cheek when he lied. "Yeah, it's at the bakery. Hours would be pretty shitty, starting at 3am and working through 'til lunch, but it would leave me the rest of the day to do whatever I want." He smiled a 'please be impressed with me' smile, like a puppy that just learned his first trick and was waiting for a reward.

"Oh yeah? Whatever you want hey? Like fucking another woman?!" *Oh shit, that wasn't meant to happen. Damn It, Skye!* Skye was utterly unimpressed with herself at this point.

Cam stared at her completely stunned. His mouth was open, and she could see his eyes glaze over as if somewhere in the total stunned silence his soul managed to black out and leave his body.

"What? Nothing to say? You obviously had plenty to say to that bitch today, 'coz she thought you were fucking hilarious! A fucking clown, Cam! I didn't know you were in the circus! Please, teach me some clown moves, Cam!" Skye was huffing and puffing and ready to blow this motherfucker down.

"Skye, Skye, Skye… chill out." His hands up as if he was dealing with a wild animal ready to maul his precious face. "We are only friends, I swear."

"Friends don't kiss, Cam!" Skye reached for the closest cup and hurled it at his head, missing completely and smashing on the wall behind him sending glass shards everywhere.

"I don't know what you're talking about, I never kissed her." His acting was truly appalling.

"Oh, fuck yes you did. I saw you kiss her! That bitch with the brown hair and the fake laugh, throwing her arms around as if you're a fucking clown, Cam! A FUCKING CLOWN!" She was starting to hear herself, and how ridiculous she sounded.

This is exactly why I did not want to do this tonight. Why don't I ever listen to me?

The tears were rolling down her face and her black mascara was running into her eyes and down her cheeks. It burned, but not as much as Cam had burned her love.

"This is bullshit, Skye. I don't need to hear this shit. I don't need to stand here and justify myself or try to make you understand that I might actually have friends out there that you don't know. You know, I am actually allowed to have friends that are female!" Cam was grabbing his wallet and keys most likely in an effort to escape the madness that was unfolding in front of him in the shape of a broken woman. Skye had mutated into something not quite from this world. Her skin seemed to turn a purplish black and her eyes were red as blood. She was screaming and Cam was petrified.

But he lied. She knew he would lie.

Cam stormed out of the house as quick as his cheating legs would carry him, while Skye raced after him shouting "Burn in hell you bitch fucker!"

It was then that a very brave Manny came up from behind her and put his arms ever so gently around her body, and rested his head on her trembling shoulder, flooding her poisoned body with warmth and support. He did not say a word, and she appreciated that. They stood there for what felt like 5 minutes while her breathing gradually slowed, and Manny breathed along behind her, almost in a state of meditation. He calmed her as she could feel herself steadily relax into the safety net that was Manny. Sanity started to return, but the pain was still there, impressively strong. And when the tears eventually stopped, she collapsed into a ball of depression, and stayed that way until the morning.

Skye sat with her coffee, curled up on the lounge of her front veranda. The morning sun burns into her bloodshot eyes that have barely calmed or slept, blinding her from the flowerpots that surround the clean space. Colours of blue, red, yellow and green form a circle of intentional happiness that she cannot be fucked appreciating right now, though she wished she could. The events of yesterday weighed her down like an elephant and the lack of sleep filled her with anxiety.

She pondered her future and was now baffled at what it might hold. She knew they had their problems, and he really is the captain of the nowhere train, but she still loved him. She feels as though she has truly given up so much of her life and patience on Cam. She has been there through thick and thin with him, and even though he can be a dick, he has always been there for her too.

Skye sat with her cold coffee cup feeling lost, broken and scarred.

Manny came out to sit next to her with a fresh cup of coffee. As he handed it over, she could feel him inhale and knew that he wanted to speak, but as much as she loves Manny, she just doesn't have the strength to talk.

"I'm so sorry, Skye." He breathed out. The cold from the morning air morphed his words into a thick fog that fled his mouth. Manny took his ripped brown cardigan off and put it around Skye's shoulders. The sun was out, but the chill sat in the air from the night, like an unwanted relative that overstayed their visit.

"This may be a silly question, but…do you want a bong? I really think it could help… you know… ease the pain."

But Skye only continued to stare at the foggy plants with her fresh hot cuppa warming her shaky hands.

"You know, when you mentioned the lipstick in the bathroom…that was hers."

"What?" Skye was shocked.

"I'm so sorry I didn't tell you, but it's not really my place. I have been choking on the inside, man. You know like drowning in the hurtful things he's been doing, but I just didn't know what to do. I love you man, and I just, you know. I mean you're like one of my favourite people in the whole world." Manny lit a joint and breathed deeply. "I mean, I don't judge anyone, but I didn't pick Cam to be the kind of guy that would give up a good bird like you to go screwing around with some blue haired chick. You guys have been together forever…"

Blue haired…

Suddenly Skye's attention was peaked. "Blue hair?" Her eyes rolled from the flowers to Manny's legs beside her.

"Yeah, weird hey? I mean, nothing wrong with blue, but just not Cam's…"

"Not weird Manny, but very fucking interesting. The girl I saw him with had brown hair. Brown."

"Shit." Manny shook his head. Though not hard to confuse Manny, even he knew they mustn't be the same person.

"So, there was more than one…"

"Look, Skye, I'm so sorry about all of this. He's an arsehole, you're better off without him." He patted her on the shoulder, "I was going down to Ted's. He's got these brekky pizzas now with bacon and eggs and cheese…do you want anything?" Skye could tell that Manny was obviously feeling too awkward for this conversation and was looking for an escape route.

She shook her head slowly.

"I wish I could escape. I wish I could focus on something other than the fact that my soon to be ex-boyfriend was sleeping around with everyone."

Gypsy

CHAPTER 7

Gypsy was exhausted already. She had tried on everything in her closet at least 20 times and her room looked like a bomb went off in it. She has some heavy metal music playing for a bit of confidence, but today it just doesn't seem to work.

"Come on Gyps, just throw on anything. Anything at all." She coaxed herself.

Gypsy is a little nervous… scratch that, she is *insanely* nervous. Because today, she will meet her biological father.

He doesn't know yet, but after receiving a reply letter to the one she sent off with Dr Inker, she doesn't think she can wait any longer. It took her three days to open the thing, but after reading what seemed to be a pretty positive response she noticed there was a reply postal address on the back of the envelope, and when life hands you information, sometimes it's just plain stupid not to use it. Skye doesn't know what he looks like, all she knows is he lives about an hour away in Kanville, the same place where Cam is from. Gypsy still wasn't sure what to think about Cam. She liked him, but it was after only their first coffee date that he had asked if he could sleep on her couch for a night. And after he mentioned he had some plumbing problems at home, that one night turned into a week. He was growing on her, kind of like a bad smell that doesn't have a job but is just so sexy, funny and beautiful, that he's a little hard not to like. And although the word 'stalker' ran through her brain at first, Gypsy thinks she may have found a guy she could really fall for. But stalker tendencies and jobless hunks aside, Cam has agreed to go with Gypsy today to meet her father.

"You know, I'm only going to introduce myself as his 32-year-old long lost daughter, so I guess, not awkward at all!" She laughed with fear in her eyes.

Gypsy dressed in fitted jeans and a blue blouse. Her hair is down and straightened and her heart is full of hope; A little anxious, but still full of hope. She eyes herself up and down in the mirror feeling well put together, and it boosts her with a little more confidence. When she looks nice, she feels confident. No one is getting in the way of her confidence today; She'll need every little ounce of it that she can get… "Damn it, I need to go pee again…"

"Gypsy!" Cam called out "I don't think I can do it."

Oh god. There is a groan in Cam's voice that crushed Gypsy's confidence just a smidge… She hoped her suspicions were wrong about this guy. *Please tell me he isn't going to bail on me!* She silently cried.

"I think that food from Frank's was, maybe, not food anymore… I don't…" And there it is. The horrendous sounds of a full-grown man exploding from each end of his body in what can only be described as the most excruciating involuntary force of nature. "Well, I guess it's just you and me" She said to her reflection in the mirror.

"Great."

Confidence Gypsy, you can do this!

Gypsy jumped into her car and took a deep breath.

Long lost dad's address: Check.

Music on: Check.

Confidence: Check?

Phone, wallet and hope: Check.

Kanville is about an hour from High Tide, and it's a pretty smooth drive up the coast. Not much traffic today and the sun is shining through the window bringing with it the smell of the ocean. Gypsy can see the seagulls flying above beachgoers waiting for them to throw chips out to the flock, while the people laugh at the scrambling of wings and beaks. It reminds Gypsy of a childhood long ago when her parents would take her down to the beach for ice cream. She always wore her favourite pink swimmers with the frill around the back which matched perfectly with her pink hat and sandals. She could still smell the air and feel the waves crashing on her little feet. They would throw a ball and chase it into the ocean dancing with the reflection of the sun on the water and be mesmerised by the schools of fish that swam around their feet like they were playing their own game of chasey. She could still remember the blue cooler that held cordial, homemade sandwiches, and fresh oranges. These were the memories that she held to tightly. These were the days that she looked forward to the most.

But like all good things, the day would soon come to an end, and the glow of the setting sun would change the colour of the sky to all kinds of remarkable beauty. Gypsy's parents would pack up the car and her collection of seashells, while Gypsy would stare out to the water and wish it could never end.

Five minutes out from Kanville and Gypsy's heartbeat was growing stronger, thumping in her chest like the beating of drums. She could feel it in her ears like a tribe of Amazonians beating down hard in a rain dance of sorts. The anxiety crept up slowly and only made her yearn for a drink. The elephant on her chest grew heavier and the belt around her throat was suffocating.

"I can't…breath." She whined.

Suddenly Gypsy's heart was beating even faster, and she could feel the unwanted sensation of tingles creeping all over her body just as she started to hyperventilate. *For fuck sake*! She hurriedly searched her car for a paper bag, any form of bag! Her eyes were growing as wide as her head and the tears started pouring from them like a fountain. *Come on Gyps, breath in, hold it, hold it, hold it, breath out slowly, you can do this, control your breaths!* As if she had split into two people, she started to throw words of encouragement at herself, she tried to convince herself that the worst thing that will happen is that she will pass out from hyperventilating. She screamed at herself that her throat is NOT going to close up, her chest is NOT going to get crushed!

"It's just a feeling, Dude. A really fucked up feeling." Her current fight and flight sensors were out of control, and she feared in this moment, she might die. She grabbed her water bottle and skulled down the fresh liquid, attempting to open her throat even just a little. The feeling of swallowing makes her feel like it is opening her throat and controlling her breathing at the same time as she held her breath to drink. Ever so gradually, Gypsy's heart rate slowed, her elephant ran away, and the belt was loosened a few notches back. Her head hurt from the tension and her body felt weak, still shaking slightly like the remnants of an electric shock.

Feeling beaten and bruised, she sat on the side of the road with her car door open and her legs hanging out. Her eyes played movies behind the closed eyelids, as she focused on regaining her strength. *That's it, Gyps, nice and relaxed...* HONK! HONK! Suddenly a truck horn shattered her relaxation as it flew by in a flurry of rude interruption.

"Thanks dickhead!" She screamed out, but the truck was already flying into the distance. "Fucker." She glared.

"Aargh" She groaned and scooted back around in the seat. The intriguing thing was, having an anxiety attack is kind of like having a good cry or getting sick with a cold... once it's over, it doesn't seem to happen again for a while. Gypsy's emotional immunity was feeling tougher than ever.

"Ok Gyps, onward and upward." She said with forced encouragement.

Gypsy grabbed the little bit of paper that she wrote his address on and clutched on to the hope that it was right. She figured there were only two scenarios; One: He wrote the correct address in anticipation of her reply, or Two: He wrote the *wrong* address in anticipation of her never *ever* finding him. She had no idea if he had simply dropped her off on her adoptive parent's doorstep 32 years ago and packed his bags for Bangkok. *Maybe it wasn't even him that sent the letter?* Her mind started to run wild with anxious thoughts.

Gypsy ran through images of knocking on this person's door, only for this man to throw her in their basement and feed her cereal through a dirt cage that's covered in his last victim's filth. All these maybes swam around her head like threats, telling her to run. Gypsy sat and tried to toggle her brain back to its logical side. She was feeling stronger than ever now…well stronger than she felt 20 minutes ago. If Gypsy could get through the hell that is an anxiety attack, then she could get through anything. Bear attack? *Pfft.* Plane crash? *Bring it on!* Meeting her supposed biological father? *No…worries?*

Gypsy rounded the corner to the address on the paper and asked herself; what's the worst that could happen? There was the cereal in the basement thing, but she knew that wasn't going to be true…*or was it?* Her eye twitched a little at the thought.

"Shake it off, you pussy!" She said.

Apart from the fact that her parents have no idea she has been trying to find her biological dad – she didn't want to upset them – she had a newfound sense of confidence and felt as cool as a very frightened cucumber.

There it is. It's a brick house with a manicured front lawn, no picket fence but the lawn is scattered with rose bushes and all types of colourful shrubs and plants. There is a front veranda with hanging pots and a swinging chair. The steps up to the front door look like they have housed many afternoon conversations with a good mate and a beer, and many morning coffees singing out 'good morning' to the mailman. The trees on the path that run alongside the road up and down the street are well matured and give the footpath a beautiful shade and sense of serenity. There is a big shed that looks too big for the neighbourhood at the back end of his driveway.

"Bradley Mains Furniture Co." the sign read. It had a phone number under the name, so of course she wrote that down just in case she chickened out.

It was now or never.

Gypsy took a breath, turned off the car that she had parked across the street from his house just in case he saw her pull up, and grabbed her keys. She wished Cam hadn't got sick, she needed him now, she needed that support. She had thought to bring Haz, but he was busy at drama school, and if Gypsy was honest, she noticed he has been extra loopy lately, and she had enough to deal with. Gypsy felt like everything was going in slow motion. She grabbed her keys, opened her door, turned and shut the door *ever so slowly,* still questioning her movements. She looked back up at the brick house that was full of all the answers to all of her questions and it was staring right back at her – beautiful, but scary. The front door was the mouth and the windows were the eyes. She walked closer and almost up to the front path when suddenly she saw someone in the window holding the curtain back. Gypsy's breathing stopped as she wondered what to do.

What do I do? Do I wave? Do I run?

Then as quick as she noticed it, the curtains closed. The little girl inside her wanted to cry: "Daddy, is that you?" But the woman she is now, with all the constant issues she already has facing her day to day existence, is wondering if this is all worth it. Was it worth throwing more issues into the fire that already burns so deep within her? Did she need to add more to those flames?

"Hello?" Bradley Mains stood at the door with a look of confusion, shock, and horror. In that instant she wanted to run. She looked at him like he was a crazy person and really regretted not bring Haz now.

Brad was a big man, and by 'big' he looked like he was 50% muscle, 50% tacos. He looked like he pumped the weights at the gym but also wouldn't skimp on pizza night. He had tattoos all the way down both arms. He had brown hair cut into a nice barber cut style and a 3-day old scruff around his chin that looked like a permanent fixture. He wore black shorts and a white shirt with red trimming around the seams. And at this exact point in time, he wore the look of somebody who feared Gypsy. He had wide eyes, a mouth open catching flies, pale skin that was turning a little green, sweat starting to bead on his forehead, eyes looking drooped as he took a misplaced step down the stairs, falling to the ground...*shit*, laying on the ground!

"Man down! MAN DOWN!!" Gypsy yelled. "Help! Someone call an ambulance!" She had left her phone in the car, so she ran over to call them herself. It's not like it is in the movies where someone falls over and all the people in the neighbourhood start scrambling over to sticky beak at the poor fella on the ground. No one came running. She dialled the ambulance while Brad laid there, out cold.

"Hi, I need an ambulance to 54 Chester Street Kanville, please hurry."

"Hi Ma'am, please explain the problem."

"Yeah, so this guy, my biological dad, but he doesn't know that, I was about to tell him, and he looked a bit green, and…"

"Ma'am, what is the problem? I can't help unless you let me know. Is someone hurt?"

"Yes, His name is Brad, and he fell over, like looked white, then fell down the steps." Her breathing was fast and strong…she may fall over herself at this rate!

"Ok," the operator said "There is someone on their way, we are sending out an ambulance right now. Now Ma'am I need you to stay calm, are you with the gentlemen at the moment?"

"Yes."

"Can you see if he is breathing? Please place your hand or ear 2 centimetres over his airway. Can you feel him breathing? Is his chest moving?"

"Yes, yes he's breathing."

"Ok, please make sure there is nothing in his surrounding area that he can hurt himself on in case he wakes and tries to get up."

"No, he's lying on the grass, but his head hit the concrete pretty hard…I think he's bleeding."

"Ok, please do not move his head, just sit with him and remain calm, the ambulance will be there in a minute."

Well, this has been a fantastic first meeting. Gypsy thought. Her biological dad is laying on the ground out the front of his house as she is patiently waiting for an ambulance. She didn't even get to say one measly word. Needless to say, she was overjoyed at how the situation panned out. Not.

As she sat on the grass, hearing the faint sounds of sirens getting closer towards her end of town, she took the opportunity to have a good gawk at Brad's face. His eyes were partly open, and his mouth was drooling. Gypsy definitely had his brown hair and blue eyes and had also been known to drool. Gypsy had an overwhelming feeling sweep through her soul and fill her with chills. It was surreal looking into the face of someone that actually had her hair, her eyes, and who also drools in their unconsciousness.

Suddenly, a man's voice broke the silence and tore her away from her visions of what life may have been like growing up in this brick house with her dad, who had her eyes and her hair. Then it hit her; *shouldn't there be a mum somewhere here too?*

"Hello, Miss. Could you please move aside so we can assess the gentleman?" The paramedic moved in to where Gypsy sat on the ground, a hollow seat flattened by her weight in the grass. She moved aside and let him look poor Brad over. Gypsy considered running for it; jumping in her car and driving back to High Tide. She hoped the knock on the head may cause a slight memory loss and he wouldn't even remember her being here. Then maybe they could start again one day when she was feeling a little more confident. Her thoughts hung her in the air on a tightrope of decisions. She swayed in the breeze going left and right not knowing which way to fall, but she was hanging on with all of her might. It seemed no matter which way she went, the intensity of the crash is going to hurt either way.

"Ok, Miss, it looks like he may have a concussion, we need to take him to the hospital and do some tests to make sure we know what we are dealing with here. Are you coming with us? You can ride in the back of the ambulance or take your own car if you have one, it's up to you, but we need to move now."

Gypsy stood there, balancing on her tightrope. All the air around seemed thick like butter, and it felt like the world stood still, if only for a second. She looked at an unconscious Brad, squeezed her eyes shut, and jumped.

Brad

CHAPTER 8

Brad was walking down for his morning newspaper listening to the sounds of the new day. Birds in the trees he passed along the footpath were feeding their young chicks' worms freshly dug up from the recently rained on dirt. It was 8am which meant the traffic was at one of its busiest times of day as everyone would be on their way to their jobs. Brad doesn't open his shed doors until 8:30 which gives him time to follow through with his morning ritual of getting the paper and a takeaway coffee from Mrs. Cray at the corner store, then walking home to relax on his back porch. Brad wondered how many more of these mornings he would get to enjoy if he was found guilty for killing the McGill brothers. He had been brooding over it since that awful night and considered that he might need to sell the diamond bracelet.

The bracelet was given to Brad and Carly 32 years ago when they got pregnant with Gypsy and had given her up after the birth. They were only sixteen and in no shape to raise a child. The people that he gave Gypsy to for adoption were fabulous and rich. All they ever wanted was a child yet could never have one, though not for lack of trying. The husband put this down to his wife's work schedule – she put it down to his. They were both so busy and stressed out all of the time that they had to schedule sex. It was a highlighted day on their collective calendar, usually with a little sparkly heart stuck to it just so none of them missed it and forgot.

When Gypsy was born and they handed her over, and Brad's tears were no longer embarrassing but necessary and uncontrollable, the new adoptive mother looked at Brad with the tears rolling from his puffy eyes, and she took off her bracelet. It was white gold encrusted with pink diamonds all around the edges. One massive bright red ruby sat in the middle of the chain of diamonds and shined so bright he almost forgot his own name. It was extremely expensive. Handing it to Brad she said

"Take this, I know it's not much, but maybe one day you can sell it. It was given to me by one of my clients a number of years ago. She was a very influential poet and has since died, so I can only assume it will be worth a lot more in years to come."

"Really?" Brad stared in awe at the blinding beauty of this bracelet. Being a 16-year-old boy with his life ahead of him he couldn't really pass up such a gift, but was it morally right? It would feel like he was selling his baby girl.

"We'll take it." Carly grabbed the bracelet off her like a lizard catching a fly with its tongue.

Brad stood there with tormented thoughts and a horrible feeling in his gut. He wanted the bracelet to start a life with his girlfriend, be able to buy a house or a car, or get takeaway whenever they wanted…but at the same time, does this bracelet represent the value of his daughter?

Thirty two years on, and here he was with the stolen bracelet sitting in his sock drawer and stuck in his thoughts; and that same horrible feeling in his gut. The whole point in stealing it back from his ex-girlfriend was so that he could give it to Gypsy, because he knew that if by some miracle it was still in her parent's locked-up safe, and he could get it back…it belonged to his daughter. The only problem was, Brad stole it back to give it to Gypsy when he received the contact letter, except now, he may need to sell it and use the money to get away. Far, far away.

It was *his* in the first place, right?

He laughed at the irony as he walked back up his front steps, paper in one hand and takeaway coffee in the other. If he had never stolen the bracelet back, then he wouldn't need to sell it to run away. He had a little bit of savings, but business was slower than he made out to Skye, and he didn't have much money in that.

Brad opened the newspaper, sipped his coffee, and what was splashed across the second page of the Kanville Times newspaper were two pictures. The McGill brothers. *Shit*.

'HIGH TIDE MEN MISSING'
Local authorities are currently investigating
the disappearance of two men who have been

94

missing from the town of High Tide, 82
kilometres from Kanville.

The men were reported missing on 22nd of
March and have not been seen since.

Local police are assisting High Tide
authorities with the investigation into the
disappearance and ask for cooperation from
the community. If anyone has any information
regarding the two men, both aged in their 40's,
please contact local police or call 000 as soon
as possible.

Brad sat and stared at the newspaper in a state of fear.
His mind was anguished as he faced the reality of this
situation in his backyard, sitting on the steps of his porch,
coffee still warm. He squinted his eyes at the paper,
screwed it up and threw it into the firepit ready to burn,
baby burn.

His thoughts would, as if uncontrollably, return to the
yellow dress. The feeling of nostalgia toward his dead wife
had become a thing of the past, but since he had gone to
visit Skye a week ago for his birthday, it was like a song he
just couldn't get out of his head. The words spin around
and around, and the chorus becomes unbearable. Over and
over he would replay the images of his wife spinning and
laughing, them dancing together, and making love. Her
smile in the freshest light and the love that tied them
together like an invisible string.

Skye has her mother's smile and her eyes; her love for life and her belief that everything is beautiful, even if sometimes she has to squint to see it. Brad was thankful that Skye was able to possess so many good qualities from her mother. But it saddened him that his love had to leave him and Skye so soon. "You would be so proud of our girl." He would smile up to the heavens with pride.

Brad opened his shed and wondered about Gypsy. He wondered if she had received his letter and if she had planned on reaching out again. The day he received the letter from her accompanied by a letter from some doctor down in High Tide was like something he had trained his whole life for.

He had always wanted this day to come, but when it did, when he realised that she knew about him and that she wanted to know him, he freaked out. He had read the letter five times before actually *reading* the letter.

So now, Brad sat in his shed after just finishing up a three-drawer study desk for Rick Baily's daughter down the road. "Whatever she wants, let her design it." Rick had said. His daughter was 15 and the desk was her birthday present. She designed a black gothic style study desk with USB ports built into the edges, carved legs and secret hidey holes. Rick questioned the secret hidey holes, but Brad stayed reserved about his thoughts behind them; that was Rick's problem.

He had the radio blaring and a thirst in the back of his throat. For Brad it was lunch time, so he strolled up his back steps and inside his homely looking brick house. The photos on his mantle caught his eye – one of him and Skye on her 16th birthday, one of his parents, one of his dead wife swinging on a tree swing with Skye in her lap and one of him and his wife on their wedding day, broken on the edge by the man with the bat.

Brad grabbed a glass of water from the kitchen sink and wandered over to his front sitting room to switch on the telly. Brad hated midday telly, but it was a distraction from current events that plagued his mind. When he heard the car door slam across the street, out of pure curiosity he turned to look. It's usually a quiet street as most people were at work so he had a habit of listening for car doors as they could be potential business rolling up to his workshop.

Brad opened his curtain and noticed it was someone walking closer to his house. He switched off the telly and went to the window to have a peek but wasn't sure who it was from such a distance. He walked to his front door ready for a new client, but when he opened the door, what he saw was the vision of a woman he had spent 32 years watching from afar. The vision of a woman that to him was still a girl – his little girl.

Brad stood on his porch in complete shock. He felt himself say the word 'Hello', but he was not ready for this; he did not realise this was about to happen. He had dreamt of the day that he would finally get to meet his little Gypsy girl, but he had never been able to comprehend the feeling of what this might bring; What this might be like. He could feel his heart getting faster and the air around him grew thick. His ears were a flurry of white noise and his head was becoming too heavy to hold. Brad was not the kind of guy to buckle under pressure, he was the kind of guy who would stay calm in the storm while everything around him fell. He was man's man! But in this moment, in this moment where all of time was standing still in front of him, he was not strong, he was not the rope that held the sails, he was the sail. He flailed in the wind of his own mind and his eyes lost all their colour. He could see her staring at him, and as he tried to take a step down, his eyes went black and his body fell to the ground.

Skye

CHAPTER 9

It has been a week since Skye's fight with Cam. And all she knew, was nothing. She didn't even know where he went. He could have gone to Timbuctoo for all she knew.

Skye always had an almost sixth sense in a way, and for some reason, she always had a hard time trusting Cam. There was something about him that she could never put her finger on, so she put it down to her own paranoia and gave him the benefit of the doubt; she shrugged it off as her love ran deep. She always tried to see the good in people even when other people can't, because everyone needs someone to be their advocate, and she believed all people are truly good on the inside, but sometimes they just have a shitty time showing it. But now, she realised there was truth behind her doubts in Cam, and she violently kicked herself for not listening to herself.

"Why don't I ever listen to me?" She would cry into her pillow. But like the beginning of a new era, she decided to start trusting her senses more, instead of putting all of her trust into slimy feral fuckers like Cam.

At first, she was so sad and angry that all she wanted was for him to contact her, come home, and explain his side of this big fucking mess so that they could fix it. Explain why he felt the need to stick his dick into other woman. Skye was baffled, she couldn't figure out what she had done wrong. Had she not given him years of her life? Had she not supported him emotionally, financially and physically? Had she not given him sex whenever he wanted it? But now that she'd had a proper think about it – and many conversations with Manny – she doesn't feel anything for him anymore. At least she didn't think she did. In fact, if he were to walk his sorry arse into her house right now, she would have to introduce herself, because in Skye's mind she has already killed him, so it couldn't be Cam could it? No, it couldn't. Because in her mind he tried to come back, and she whipped out the old 1, 2, and chopped his fucking penis off. And in the comfort of her own mind, Manny and Skye stood there and watched him bleed to death, and they laughed and laughed…

Ok, maybe she felt something. And that something was definitely hatred.

"Skye, you're doing it again, aren't you?" Manny was standing above her passing her a mug of coffee. *The dude loves to caffeinate me…* she thought.

"Doing what?" Skye mocked, then turned her gaze. "Maybe."

"Do you know how funny it is to look out the kitchen window and see you sitting on the grass out here with this angry face, then it laughs, then it's shaking, then it's laughing again?"

"Are you referring to me as 'It'?"

"I'm referring to your face as 'It'. It has a mind of Its own, ya know." He laughed.

"Argh, I just can't stop thinking about it, Mann. Years of my life just thrown away. I really thought I could put up with his crap, ya know, never coming to bed, never getting a job and all the rest, because I thought he was the one. I thought one day we would get married and he would change, I thought we would have kids, you know…apart from you." Manny laughed and nodded in agreement.

"I guess I just wanted to put up with his crap until he grew out of it because I didn't want to have to start all over. I was comfortable. And I loved him."

Manny put his arm around Skye and rubbed her shoulder.

"Skye, he's not worth it. He's not worth all the hurt and the tears. Fuck him! You can do better anyway, I always thought that."

"Thanks, Mann. But why didn't you tell me?" She turned to him with tears welling up in her eyes.

"It wasn't my place, Dude. When I found out he had started seeing random chicks I had a massive fight with him, like we were fully blueing. You were at work one day and some chick came over, I got really confused and asked her who she was and what she wanted, she basically stabbed me with her eyes and then they left together. So many times, I had told him to tell you, you know, show you the respect you deserve. I mean, I sleep with different chicks all the time, but that's me. I am not in a long-term relationship with anyone but myself, and I like it that way. I like to sell my toothbrushes and smoke my cones and have meaningful connections with chicks that only last the night."

"Still, it would have been nice to know this a long time ago, since you are supposed to be my best friend." The anger was back, she could feel it creeping into her soul like a virus. Stabby thoughts and severed penises. Blood everywhere. Manny, quite unsettled, could see her face growing darker and shifted in his seat of grass.

Suddenly, even though they were in the backyard, Skye could hear the sound of high heels walking down the footpath past Old Clickety-Clack's house.

"God they're loud." Manny noticed too.

"CLICK CLACK, CLICK CLACK!" That wasn't the sound of the heels, that was Old Click Clack, and she sounded terrified!

"What the hell is going on? I thought she was going to be gone for weeks?" Their attention was drawn to the sounds coming from next door.

Manny and Skye jumped up from the ground and walked around their side fence to peer over at the half-burned house. In absolute horror, they saw Click Clack laying back on her front steps with a blue haired woman shoving her high heel up to Click Clack's throat.

"Not one fucking word, you bitch." She hissed the words from her bright pink lips. "Haven't we been through this before? You're already half dead, don't make me help you the rest of the way to your grave." She foamed at the mouth.

"Hey!" Manny yelled "What the fuck are you doing?" They both started running around to the other side of the fence, hearts racing, bolting towards the crazy lady. The pink lips looked up at them and jumped off Click Clack's front steps. She high tailed it down the road in a flurry of blue hair and cleavage.

"Oh my god, are you Ok?" Skye panted at Click Clack as she raced up the front step. But the old woman only shook and muttered:

'Click Clack, Click Clack'

"Holy fuck, I know her!" Manny stood wide eyed staring at the dust left in the air by this lady, who was well and truly too done up for a Thursday morning stroll.

"Who was it?" Skye gawked at Manny "Well?" Then it hit her – *Blue hair.*

"Click Clack, Click Clack." The old woman continued. Manny's eyes fell to Skye's like a magnet to a fridge.

"Skye, she was…she was one of the chicks Cam was seeing. She was the one that left the pink lipstick." He looked like he was still in shock, and Skye could feel the pain of it as it all became reality. This wasn't just some thought in her head, some story she was told. The bitch was real. But the thick cloud of confusion still lingered over their heads.

"So why the fuck was she threatening to stab Click Clack?"

Oh. My God. Click Clack knew.

"Have you met her before?" Skye threw away her scorn ex-girlfriend hat and put on her detective hat. *Like a glove.* She sat next to Click Clack and tried to get some words out of her other than the usual. "Click, Clack?"

"Anne."

"Anne?" Skye questioned. "Is that her name?"

Click Clack shook her head and pointed a 200-hundred-year-old bony finger at her chest. "Anne."

"You're Anne?" Manny sat on the other side of her. She nodded her head.

"Anne, do you think you could tell us about the blue-haired bitch… sorry, *lady*?" Skye sat uncomfortably next to her and watched as she fiddled with the buttons on her brown cardigan. One single tear was drying up in between the wrinkles on her cheek. "Why did she do that to you? Did it have something to do with Cam?"

"She…" Anne stammered. "…No, no, no." She started looking scared again and shook her head. She started looking around, up and down the street, searching for the blue haired lady. Shaking and rocking, shaking and rocking, fiddling with buttons. Her anxiety hung around them like a two-week-old casserole, stinking up the yard.

Skye looked to Manny for answers.

"So, Manny, you've met this crazy bitch before, she was obviously one of Cam's sluts?" He nodded. "Whatever the fuck her reasoning, she has really done a number on Anne." Skye usually had more respect than to swear so much in front of an elderly lady, but in this circumstance, it was justified. She looked back at Anne.

"Anne, do you want me to call the police?" But her fear only grew stronger. "Or I could make you a cup of tea?" Anne nodded and continued picking at her buttons, that Skye figured by this stage must be made of titanium the way Click Clack was hacking at them. As she didn't know her way around Anne's house, she decided to leave Manny sitting with her so she could walk next door to fetch the cup of tea. Skye walked into her back door and into the kitchen as if in a daze. She stood leaning against the kitchen bench while waiting for the kettle to boil, noticing every tile on the floor. There were little strange faces all throughout the patterns in the tiles, ones she would make up with her own imagination. Some were happy, some were sad, and some were more alien like than the nightmares she would have as a child. One particular spot was cracked, and if you were to look at it at the right angle it looked like the happiest face in the crowd. Cam and Skye were cooking one night, and Skye dropped a cast iron frypan on the floor. The tiles cracked instantly, but at the time they didn't care. It was with brilliant timing that Cam and Skye had gotten into Manny's weed and were so stoned that all they could do was laugh. They sat on the floor surrounded by minced meat and crushed tomatoes and laughed at the happy face staring back at them. And as they pretended to feed the tiled face their pasta sauce, they were sure to sprinkle some salt and pepper for taste. Skye knew how stupid they were being, but at that time, that amazing time when the rest of the world didn't matter and she could look into her beloved Cam's face crying tears of laughter, she didn't care. All she cared about was their love for one another, and the face in the floor.

It was only when Skye heard the front door shut that she remembered what she was supposed to be doing.

"Skye, what's taking so long?" Manny came walking down the hall into the kitchen.

"Sorry, I got distracted." Skye turned to fill the cup with hot water, and only then did she realise how long she must have been standing there. The water was nearly cold again.

"Dude, I think you're going to want to hear this." Manny's eyes were full of seriousness. A seriousness that was as common as a blue moon on someone like him.

"What? Actually, hold on, let me make Anne this tea and take it around to her. Is she alright?"

"Dude don't worry about the tea; she's gone to sleep. I laid her down on her couch and she's Ok, but you need to hear this!" Manny grabbed Skye's arm and sat her down at the kitchen table.

"She spoke to me."

"See! I tried to tell you guys that the other…"

"No, just listen, it was more than one word."

"What?" Skye's jaw dropped a little. "Like how much? I have only heard her say two words, and I thought *that* was a lot." She looked at him quizzically.

"No Dude, more than two words, like she fully spoke to me."

"This is crazy, did she say anything about the blue haired bitch?"

"Oh yeah. Man, I knew that chick was crazy when I met her the first time…" Manny's head shook like he couldn't believe it himself.

"How many times have you seen her?"

"Only the once, but it turns out, that wasn't the only time Cam saw her." He grabbed Skye's hand from across the table. "That chick is fully crazy, Skye, I don't know what he thought he was doing with her, but she's nuts. I need a cone. Hold on." Manny jumped up and walked back down the hall to his room. Skye could hear the pulling of the bong from the kitchen. Like self-medicating away the reality, he only feels normal once he has his bong. Manny came walking back in a cloud of smoke like the wizard coming out from behind the curtain.

"Ok, so hurry up, what did she say? And why would she speak to you and not me?"

"The 'Clickety Clack' I figured out myself was her recreating the sound of the bitch's high heels walking down the street… It's like she is fucking traumatised! It's like this chick had tormented Anne so much that that's all she'll say now. She didn't give me full detail, it was hard enough getting the little bits out of her that I did get, but that chick has been threatening her for ages. Now, don't freak out, but apparently when Click Cl…sorry, *Anne*, saw her going into our house over a year ago…"

"A YEAR ago?!"

"Yeah, sorry…" He paused before continuing, "Anyway, she noticed what was happening between her and Cam and threatened to tell you about it. Even though we had never spoken to her before, because she said she likes to keep to herself, but she told me she was looking out for 'the sweet girl next door'… Her words not mine." He winked. "Then, the 'click clacking' started."

"Ok, Mann, get to the point." This was intriguing, but Skye was getting impatient waiting for the punchline.

"Ok, so when Anne spoke to her the first time, the blue haired bitch shoved her heel into Anne's throat, just like she did today, and apparently that night a couple of weeks ago when Anne was going off her tree with the 'click clackety clickety clack' and her house was burning down? Remember?"

"How the fuck could I forget, Mann?"

"That was her! That was the blue haired bitch that tried to burn her house down!"

"Holy…" Skye was completely wide eyed and dumb struck. "What the hell?"

"I know right? Bitches be crazy!" Manny was full of so much enthusiasm telling the story and excitement over figuring out why their neighbour had gone mad, that he had forgotten the severity of this situation. The very bad situation.

Skye now realised that Cam hadn't just been seeing some random chicks on the side (as bad as that already was), but he had been shacking up with a fucking psycho for more than a year. A Bat Shit Crazy Fucking Psycho. But what Skye couldn't figure out was: *if she was that obsessed, then why would she even care if I found out? Wouldn't she want to break us up?* But all she could conclude was that Manny was right – bitches be crazy.

"You going to say anything, Skye? Maybe we should ring the police?"

"I'm not really sure what to say, I don't even know what I'm feeling right now. I can't believe this has actually happened and I can't believe it's been over a year since he started jumping ship. How can someone be so obsessed with Cam that they would want to burn down Anne's house just to save me from finding out about it?" Skye was looking at Manny in disbelief at the whole thing. It was like a tornado had come into her life and in just over a week torn everything out from under her. Like everything she knew and everything she was had been torn to shreds leaving nothing but a confused and broken heart. No, she wasn't going to do this. She was *not* going to feel sorry for herself, and she was not going to obsess over some random chick with blue hair. Then it dawned on her...if she came here looking for Cam, then where the hell has Cam been? Who has he been shacking up with for the last week? Because it certainly mustn't be with her, or she wouldn't have come here looking for him. Her mind ticked with questions. The loud ticking of a clock.

Skye let her mind drift back to unhealthy thoughts. She convinced herself to go back to that happy place where she was chopping off his penis and watching him die.

I can't take this anymore.

"Mann, I'm going for a walk. You want to come with me?" Skye stood up and grabbed her bag from the kitchen floor, searched for her wallet, her keys, and her sanity.

About a kilometre from Skye's house is a peaceful lush park. It has massive iron gates at the front of it, which she never understood as there was no fence around the perimeter of the park. But they looked pretty, nonetheless. The perimeter however was lined with trees. There were willows and pines and a big fountain in the centre. Off to one corner was a playground for little kids, and another corner had a pond where ducks would scatter all around awaiting their afternoon snack from the oldies that fed them bread. There were patches of shadows from the trees that danced in the sun light and swayed in the breeze. Lovers sat under willow trees on blankets and fed each other strawberries, while children chose the sunlit sections to kick their ball and play chasey with the butterflies.

Through to the other side of the park on the parallel street was the café that Skye had breakfast in with her dad last week. She didn't want to go there. She would rather shit her pants in public than be anywhere that reminded her of Cam and *that incident*.

"You're imagining hurting Cam again, aren't you?" Manny looked at her with an 'I know that look', look.

"Maybe. Cheer me up."

"You want a joke?"

"Hit me." She said, throwing on a smile like an old jumper. Manny took a deep breath and looked around, searching his memory for a good one.

"Ok, so today at the bank, an old lady asked me to check her balance. So, I pushed her over." Manny started laughing hysterically. Skye chuckled.

"That's fucking horrible, Mann," shaking the smile off her face. "Ok, I've got one. Where do you find a cow with no legs? Right where you left it!" And with that they were both in fits of laughter at the ridiculousness. Manny wasn't too hard to get giggling, but once he starts, his laugh is as infectious as gastro.

Skye and Manny walked around laughing and telling horrible jokes, until out of the blue, something happened; a shift, a strange shift in the universe that neither of them could quite explain.

Skye's blood ran cold. *Was I...no, I couldn't be? Could I be, feeling something for Manny?*

Suddenly her laughing stopped. Suddenly a strange awkwardness came over her like a wave at the beach that she didn't see coming. It hit her in the back and threw her head under the water, tumbling her around and around as she struggled for air. This was Manny. Her best friend, her housemate, the man who has been helping her through a really fucking hard week. She always saw him as a gorgeous looking creature, and an amazing friend, *but it's Manny.*

You're being stupid Skye, stop thinking stupid thoughts.

Manny looked at her with a sideways smile "You alright, Dude?"

Could he tell? Were her thoughts that obvious?

"Yeah, yeah I'm totally fine. Just off with the fairies again." She waved her hand in a gesture of dismissal and had to remind herself to breath. Remind herself that she was just going through a shit time, she has gone through worse, and she didn't need any more penis in her life right now. Skye did a little laugh and a shake of her head trying to jiggle the thoughts away. But, oh, how she found those thoughts captivating …

They got to the other side of the park and sat down on a bench to chill, when Skye's phone started to ring. It wasn't a private number, but unknown anyway.

"Hello?"

A strange voice on the other end asked, "Skye? Is this Skye Mains?"

"This is she." Skye replied, unaware of who the man was at the other end of the phone. He had a deep voice that flowed in a very important fashion. His voice oozed 'I have a very big vocabulary.' All Skye could think was: have I paid all of my bills? Did I get a speeding fine? Who are you?

"This is Doctor Stone from Kanville Hospital, we believe you are the next of kin and contact person for Bradley Mains?"

"Yes." Skye's voice became shaky and confused. Worry took over each limb and numbed her senses.

"What's happened to my dad?"

"He has had a fall which caused a slight concussion on impact, I assure you he's ok, but could you come to the emergency department at the hospital please?"

"Yes, yes sure, I… I am coming right now."

"Thank you, Miss Mains, goodbye."

Skye hung up the phone and turned to Manny who had a look of worry on his precious face.

"What is it?" He had his palms turned up as if he were feeling the first of the summer rains.

"It's my dad, I have to go, he's at the hospital."

Manny stood up, "Do you want me to come with you? I don't care, I'm coming…"

"No, Manny, it's all good, you stay here, or go home, it's only a couple of blocks, I'm just going to run around and make sure he is ok." She didn't want him to come, but Manny looked concerned.

"It's ok, seriously, I will see you later at home. Thanks Manny." Skye gave him a hug and left him standing at the bench in the park, watching her run towards the hospital and leaving behind the events of the day, crashing towards the next thing that she hoped wouldn't break her heart.

Gypsy

CHAPTER 10

Well, this was not how Gypsy expected to see her dad for the first time. He was currently laying in a hospital bed, awake, and wanting to get the hell out of there. Gypsy could totally understand. She didn't want to be there either. But she was the one that jumped. She jumped off her tightrope even though she knew she didn't have a parachute, she still jumped. Gypsy made this choice, now she had to live with it. She sunk deeper into the filthy hospital chair beside Brad's bed. *Shit, I need a drink.*

"I'm fine." He said to the nurse for the fifth time "Just let me go!" Gypsy was starting to wonder if it was the hospital or *her,* he was trying to run from. But then the thought came crashing down on Gypsy like a welcomed tidal wave…he didn't know who she was! Gypsy relished in the realisation that he wouldn't know she was the one that sent the letter. For all he knows, she was just some random person walking by his house and happened to see him right before he fell down the steps. Then followed him to the hospital…

Creepy much? No, fuck it, I'm in the clear. I'm feeling better. I can do this. The ball is in my court, this court is my bitch. I am the queen of this motherfucking court! But little did she know...he knew exactly who she was...Gypsy was so wrapped up in her own thoughts that she didn't realise he was still talking to the nurse.

"Look, Mr. Mains, you suffered a concussion when you fell. We can't let you go until the doctor has cleared you. If you insist on leaving before that, then you will need to sign an AMA form stating that you understand you are leaving against medical advice."

Gypsy started to stammer, she didn't know where the words came from, but suddenly they were flowing out of her mouth like stinky tap water, "Dad, I mean Brad! ... I meant Brad..." *Wow,* "I don't think you should go unless they say you're fine to leave."

"She's right." The nurse said. "We have contacted your next of kin and she should be here shortly."

Brad's face turned white as the nurse left the room. He was staring at Gypsy not saying a word. He looked like he was in pain.

Fuck it Gyps, you're the one that jumped.

"So, um, hi." She waved, like an idiot, and continued on, "This might come as a bit of a shock, but considering you are already in a hospital bed, you won't fall far, will you? Haha" She attempted to joke and brighten the mood with her awkwardness, but Brad only continued to stare.

"So, um, my name's Gypsy..." She pushed her hand towards his to exchange what could only be described as the world's most nervous handshake, and waited for the shock to set in.

"I know." He said, staring. Just flat-faced staring.

"So, you got my letter then?" Gypsy instantly felt like a dickhead. Of course, he got her letter, he replied to her letter. So here she was, feeling like a complete knob, yet again.

"Yeah, I did." He paused. "I was shocked, I really wasn't expecting it." He smiled at her, but she was so confused, she didn't know if he wanted her there, or if she should go.

"I'm sorry for dropping in out of the blue, do you want me to go?" Gypsy was so uncomfortable. She just wanted him to say yes, *begged* him to say yes, that he wants her to go.

"No, not at all, please stay." He smiled again. Gypsy's insides just blew up.

Whatever I'm made of, it's everywhere now.

"Hold on, how did you know who I was?"

Now Brad was the one that looked uncomfortable. He looked at her for the longest moment. The sounds of the hospital, the beeping of machines, the cries, the nurses chatting quietly at the nurse's station, and doctors whooshing past their open door; they all sounded clearer at this moment. Gypsy could hear a mosquito buzzing around the window to the outside world, a world that had not seen nervousness like this. She didn't even know Brad, so she didn't feel comfortable staring at him while he waded through his awkward moment. *Look away, Gyps.*

"You look like your mum." He said, finally.

Your mum. The words floated around in her head looking for a place to land. Should they land on her hopeful heart? No. Should they land on one of her dying brain cells? Yes, please. She didn't know why, but for some reason she had never felt unhappy towards her biological father for giving her up, she had saved all of her abandonment issues and the pain that goes with it, for her biological mother. She felt crazy feeling this way, because she never even met these two strangers. But there was a strong feeling inside of her that felt a mother should be the one that never lets go. Gypsy grew up with a lot of kids at her school that only had a mother, and the father went god knows where, maybe down the shop for a pack of smokes never to return, maybe found their secretary a bit more enjoyable and skipped town, or there simply was no story, he just wasn't there. So, in her mind, she was more hurt that her mother gave her up. But she never blamed the dad. And she didn't know why. She understood that they shouldn't get away with being pricks just because they are men, but society had made her believe that 'boys will be boys', and it's a ridiculous concept. Why should they get away with everything because they have different genitals? A male and a female should be treated the same no matter what the crime. She could feel the anger pushing towards the surface and forced it down. Maybe she was just protecting herself by focusing all of her energy on one parent just so that she could let her emotions loose, but still be able to hold on to the other parent, because she didn't want to hate them both.

"Oh, ok." Gypsy sat awkwardly. "So, you have someone coming for you?" She questioned.

"Yes. My next of kin is my daughter, Skye. I would have liked to spend a bit of time getting to know you before introducing you to her. She doesn't actually know about you, I never mentioned you before. But she was an only child and I think it will be a really fantastic surprise." Brad looked hopeful. "She always wanted a sister." But behind his eyes Gypsy could see doubt smothered in fear.

"Look, Brad, I'm not sure about this. I mean, I only just met you, I don't really think I am ready to be somebody's unwanted surprise…"

"No, no it will be fine," he waved his hands dismissively, "She's going to meet you one day anyway, why not today? I'm excited to have had you drop by my house; I have waited so long to meet you. Yes, I fell down like a fool, and yes, I got a concussion from the fall, but trust me, this is still one of the happiest days of my life."

Brad actually had a tear in his eye. Gypsy wondered if maybe he was serious. She didn't feel special. Was she? *Ok, focus Gypsy. This can go either way.*

"Brad, thank you, but I don't think I'm ready."

"Please, Gypsy? This would mean the world to me?"

Gypsy knew puppy dog eyes didn't affect her. So why were Brad's puppy dog eyes affecting her now? *Damn it.*

"Ok, as long as you are sure it is going to be ok. If she looks even slightly unhappy, I am leaving, ok? I haven't even had a chance to talk to you properly yet."

Brad laughed "True, true. Gypsy, just breath, you will be fine." His words were followed by a very supportive smile. Strangely, in that moment Gypsy felt at ease. She felt as if there was some spiritual connection, as if she had known him her whole life.

"Do you want to have a chat with her first and make sure she even wants to meet me? I can go down to the cafeteria or something?" Let's face facts, Gypsy was shitting herself.

Brad looked away and thought for a second. Turning back to her he said, "That might not be such a bad idea. I can get one of the nurses to come get you after I have spoken to her."

Suddenly the door opened. *Fuck. Too late.* If there was anything in the tank, Gypsy would have actually shit herself.

"Dad! Oh my god, are you Ok?" Skye, a girl with long blonde hair that looked sweaty and stressed, ran into the room and Gypsy could swear she could feel all the blood in her body thumping through her skin. Gypsy's face went red and was now the one that felt a little faint. Skye didn't even notice her as she ran towards her dad and gave him a massive hug. She hugged him so tight he let out a little squeak. Gypsy looked at the door and considered sneaking out, manoeuvring around the furniture like a lizard in the night before anyone noticed she was even there. But just as she went over her escape plan, she heard Brad speak, still squished under this blonde girl he called Skye.

"Skye, Honey, I'm fine, but I want you to meet someone..." He rubbed his forehead, "This is Gypsy."

Skye let loose her dad and stood up slowly. Gypsy took a deep breath, put on her best inviting smile – *I am a lovely person, sorry for the surprise* – and put her hand out for a handshake.

Skye turned towards her.

Gypsy smiled. *Holy shit, I have a sister. My heart is thumping…*

Three Worlds Collide

CHAPTER 11

Skye turned to Gypsy, and as if in slow motion her face turned into that of a stunned fish as it gets ripped out of the water. Her world stood still as she saw Gypsy standing in front of her, next to her dad's hospital bed. *Holy fuck*, she thought, *it's the girl from the café! The girl Cam was with!*

Skye dove over the bed towards Gypsy "Who the fuck are you?!" She screamed, grabbing Gypsy's shirt and ripping her towards herself trying to slap Gypsy as she struggled and fought to get away. Arms were being slung in every direction and eyes were burning with rage.

"Woah, hold on, what the hell is going on?" Brad tried to pull the two apart.

Gypsy was in total shock, *what is this girl's problem?!*

"What? You're here to fuck my dad too?!" Skye screamed.

"What the hell are you talking about? You're fucking crazy, bitch!" By this time Gypsy was panting, Skye was panting, and Brad was using all of his strength to keep Skye from ripping Gypsy apart.

"Sit down! Both of you!" He yelled.

The nurse came into the room in horror, "What is happening in here? Pull yourselves together! We have sick people trying to sleep. If you can't control yourselves, I will throw you both out, right now!" The Nurse was about 50 and looked like she would have no trouble at all grabbing both girls by their ears and tossing them out onto the street.

Gypsy took a step back from Skye and Skye grabbed her bag and ran out of the room.

There was complete and utter silence as looks were thrown from Brad to Gypsy and both of them to the nurse.

"Are you done?" She demanded.

"Yes, done." Gypsy said as she sat down and put her head in her shaking hands.

The nurse left the room in a huff, but not before throwing a glare of warning in Gypsy's direction.

"What was that all about?" Brad asked

"I honestly have no idea!" Gypsy said, feeling defeated and confused. She shook her head and got up. No, she couldn't do this.

"Have you two met before?" Brad asked clearly interested and just as confused as Gypsy. They both thought back to their conversation only minutes ago. Gypsy should have left the room sooner. But why was Skye in so much shock? *Why did she want to kill me?* Gypsy thought.

"I've never seen her before in my life, but she seemed to know me! Or am I crazy? You hadn't even told her I was your daughter. I am so confused…" Gypsy trailed off. She had had enough. She wanted out.

Brad tried to calm her down. He wasn't about to lose her again. "Please don't go, I will give her a call, I will ask her to come back and talk to me. I want to figure this out. I can't leave things like this Gyps; I have just got you back after 32 years." Brad could hear the cracks forming in his heart.

Now Gypsy felt that unusual feeling again, she felt sadness overcome her. She didn't want him to be sad, and she certainly didn't want to leave things this way either because she probably wouldn't see either of them again. No, she would go to the closest pub and drink herself into a stupor. *Fuck yes*, she thought, *next stop – oblivion.*

"Can I get your number please? I will ring her, and I will see why she did that, I swear she is not usually like that, I mean, I have never seen her like that before. She is usually the sweetest person and it takes a lot to even get her slightly upset with someone, so trust me, I am just as mystified as you."

Gypsy breathed in deeply. She wasn't sure if it was such a good idea, she felt as if she had just destroyed someone's life, but she had no idea how. Her day started off so much better than this. She reached into her bag and pulled out a scrap of paper and a blue pen. She scribbled her number on it and handed it to this man who had given her up at birth, a man whom she had just met, and she kept reminding herself – *I chose to jump.*

"Thank you, Gypsy, I will call you once I figure out what just happened." He paused. "I'm really glad you turned up today, even if it did turn into a catastrophe." Both

Gypsy and Brad laughed together for the first time in their lives.

Skye was in a state of fury. She was running and running trying to find her way home through the crowds of people on the street. They all seemed so happy, and a few of them took the time to look at her like she was some kind of crazed person as she fled past them in a cloud of sweat and anger.

All she could think was – *why the fuck was Cam's mistress in my dad's hospital room?*

The tears were flowing furiously from her eyes and were thrown off into the dust she left behind. She ran from street to street until she reached the park. Here is where she will stop. Here is where she will stop and gather her thoughts, her breath, and her sanity. Skye thought that this woman who had taken her Cameron from her was now trying to take her dad. She could feel that this woman must be out to get her. "Why is she doing this to me?!" She breathed the words out in a silent cry as she flopped to the ground.

"Holy shit, Skye, what happened?" She heard Manny's voice like it was a gift from above.

"Manny? You're still here?" Skye looked up to see Manny walking towards her. Manny laid down beside her on the grass and grabbed her hand.

"I was still over on the seat, Dude, I was talking to my mum on the phone when I saw you flying across the park in a hot mess, how's your dad? Is he ok? What's happened?"

Skye was still trying to catch her breath. "He's fine."

"Are you sure? You don't look like he was fine." Manny looked at her like she was crazy.

"Well, he might not be fine once I'm done with him. The nurse told me he fell and gave himself a concussion when he hit the ground, but when I went into the room, you wouldn't believe who was in there."

"Am I supposed to guess?" His eyes were glued to hers in a state of confusion.

"That fucking slut I saw Cam kissing in the café last week!" Skye started crying again, she felt like maybe she *was* going crazy. Manny sat up in shock.

"You're shitting me?! What do you think that means? I mean, like, how would your dad know her?" Manny was shaking his head back and forth staring at the grass. Apart from his head uncontrollably moving, the rest of his body was motionless. "Is your dad… is he…?"

Skye swung her head in Manny's direction "I don't know! It certainly looks that way!"

"Hold on, hold on, now I think you should probably talk to your dad before you go jumping to any crazy conclusions. Come on Skye, you are the queen of giving people the benefit of the doubt. Do you want me to ring him for you?"

"No. It's up to me. Just give me a little while."

Manny looked at her "Skye, the longer you wait, the longer you will be sad. Honestly, it's probably nothing and you're going to spend your whole day upset over something that may not even be right. Dude don't bring bad vibes into your soul where they don't belong. Ok?"

Skye thought Mann was right. She wished she could think as clearly as him. As much as she tries to stay positive, sometimes where Mann sees a sunny day, Skye struggles through the clouds.

"Ok, fine. I'll ring him. But you're not moving!" She said grabbing Manny's hand and keeping a firm grip.

"I'm not going anywhere" Manny smiled at her. *Those beautiful white teeth.* She was feeling that odd feeling again. *Look away Skye!* She looked away.

"Ok. Shh" Skye dialled the number to her dad's mobile and laid back down on the grass, watching the trees above her. The sky was growing darker with grey clouds and she thought this appropriate for the situation. She was still seething at the thought of that woman standing next to her dad. *Gypsy. What a stupid name*, she thought.

The phone rang and went to message bank. Skye decided she didn't want to leave a message; Fuck that! It's obviously a sign that she needs to give it some time, she needs to calm down first. But all she could taste was metal. She could taste metal in her mouth and feel acid in her brain. Her head hurt and her eyes burned like a fire. Skye put down the phone just as it started ringing again.

Shit. Ok, deep breaths.

"Hi Dad." She said solemnly.

"Skye, how are you?" Brad sounded deeply concerned.

"I don't know. You tell me."

"Skye, don't be like that."

"Seriously Dad, who is that chick? She doesn't look much older than me! Are you having a midlife crisis or something?"

Brad realised what Skye was getting at and desperately needed to address the elephant in the room. The elephant that wasn't even there but Skye seemed to think it was.

"She's not who you think she is," Brad said, "she's your sister." And just as Brad said it, his entire body filled with pins and needles. "I wanted to tell you when you got here, you know, without her in the room, but it all fell apart and I guess the timing was really shit."

Sister?

"Hold on, I have a sister?" Skye's head was swimming, or more floating, slowly losing momentum. She could drown quite happily right now. Fuck it, she could stick a fork in a power point and call it a day. Her supposed 'sister' was the woman who Cam was cheating on her with? *No, it can't be right. No way.*

"Yes. She's 32 and I wanted to have this conversation in person with you, Skye. Can you come back to the hospital? Please? Gypsy has gone."

"Is she coming back?"

"No."

Skye looked to Manny and felt a sense of security. "Okay," she said. "I'll be there soon." She hung up the phone.

"Manny, you're coming with me."

"Where?"

"The hospital."

"Hi Dad" Skye said as she entered the room that had not long before been the stage for a one-on-one brawl.

"How are you feeling?"

"Fine" He said.

"You remember Manny?" Skye said as Manny waved and sat in the chair in the corner.

"Hey, Mr. Mains."

"Hi Manny, how are you going, Mate?"

"Better than you by the looks of it." Manny gestured towards Brad and his hospital bed.

"So, tell me Skye, what the hell was that all about? You treated her like she killed your cat."

"I'm sorry Dad, I thought she was your girlfriend or something..."

"Really, Skye?" Brad shook his head. "What do you take me for? Is that why you jumped her and tried to rip her teeth out?"

"No, actually..." Skye looked at Manny for support and strength, then continued "...Cam has been cheating on me..."

Brad's left eye started twitching. "What?! I'm going to kill him." He seethed. His teeth gripped shut and a vein started popping out of his forehead. Skye and Manny probably think he is joking, but he knew damn well that he wasn't.

"...With her, that Gypsy girl." Skye continued.

Suddenly the room filled with a chill and the nurse came running in to shut the windows. "Rains-a-coming." She said in a jollier voice than before.

No-one moved for fear of spooking the beast that was Brad Mains. Manny sat awkwardly across from the bed and stared back and forth from Brad to Skye, and then back to Brad, while Skye stared at her father waiting for a response to what she had just told him, while also trying to process the new information she had learned herself. *What a fucking day*, she thought, and assumed everyone in the room was thinking the same thing.

"Well, do you think she knew he had a girlfriend?" Brad questioned, playing devil's advocate.

"How am I supposed to know?" Skye said, completely honestly, how would she know?

Brad was tormented with the thought of having to talk to Gypsy about this. He had already lied to her about how he knew her instantly when she stood on his front lawn – he wasn't exactly going to admit that he had watched over her for the past 32 years, without making any form of communication, because she would probably never want to speak to him again.

"Let me talk to her" He said. Not that he wanted to bring such negativity into such a new and raw situation.

"No. Stuff that. Let me talk to her." Skye was running on adrenaline still. She wasn't scared of anything right now.

"Seriously? Is that such a great idea?" Manny jumped into the conversation from his corner seat.

"Yeah, why not? I've got nothing left to lose. Anyway, aren't I the queen of fucking optimism?" Skye shrugged her shoulders and left her face as straight as the line she was about to walk.

Brad sat uncomfortably in his bed. He wasn't sure if he wanted to side with Manny or Skye. Was it a stupid idea? Was it ludicrous? Or was it brilliance disguised as surrender?

CHAPTER 12

Gypsy was full of emotion. Not good emotion, but the kind of bad emotion that really made her want to scream at the top of her lungs. She had the windows down and it was one of the vary rare occasions that she didn't have music playing in her car. She stared at the road as if there was nothing but the white lines, broken then straight, doubled then gone.

She drove from Kanville back to High Tide in a daze as if her emotions were so scrambled that she herself could not even decipher which was which. Her body wanted to scream, and her heart wanted to cry. Her mind was a mass of images – claws grabbing at her, and strangers made of the same blood as her but from another space in time. The same genes, the same eyes, but did they have the same hearts? She felt like an idiot as she let her car go faster than the speed limit across the western road home that curved and swung with the body of the edge of the world. The ocean beyond the trees reminded her of that peaceful time throughout her childhood and brought a little harmony to her shaking hands, and the wind in her hair helped wash out some of the hurt that plagued her mind.

Could this be fate? She thought to herself - *could this be the universe telling me I was better off not knowing, and just being happy with my adoptive family who so caringly took me in when I was an infant and couldn't make such stupid judgment calls for myself?*

Almost twenty minutes from home and Gypsy needed a distraction, so she decided to stop at the pub for a white wine and some food. Now usually pub food would bring the mouth-watering feeling before she even got there, but today, she got the salad. She knew when she got back home Haz would most likely drag her to Frank's for a burger, so she needed to stock up on healthy food.

Gypsy sat across from a little family playing with their two small children that looked around 2 and 4 years old. They were giggling and kept running back to steal another chip from the bowls on their table as their parents would tickle them under the arm and pretend it wasn't them who did the tickling. Gypsy watched these kids, who looked so loved and free, giggling and running in circles around their parents while their parents wore smiles of joy and happiness. Not just happy smiles, but the kind you see on billboards with pure white teeth and hair groomed to perfection. If anyone was to sell happiness, this family was the picture-perfect brochure.

Kids don't have the stresses a normal adult does - not that Gypsy considered herself a normal adult the majority of the time, not for lack of trying, though - she still had bills and responsibilities, kind of. Her parents bought her house and give her a weekly wage as they say she is 'in between jobs', even though they know that's bullshit.

Gypsy knew that she was lazy, and she knew that she had problems that needed to be fixed, but she didn't really feel that she needed to push herself to change as her parents didn't really care. They felt that if they just gave her money then she would feel loved and looked after. They were very busy people, and anyway, they had no time to give her real attention.

Gypsy was interrupted by a plate being shoved under her nose.

"Caesar Salad?" The young girl said as she put the bowl down.

"Yeah, thanks" Gypsy said, not even looking at the girl.

"Are you ok?" The girl asked.

"Fine, why?" Gypsy threw back.

"Well, you're, umm, crying?" The girl said as if it were a question.

It was only then that Gypsy realised she had mascara filled tears running down her face. Her face was as motionless as a lake on a full moon night, but her eyes had been pouring without her even noticing. The little kids had stopped playing and were sitting on their parents' laps eating their chips in quiet all the while throwing sideways looks at Gypsy. How did she not even realise this?

"I'm fine, thanks." Gypsy said, shooing the waitress away. She grabbed one of the napkins from the middle of the table and tried to wipe her tears away as casually as she could without bringing any more unwanted attention to herself. *This is ridiculous*, she thought. She's sitting in a beautiful beer garden with trees, and happiness, and Caesar salad, and wine. What more could she want?

Out of nowhere, to break the sounds of music in the background and croutons crunching in her mouth, came the sound of her phone. *For fucks sake.* She wished everyone would just leave her alone. She wished that a giant whale would swallow her up whole so that she could be consumed into its belly with her salad and be able to eat and drink in peace.

"More wine?" the waiter would ask inside the whale's belly.

"Yes please, Sir, I would love another." Gypsy would say courteously. And she would watch the little mini whale waiter waddle off back into the whale throat to fetch her some more wine. *If only life were so simple*, she sighed.

"Hello?" She said, impatiently.

"Gypsy?"

"…Yeah?" Gypsy cocked her head. "Brad?"

"Yeah it's me. I'm sorry things got so bad at the hospital. Look, I've had a chance to talk to Skye…"

Here we go. "And?"

"…This is going to be a strange question. I'm not really sure how to…"

"Just ask it Brad."

"Have you been seeing anyone?" Brad shot the words out like a bullet.

Gypsy scrunched her face.

"What? Yeah you weren't wrong there. Why the super strange question, Brad?" She was mystified.

"I'm just… well I need to know if you have been, and if his name happens to be Cameron?"

There was a silence on the phone from both ends. They could hear each other breathing deeply. Gypsy spoke quietly and slowly.

"Umm, yes. Ok, you're weirding me out, do you know him? He's just some guy I met like a week or two ago…what's the problem?" Now Gypsy's ears were pricked, *what the fuck is happening?*

"Ok, so this is going to be a bit strange, it's a very fucking small world." He laughed nervously, almost like it was a joke "Look, Skye is here, and she wants to talk to you. Can you talk to her? Please, Gypsy?"

There was a muffled noise on the other end of the phone like it was moving around. But before Gypsy had the chance to respond she was thrown into the snake pit.

"Gypsy?" Skye said.

"Hello?" Gypsy's heart was racing, bringing back the feelings of only a couple of hours ago when Skye was clawing at her.

"Gypsy, how long have you been seeing Cameron for?" She asked.

"Like I just said to Brad, like a week or two, why? Is there some kind of problem? And why the hell is it any of your business?" She snapped

"Because he's my fucking boyfriend!" Skye yelled into the phone.

"No, he's not." Gypsy snapped back "He doesn't have a girlfriend!"

"Of course he's going to tell you that!" Skye yelled "Why the fuck would he say he has a girlfriend while he is trying to get into your pants?"

"You're fucking crazy." Gypsy said. She had to remove herself from the beer garden and walk around the side of the pub as she was creating a scene in front of the picture-perfect family.

"Then do one thing for me, I think you owe me that." Skye said.

"Why should I do anything for you? You're accusing me of sleeping with your boyfriend!" Gypsy said.

"And imagine if I'm right! If it is my Cam that you have been seeing then I want you to ask him if he knows a girl named 'Skye' and trust me, just watch his reaction. I'm telling you now, he will scratch his face." Skye was on the other end shaking her head in disbelief at the absurdity of the situation.

"Look, if you're right, then I am sorry!" Gypsy said. "I didn't know he had a girlfriend. But I think you're wrong, and if you're wrong then I want a fucking apology." *The nerve of her…*

"Gypsy, did you meet up with him in a café in Kanville last week?"

Gypsy's jaw dropped. How would she know that? *Has she been watching me?* Now, she started to believe Skye and everything she was saying. *Fuck.*

"Ok, fine, whatever, I'll ask him if he knows 'a girl named Skye.'" Gypsy huffed into the phone. "Look, I got to go. My Caesar salad's going cold. Bye."

Gypsy hung up the phone and walked back to her table in the beer garden. The family had left, and the waitress was cleaning up the tables.

"Hey," She grabbed the girl's attention "Where did my salad go?" Gypsy gestured towards the table she was sitting at 5 minutes earlier.

"Oh my god, I'm so sorry, I thought you had gone." The girl looked a little distraught.

"Are you fucking kidding me?!" Gypsy looked at her all saucepan eyed and threw her hands in the air. She was having a terrible bloody day.

When Skye got off the phone, she handed it back to Brad and said, "It's absolutely Cam."

"Are you sure?" Manny said, still sitting in his corner.

"Yeah, are you sure?" Brad asked.

"I can feel it in my bones. Too many things add up. The proof is in the asshole flavoured pudding. I know she was definitely the girl I saw him with. But the thing is…I don't think she realised he had a girlfriend. So, there's that."

"So really it's not her fault? I mean you can't get angry at her when she had no idea, right?" Brad said. But even though Brad was right, it still sat better with Skye to hate Gypsy as well, since she was the person he cheated on her with. She thought about Gypsy and wondered; *why her?* The pain was all too much. She thought she was slowly getting over it all with her daydreams about snapping his neck and boiling him alive in hot lava, but it seems the pain was still there. The hurt and the torment of years of her life wasted on someone she thought she loved. And as much as she tried to fight it, her brain would always lead her towards those memories of laughter and love, looking into each other's eyes as if the rest of the world didn't exist. She thought he only saw her. How wrong she was.

"I don't know anymore." Skye sighed. "Dad, are you going to be alright if I go home? I'm so done with today. I will give you a call in the morning." Skye was exhausted.

"I'm fine, Honey, you just go home, have a sleep, and we will sort all of this out in the morning. I mean it has been a massive day, I really am so sorry, but I never really knew if I would get the chance to meet Gypsy, or if I would ever have the courage to introduce you to her. It all just went out of my control today. I just wish it had all gone a different way; A better way." Brad reached out to give her a hug from his hospital bed.

"Look, I know it ended up being a tremendously shit situation, but we have time, you know? We have all the time in the world for you two to meet again and maybe settle your differences. I would really like for us both to get to know Gypsy, and I guess give her a chance to be part of our family." He sighed. "You always did want a sister, Skye."

"What happened, Dad? Like, she is a lot older than me, but she's not Mum's, is she?"

"No, Skye, she wasn't your mum's. I had her with a girl I knew when I was 16 years old. We gave her up for adoption because we were simply too young. We couldn't give her a life worth living at that age, and it was one of the hardest things I have ever done."

"Aside from losing Mum." Skye said sadly not moving her gaze from the floor.

"Yes." Brad nodded and looked down as well.

"What happened to your girlfriend?" Skye asked.

"Drugs." Brad simply said like it explained everything. And it did. "Giving up a baby is an extremely hard thing to do, even when you know it is the right decision. It was hard on the both of us, but where I threw myself into a carpentry apprenticeship, she found other ways to numb the pain. But," he continued, "when I met your mother my world exploded. She was the light at the end of a tunnel that I didn't realise I was stuck in until I saw her at the other end."

Skye got a little smile remembering her mother's face.

"Look, I'm thinking about taking a little trip. I think it would be good if you both came with me. It would give you guys a good chance to get to know each other." Brad had settled on the plan that he needed to get out of town. Since the men he had killed were officially missing, he needed to flee the scene of the crime. Gypsy had just come back into his life, so now he had two daughters he was obligated to protect from seeing his face splashed across the six o'clock news. He had to get out, go somewhere safe until the whole thing settled down – *right out in the middle of the bush where no one could find me*, he thought.

"A trip? Where?" Skye probed.

"I was thinking we could go on a camping trip." Brad said this with fake enthusiasm knowing that Skye wouldn't want to go camping, but he had to be convincing. There was a part of him that didn't want them to go with him in case things went sour, but his selfish side took over, and he needed as much time with them as he could get before his world fell apart.

"Serious? Dad, you just got a concussion from falling over and you want to go camping? With bugs and wild animals and spiders and snakes and…"

"It will be fun!" Brad cut her off with a big smile.

Skye was not into camping, nor was she into snakes and spiders and bugs.

"I am going to call Gypsy tomorrow and invite her."

"Dad, no."

"I don't want to hear it Skye, this will be fun. Look, she is not the villain in your life, she is the victim. She had no idea Cam was with you, it's not her fault, and she is now realising that some guy she may have liked has turned out to be a piece of shit. The sooner you get that through your head the sooner you can get over it. What Cameron did to you was unforgivable, he is slime, he is the chewing gum stuck on the bottom of your shoe, and he is certainly not worth wasting anymore of your breath over." Brad said this sternly but powerfully.

"I don't know." Skye said "I need time to think. I'm going. I will call you in the morning."

"Love you, Honey." Brad said and hugged her goodbye. "You look after my girl, Manny" He said to Manny as they shook hands.

"Will do, Brad. Get better soon."

And with that Manny and Skye were gone, leaving Brad to his thoughts; Too many thoughts crawling around in his head, scratching at his skull and flashing images of his future.

Gypsy walked into her house in a daze. The sun had gone down, and the house was all lit up with fairy lights and candles.

She walked through her front door and called out to Haz. "Haz, Mate, I'm home!"

"Gyps!" Haz called out from the lounge room "Come here Mate, I missed you!"

Gypsy rolled her eyes but accompanied it with a smile. She walked into her loungeroom ready for a beer or ten and saw Haz sitting on the floor with Cam playing cards and drinking scotch.

Damn, I almost forgot he was here.

Cam looked up to her and beamed a big smile "Hey, how was your day? I have a surprise for you." He got up and grabbed her hand, walking her into her bedroom. The room was full of flickering candles and he had strung fairy lights all over the ceiling above her bed.   Her bed was covered in rose petals and there was a funny smell wafting up her nose.

"What's that smell?" She asked.

"Ahh, that's part of the surprise." Cam opened a brown paper bag that was sitting on her bed. He pulled out a bottle of white wine, two boxes of fried chicken and some hot chips wrapped in paper. It looked as though it had been sitting there for a while because she could see the grease had soaked through the paper making it almost transparent. Gypsy thought back to her Caesar salad and wished she had got to finish eating it.

"Why?"

"Just because, I wanted to hear all about your day, I thought this might be romantic?" He said this like it was a question.

All Gypsy desired right now was to get to the bottom of this whole Skye thing, and figure out what was happening. Was Skye right? Was this her Cam? She didn't know, but she felt sick. Fuck it, she didn't care, she had only known this guy for a little over a week, and if Skye was telling her the truth then she wanted to get him the hell out of her house.

"Cam, I need to ask you something…" Gypsy said.

"Hold on, let me get some plates." Cam ran off to the kitchen and Gypsy stood biting her lip like it produced morphine to help get her through this awkward conversation.

"Here." Cam came back into the room and handed her a plate. He looked so innocent she wasn't sure if she wanted to question him, because what if she was wrong?

What if Skye was hallucinating them together in the cafe? Though, she *was* in the café… But it would just make it seem as though she didn't trust Cam, and she really liked him. Gypsy was full of anguish, but she soldiered on. Mumma didn't raise no quitter.

"So, Cam, I need to ask you something." She said not looking at him, but then realised it's better to see his face expression, and if he scratched. Skye told her to watch for that. "This might seem stupid, but just be honest, please." She was feeling nervous. She grabbed the white wine and drank straight from the bottle. *Argh, its warm. But still better than nothing.*

"Just ask, its ok, I won't bite." Cam chuckled "Unless you want me to."

Gypsy watched him wink at her and felt herself cringe. *Maybe this guy is a creep.*

"Do you know someone called Skye?" *Don't look away, don't look away.*

And just like that, BAM! she knew the answer. He didn't even have to speak any words; she could see it all over his face. His face that seemed to drain of all blood cells in a matter of seconds. He was as white as a ghost and his hand went straight to his cheek as if scratching an itchy spot that wasn't there. His eyes darted like ping pong balls back and forth, to her and to the door of the room. Was he trying to escape? This was incredible to watch. Cam opened his mouth and then shut it again. Then it was almost like something clicked, he changed his entire persona and spoke.

"Skye? No, I don't know any Skye…" He scrunched up his nose, squinted his eyes and shook his head as if in utter confusion. "…Why are you asking that?"

Gypsy looked at this guy she hadn't known for very long and felt in this very moment that she didn't even know him at all.

"Wow," she said shaking her head, "Get the fuck out of my house."

"What? Why? Because I don't know someone called Skye?" Cam said, his voice rising with the heat of the room.

"I met my dad today Cam, and guess who else I met? Go on, have a guess." She laughed.

"I don't know. Some person called Skye?" he said raising his shoulders pretending to be confused, but he was such a bad liar.

"BINGO! I met my *SISTER*, Skye!" She said emphasising the word 'sister'. "I also found out that you cheated on her with me!" She laughed again as if insanity was taking over.

Cam looked at her stunned. No words were coming out of his mouth and he looked completely defeated. As his body fell back on the bed and he sat with his hands curled up in his lap, Haz walked into the room. "What's all the yelling?... Wow, this looks nice!" He stared at all the candles and fairy lights. "Ooh, food…"

"Not now Haz." Gypsy said and shook her head at him. "Actually, you know what? Yes, now. Can you help me get this piece of shit out of our house?"

Cam looked at Haz and then over to Gypsy.

"But, I've got nowhere to go." He said this almost pleading. She could see his eyes start to glisten as if tears were in the early stages of creating a mess all over his face. But she had no care at all. She had lost all compassion and only wanted him gone.

"So, this is why you asked to stay with me? Because you got kicked out of your house?" The penny had dropped, and Gypsy had figured it all out. "There was no plumbing issue was there? You fucking SCUM-bag."

She looked to Haz, "Haz, I want him out!"

Haz walked over to Cam and looked him in the eyes for half a second. "Sorry, bro."

"He's not your bro Haz, he's not anything." She looked at Cam and pointed her finger to the door "NOW!"

Cam got up off the bed and grabbed his bag. He started filling it with all his dirty clothes and other possessions.

"Fuck both of you." He mumbled and walked towards the front door. Haz glared at him as he held open the door for Cam to go through.

"Hold on." Gypsy said, and she ran back into her room grabbing the oil-soaked paper bag, "And take your crappy food!" She said hurling it at his head, letting loose fried chicken and chips all over her front steps. She didn't care, why would she? "And stay the fuck away!" She shouted.

Haz and Gypsy stood there and watched him walk away mumbling obscenities under his breath.

The night was otherwise peaceful. The air was crisp and the sky was full of so many stars it was enough to distract Gypsy, if only for a moment. They stood in silence as the madness in Gypsy's head calmed and her heart slowed back to normal. "Skye was right."

"So, are you going to tell me what that was all about?" Haz spoke.

"Another day, Bud. For now, I need a fucking drink."

Haz and Gypsy walked back inside closing the door behind them, like closing a chapter of her life. Though it was only a small chapter, she couldn't believe it turned out the way it did. She really liked him until it all fell apart and he turned out to be an arsehole, but she was glad it only took her a week to find out. She couldn't imagine being Skye and having a long-term relationship before finding out he was such a fucker. So, she decided to unfold the dog-eared corners of this chapter and not look back. She will look at this as only a week or two of wasted time. And she will talk to Skye tomorrow.

CHAPTER 13

Brad woke up in his hospital bed and listened to the doctor tell him he was free to go. It was sunny again and the lack of clouds in the sky brought him fresh hope for a new start with his daughters. He was excited to get the fuck out of this bleach filled hospital room and get organised. He made a mental list of everything he would need for this façade that he called a 'camping trip'. But the one thing he had to convince himself to leave behind, was his fear. Skye could read him too well; she would sense something was wrong and would not give up until he spilled the beans.

The authorities hadn't found him yet to ask any questions, which had Brad holding back on feeling any form of relief, as he knew that eventually they would find his connection with the McGill brothers. He knew Carly - Gypsy's biological mother - had two good reasons to dob him in; the bracelet and her comatose boyfriend that Brad so lovingly belted to near death. The bracelet had been kept at her parent's house all these years and was saved for them both as an incentive for Carly to give up the drugs. Even once Brad had split up from her, his efforts to convince them to sell the bracelet so he could get his share only fell on deaf ears. He was refused time after time and told the bracelet would not move until their daughter was clean and sober. But when he first received that letter from Gypsy wanting to get in contact, he knew he had to take it – he wanted it to be hers. He wanted to give it to her as, what? An apology for giving her up? He wasn't sure, but he felt it only seemed right that she be the one to end up with it.

Brad had watched the house for a few weeks, waiting for the right time to break in. His opportunity had come when he noticed Carly's parents packing for what looked like a mini getaway. But what he hadn't planned on, was Carly and Jeffery house sitting. The fight was a furious one leaving both men battered and bloody, but luckily for Brad, he wasn't the one who ended up in the coma. So as Jeffery lay on the ground unconscious and Carly screamed after Brad to come back, Brad silently kicked himself for not even seeing them enter the house.

Brad stared out the window of his hospital room and considered the change in circumstance. Questions plagued his mind like a gang of village folk, yelling their demands, wanting this, questioning that, throwing rotten tomatoes at his head. Should he sell it? He would need the money now more than ever for his obvious escape; he might just go into hiding forever and never return. What if the bitch squeals and he becomes a suspect? What if she doesn't and he is being paranoid? So many things could have happened to the McGill's…they were druggies, after all. They could have gone on a bender somewhere and got lost or overdosed. But, if he sold it to fund his get-away, then how is he any better than Carly wanting to sell it for drugs?

Before all of this, he hadn't spoken to her in years; the last time was in a crowded bar in a little suburb out of town. She was so high she couldn't even recognise him as two men groped her in a dark corner of the bar. He had tried to intervene and remove them from her body parts, but she told him to fuck off. It was then that he had noticed how age and a lifetime of drugs had dissolved her into nothing. Her eyes were dark and sagging down towards her lipstick smeared lips. Her hair was messy and her unbuttoned dress almost non-existent in the men's hands. It was apparent that she never did get out of that world, and she didn't seem to mind being there.

Brad felt a sadness seeing what he did, as even though they were not in each other's worlds anymore, and there was not one similarity between the two of them, he could still see the sixteen-year-old girl he once knew, full of life and dreams; she was going to be an art teacher.

After finally being discharged from the hospital, Brad sat in the taxi and picked up his mobile. He had asked Skye to go on this trip, but he hadn't asked Gypsy. The houses of the suburban area were flashing by the taxi window like pages of his life. Some moments were pristine and colourful, others dry and unkempt. Brad sighed buckets of worry into the comfort of the taxi, loud enough to make the Indian man in the front reflect his vision towards Brad in the rear-view mirror.

"Are you ok, Sir?"

"Yes." Brad uttered. "Just here, thanks."

Brad pulled up to Skye's house and found her on her front steps watering her plants.

"Morning." He called out to her.

"Morning, Dad, how are you feeling? I was going to give you a call shortly."

"It's all good, they let me go, I just thought I would drop in for a coffee, if you're not busy?"

"Not busy, come on in." Skye smiled and put down her watering can. "The place is a bit of a mess, sorry, I'm cleaning today."

"Where's Manny?" Brad questioned.

"Ahh, he's still in bed." Skye said, feeling herself blush a little at the sound of his name. *Stop it!* For crying out loud…she was still having random little thoughts about Manny. Random thoughts about jumping his bones. She has been trying to shake them since yesterday, but they just keep coming, coming like a fucking train ready to run her down.

"Ok, cool." Brad noticed her getting uncomfortable, he wasn't sure why. They walked into her kitchen that was filled with light. "Where's your coffee?"

"Oh, sorry, all good, I've got it." Skye jumped at the kettle and punched the button down.

"So, have you thought any more about this camping trip?" Brad said.

"Um, yeah, I don't know Dad, I've got my job, and all this other stuff…" Skye gestured towards all her other stuff, which was literally nothing but her kitchen. "Plus, I don't want to be stuck in the middle of the bush with Gypsy. I don't really care that she is my half-sister, she is a bitch and the reason I'm single."

"And I think she did you a favour." Brad said, "You're better off being single than being in a relationship with that moron."

"You didn't know him like I did, Dad." She said as if defending his honour, then remembered who she was talking about. "But you're right, I know you're right."

"You shouldn't defend him, Skye."

"I'm not. What he did was unforgivable and makes me wonder if I even knew him at all. Shit, maybe you did know him better than I did." They both laughed. A sad laugh, but still a laugh.

"Think about the trip, Skye. I will be leaving in the morning with or without you, but I really do hope that you decide to come with me." Part of him wondered why the hell he would want to drag his girls along on the magical carpet ride that was his run from the law, but the other part of him… well the other part of him was just naïve.

Brad and Skye went to sit in the backyard to drink their coffee. They sat in silence for the remainder of their cups and listened to the sounds of the world. Anything was better than listening to the sounds in their heads. Then a very loud noise broke the silence. It was Brad's phone receiving a text message. He pulled out his phone and checked the number – Gypsy. Brad looked at his phone, gasped and turned the phone towards Skye:

Skye was right, it was her Cam.
I didn't know. I kicked him out.
I am so sorry :(

"Holy shit" Skye shook her head. "I knew I wasn't imagining things that day."

"Well there you go. Gypsy said she had no idea." Brad shrugged.

"I'm just so pissed off. I'm pissed off with Cam, I'm pissed off with Gypsy. I'm just pissed off!"

"I know, Honey," Brad said putting an arm around Skye, "I know."

Skye didn't want to think about it anymore.

"Ok, I've got cleaning to do. Do you want to hang out and help me?"

Brad laughed, "No thanks, I've got to go and get my morning paper or Mrs Cray will start to get worried." He joked. Skye breathed a laugh and hugged him goodbye.

"Ok, see ya Dad, have a good day, and no more falling over!" She said sternly pointing a finger in his direction.

"I will call you later about our trip" He called out.

"Yeah, yeah…" She waved him off.

Skye went back inside and laid on her couch. She switched the TV on and searched the channels like she was trying to find something in particular, but nothing appeared to hit the spot. Infomercials that reminded her of Cam, midday movies that reminded her of Cam, and cooking shows that reminded her of Cam. She contemplated her dad's offer of a get-away. It was strange of him, as he was never the kind of man that liked to camp. Not that she knew of anyway. The closest she ever came to be camping with him growing up was on the very rare nights when he would get a little bonfire going in the backyard and they would roast marshmallows. *Camping?* She thought, *how strange.*

She imagined being stuck in the bush with no toilet, bugs all over her face, and the half-sister who had just fallen into her life. *Now that is strange.* She has always been an only child, and since her mum died when she was five years old it had just been her and her dad. She tried to imagine what it would have been like to grow up with a sister. Would they have gotten along? Would they have been best friends? She knew a lot of girls growing up that had sisters and they always seemed to get along well. But she knew other girls who fought with their sisters like they were fighting over their parent's attention, and everyone else's for that matter.

Skye sighed and stared at the ceiling. Cobwebs, everywhere. *Shit, I need to clean.* But who can be bothered?

All of a sudden Manny was at the entrance to the lounge room.

"Morning Dude." he sat down on the end of the couch and pulled a lighter from his pocket, ready to smoke the bong in his hand. He sucked it down like a champion and blew smoke into the air, filling up the room with one puff. The smoke settled in a straight line in the centre of the room like Skye believed the clouds would look if you could see them side on. She stayed on her couch below the fog and breathed air that slowly became thick with the swollen puffs of smoke.

"How's my main man, Manny, this morning?" Skye said.

"Good, man, good. Was that your dad I could hear?"

"Yeah, he's still at me about this camping trip. I don't want to do it, Mann."

"Then don't do it, you're not obligated to go" He said, pulling another cone.

Skye looked at him. What was this sudden fascination with Manny? Could these feelings have been here all along and she just didn't notice them until Cam was out of the picture? Or was it *because* Cam was out of the picture? She didn't know. But she did know that she needed another coffee.

"Want a bong?" Manny pushed his glass bong towards her, his hair still messy from sleep and his eyes already turning red. Manny had a smile that could stop a crowd, and at this point in time, right now, it was stopping Skye's heart.

"Yeah, fuck it, why not?" Skye grabbed the bong off Manny and put her mouth to the hole. He packed the cone and she put her thumb on the shotty. Skye let Manny light the lighter for her, because, though she didn't want to admit this, she was feeling quite faint.

"You ready?" Manny asked.

Skye only nodded as her mouth was preoccupied with the anticipation of weed making its way into her body. He lit the lighter and she breathed deeply, sucking hard, letting her lungs fill with the sweet relief of numbness. She let go of the shotty hole and drained the pipe of any traces of smoke.

"Hold it...hold it..." Manny said with a big glorious smile.

And as if in a big explosion, Skye released all of the air in her lungs and watched the smoke depart her mouth. It seemed crazy that so much smoke could have been in her tiny little lungs. She made a circle with her mouth and let the last remnants create rings in the air, to float away into the house – *the left-over parts of me.*

"Good work, Dude." Manny said with a chuckle.

Skye instantly laughed and barrelled herself towards Manny so they could laugh in fits together. Like one person, one piece of the earth moulded together, one soul intertwined in a fit of pretend happiness. Or was it real? She didn't know anymore. All she knew right now is that her face had gone and was replaced with playdough. She giggled and poked at her cheeks with her fingers and Manny laughed because he wasn't sure what she was doing. It had become harder to see through her eyes as her eyelids were insanely heavy and she had been smiling so much that her cheeks had risen up to nearly cover her eyes. There was a muffled noise that she had just noticed, so she turned to Manny and said "What?" But he looked at her and laughed – Manny hadn't said anything.

"Dude, you're smashed."

"What?" She said again. Then they both started laughing again.

Skye was so relaxed; she could feel all her worries washing away. As the laughing subsided, she sat in quiet looking at the room like she hadn't looked at it before. She studied every corner and every crack in the wall. She would have the odd smoke on rare occasions, but she was starting to wonder why she didn't do this more often. *Sister? What sister? And who is Cam? What a funny name.*

"Cammmmm." she said out loud.

"What? Hahaha." Manny giggled at her.

"Say it with me; Cammmmm."

"Cammmmm." They said in unison.

"Want to hear something funny?" Skye said.

"Is it the name 'Cam'?" He said, "Anyway, when do I not want to hear something funny?"

The air tickled Skye's toes and played games with her arms. They were weak but tingling like the weight had been taken from them and thrown away. She was absorbed in the feelings of her body and the thoughts that swum around in her head.

"Wait," she said, "What was I saying?"

"You were going to tell me something funny. Dude, how stoned are you?" Manny looked at her in amazement at how terribly easy she got stoned. He was laughing, but he was always laughing. It didn't matter anyway, Manny knew that Skye needed a chance to just chill out, especially after the week she has had.

"I have these thoughts, and these thoughts keep popping into my head." She said while pointing at her head and scrunching up her face, "And I don't know if I can control them, you know?"

Manny stared blankly at her while she continued.

"I want rainbows and turtles and funny faces in there, but they're not in there, they're gone!" Her hands did that of a magician, her trick was complete, she had made no sense whatsoever.

"Skye, what the hell are you talking about? I'm grabbing something to eat…"

"No! Don't… stay here" She grabbed his arm. "You see, I like this arm. I like this arm and this hand and these fingers." She traced the lines on his hand with her fingertip.

"Skye… umm." Manny was getting uncomfortable. He desperately needed to get up. He rubbed his forehead with his free hand and looked at her. "Whatever you're doing right now Skye, I can't do it." Suddenly he was a picture of stoned seriousness.

"What?" Skye felt everything in her fall over. "I wasn't doing anything; I was just admiring your hand. Geez, not everyone wants to sleep with you, Dude. Fuck, what an ego!"

"Calm down, Skye." Manny said quietly. "It's all cool, just chill."

"Pfft, calm down? You want me to calm down? Whatever, Dude." Skye jumped up and walked out of the room and into the kitchen. She slammed open the fridge in search of liquid, any form of liquid. "Skye," she addressed a jar of pickles, "why so annoyed, young warrior?" *Hold on, what was I doing?*

Manny walked in. "What the hell Dude? Why are you so annoyed?"

Holy fuck, he can read my mind!

"Skye, it's me, remember, your best friend Manny?"

"That's it, you are my best friend, nothing else."

"What does that mean?"

"I don't know…I really don't know." She said with her head still in the fridge.

"Dude, the weed is supposed to make you calm, it's supposed to chill you out, not turn you into a crazy person"

"I'm not crazy, Manny" Skye said, her body and mind calming back down like it had just escaped the fires of hell only minutes ago.

"I know you're not. Mate, you've had a shit week, I get it." Manny put his arms out, "Hug?"

Skye couldn't believe she actually said what she had said and acted the way she did. She was wondering who this person was that she had become lately. Shit, she couldn't even have a nice happy buzz without flipping out. *I'm a flippin' maniac*, she thought.

"I'm a maniac, aren't I?" She took her head out of the fridge and looked at Manny.

Manny laughed and said, "Yes, yes you are." They both laughed and Skye slapped him on the arm.

"Now, let's go get some food, there's nothing in this bloody house."

"Look, Skye…" Manny started then paused. "Actually, it doesn't matter."

"What?" She asked.

"No, really, it's fine."

"Whatever." Skye waved a hand and smiled back at him. She grabbed his shoulders and shook them, "Food, Mate, let's go." But Skye could feel there was something in the air other than stale bong smoke. And Manny felt a familiar old feeling that he had pushed down deep inside himself for all the years he had known Skye.

"Hello?" Gypsy answered. Her phone had rung three times, and she was still half asleep. The events of the other night and the events of that whole day were enough to drain her mentally and physically, and she was still recovering two days later. She had slept over ten hours that night and woken up with no recollection of any dreams. Haz had sat up with her having a drink and listening to her fill him in on everything that happened; Her dad, her sister, her sister's connection to Cam. Haz didn't have much to say, but she didn't mind, he was a good listener, and that's all she needed, a listener and a drinking buddy. Marcy was out of town with Nicki on a wine tour and she obviously didn't have her parents to talk to – plus she hadn't even told them about finding her biological dad, she wasn't sure how they would take it.

"Gypsy, it's Brad. How are you going?"

"Oh, Hi Brad. I'm ok, how are you feeling?"

"I'm good, all recovered." She could hear the smile in his voice from the other end of the phone. "I know this is going to be pretty straight forward of me, and maybe too presumptuous to assume you would even say yes, but the thing is, I am going across the county on a little camping adventure, and I thought it might be nice if you and Skye came with me? It would be such a great opportunity for you both to get to know each other, and for you and I to get to know each other. I, myself will be going for quite some time, but I thought if you wanted to come with me on the first part of the trip, I am happy to pay for a plane ticket for you to get back home again once you are bored with it…"

"A camping trip?" Gypsy interrupted, "Where?"

"That's the fun part," He said enthusiastically, "I don't know yet! I plan to get in the car – I will be coming past your neck of the woods – and just driving out bush. It's good for the soul, Gyps. I would really love for you both to come with me."

"Is Skye definitely going?"

"I don't know yet." He said honestly. Probably the most honest thing he has said about the trip – he isn't going to tell them why he is really going far away into the middle of the bush. "I am going to give her a call after I have spoken to you. It looks promising though."

"Brad, I don't know. Camping? It's not really me. And honestly, I don't really think it would be such a good idea for me to go along with you guys. I mean, I'm really glad we have met, and I want the chance to get to know you both a lot better, but it just feels way too soon for me. You know?" *What the fuck? Camping? Who does he think I am? Shit, no.*

"Oh. Ok, that's ok, I understand." Brad was feeling a little deflated, but he understood. It wasn't really the happiest of days when they met. Plus, they *had* only just met.

"Sorry, I really do appreciate the offer, but I can't just kind of pack up and go, you know?" All Gypsy could think was, that would be one uncomfortable camping trip. Not that she knew what a camping trip entailed, but she could be sure of one thing – she didn't want to go.

"No, no, it's seriously all good, I understand. Look, when I get back home, I will give you a call and we can catch up for a coffee and get to know each other better. I am so glad that you came back into my life, Gypsy, I feel like we can have a fresh start. Did you tell your parents?"

"No." Gypsy said.

"Are you going to?"

"One day."

"Ok, well, I've got some packing to do, so I will give you a ring when I find a camp site with signal if you want?" Brad hoped he hadn't blown it and felt extremely guilty thinking about the bracelet that was rightfully hers. He still hadn't decided what to do with it.

"That would be good." Gypsy smiled. "Have fun."

"I will, talk to you soon." Brad wasn't sure if he would ever be able to catch up with her again. But he had to stay positive.

"Bye." Gypsy hung up the phone and said, "Well, that was odd."

CHAPTER 14

"Hi Dad" Skye said. "You're calling about the trip, aren't you?"

"Yeah, how did you go? Have you decided to come? Please say yes. Gypsy isn't coming." He said, thinking this might make Skye want to go with him more than if Gypsy was going.

Skye was sitting on the grass, leaning up against the big willow tree in her backyard. She had been for a walk with Manny this morning and rustled up some ingredients for omelettes from the fresh food market down the street. She could see Manny through the kitchen window bopping along to the radio and chopping the mushrooms and onions for their late breakfast. She thought back to her stoned antics yesterday and how it took her most of the day to not feel weird around him again. She thought he looked so cute cutting up veggies and dancing – why had she never noticed his beauty before? His charisma? She still wasn't sure if she knew the answer to that. But things were going well with her secret admiration and she didn't want to leave him behind until she could muster up the strength and courage to see if there was anything there; to see if he felt the same way. *Shit, I can only try, right?* She thought. She couldn't quite put her finger on it, but since she had secretly fallen for Manny, everything around her had changed. The air tasted like spring and the birds all sounded sweeter. They sang songs of love and everyone around her glowed with a light she hadn't seen since her mother was alive. The days started to sweep around her like a perfectly fitting jumper, filling her with warmth and encouragement. Her days of wishing harm on Cam had gone, and her thoughts were filled with Manny; wrapping his arms around her, kissing her and making love to her. She couldn't leave this possibility behind to go and sit in the middle of the bush somewhere.

"Sorry, Dad, I don't think I can do it. I've got my job, and, yeah, it's not glamourous, but it pays the bills. I just don't think I can get any time off work. Sorry." She lied, but she wasn't going to confess the real reasons she wanted to stay.

Brad sighed inwardly. He especially wanted Skye to go with him. She had been his best little mate since the day she was born; they were a team. And she was all he had. Gypsy had just come into his life, so he could understand that it was all too soon for her to just go galivanting around the countryside with him. But it was a lot harder for him to hear that Skye wouldn't go.

"That's ok, Skye." He said. "There was no pressure, it was only if you wanted to, I can understand you have your life to live. I may not be able to call you and let you know where I am all of the time, but just know that I will be thinking of you every day."

"Geez, Dad, you sound like you're never coming back."

"Sorry." Brad laughed a little fake laugh "I'll be back soon; I just want you to know that I love you."

"I love you too, Dad, and I hope you have fun on your adventure…the adventure that was totally out of the blue." Skye added her sarcastic remark, but she wasn't sure if it was a statement or a question. She didn't really understand his reasoning for this abrupt trip.

"I know, it's a little out of the blue, but maybe I'm having a midlife crisis?" He said.

"Oh, you're not old enough for that, Dad!" Skye scoffed.

"Never too old to start, I say."

They both chuckled and said their goodbye's. Brad promised to call her along the road and Skye promised to stay out of mischief. She stayed by that tree and watched the branches hanging around her sway in the breeze, she could smell the omelette cooking through the open kitchen window and heard Manny call out to her to let her know it was ready.

Ahh, but are you ready? She thought.

Just as she got up to go inside, she got a message off Gypsy:

Hi, it's Gypsy. Just wondering if you want to talk?

Skye looked at her phone and pressed the 'Off' button. No, she did not want to talk.

"Hey Bud, are you ready for the best omelette in the whole entire world?"

"Haha, bloody oath I am." Skye said, sitting down at the little round kitchen table. The food smelt delicious. Manny sat across from her in a plain black sleeveless shirt and blue jeans. His toned arms glistened in the morning sun light that shone in through the window.

"What are you looking at?" Manny asked, wondering why her focus was on his arm.

"What? Oh, nothing." She said flippantly.

"Oh, would ya look at that?" He laughed and picked a piece of capsicum off his bicep.

Skye looked whimsically at his beautiful bicep while she got the chance, then looked back to her eggs before he could notice.

"I got a message from Gypsy." Skye said, breaking the tension she was creating in her own mind.

"Really? What did she say?"

"Just wondering if I wanted to talk."

"Are you going to talk to her?" Manny asked.

"I don't know." And Skye didn't know. She didn't know if she could look at her and not feel pain. She really was trying to move on, her heart and mind have surely moved on, but will Gypsy bring it all back? She wasn't really sure how to feel, and it became clear when she spoke of Gypsy out loud.

Her pain could be perceived as a longing for Cam, and an intention to have him back in her life. But that wasn't the case. She had her sights set on someone else, and he cooked a mean omelette.

"Hey, I just realised something!" Skye said. Manny's ears pricked up. "She said she kicked him out… *Kicked him out*," She emphasised, "That means that he must have been staying with *her* when he left here, because he never came back, did he?"

"I never saw him." Manny shook his head, "Well, holy shit, there you go."

"It's a bloody small world." Skye said.

"I think you should call her." Manny said. Always the one to encourage a good opportunity, whereas Skye lately had been losing her optimistic personality and had been looking too much on the negative side of things. This wasn't like her.

"Skye, usually you would look beyond this stuff, it's one of the reasons everyone loves you so much; you're such a glimmer of hope. Your glass is half full, Dude, it's full of wisdom and optimism and truth. You always give people the benefit of the doubt. And here is your blood, she's your blood, Skye, and she wants to make amends with you for something that was out of her control.

Bullshit. Skye thought.

"She didn't know that he was with you, she didn't even know that you existed! She is not a homewrecker, and the sooner you start to see that, the sooner you can start to forgive her, and yourself."

"Myself? Why do I need to forgive myself?" Skye was confused.

"Because. You've lost your way; you haven't been your beautiful caring self lately and I think it's getting to you." Skye blushed a little at the 'beautiful' part. "The anger that has been inside you is oozing out of every one of your words and emotions. And I think you're hating yourself for it."

Skye was watching him talk, and somehow, he made sense. She understood what he was trying to say.

"So, first things first; forgive yourself. It's ok to be upset, there is nothing wrong with that, it's part of being human. But, don't lose yourself in the process. Once you're done looking after number one, I think you should ring Gypsy. She is your blood, and she obviously wants to see you. So, number one: you. Number two: Gypsy." Only Manny could be so profoundly philosophical and then say what he said next. "Now, finish your eggs. I've sold all my toothbrushes, I gotta go buy some more. Wholesale prices, Baby!" He walked out of the kitchen doing the 'rock on' hand signal.

Skye sat and remembered being a teenager. All the other girls had mums and all the other girls had sisters. All she had was her dad, and for most of the time that didn't bother her. She got along with her Dad fantastically, so she never really felt like she was missing out – only occasionally. She had many friends and had always fit in with the 'cool' kids. But one day she got in a fight with a girl at school because her hair wasn't straightened – she didn't have the new hair straightener that all the girls were going on about. They laughed and pulled at her hair and called her a mess. The fight escalated so badly. They told her she was a feral and a polecat. They brought so much attention that a group had gathered around in a circle and laughed while these girls picked on her, kicking her shins, and throwing food at her school dress. She was so embarrassed that she could feel the tears start to come out of her eyes, and she didn't want them to see her tears, for they reflected her weakness. Her dad had always taught her to stick up for herself, but in this moment with an audience of all her peers, she hadn't the power to stop. The tears started flowing and the girls grew meaner with every drop that fell from her eyes. It wasn't until a teacher heard the noise and came to investigate that it all got torn apart. She had been taken to the principal's office and her dad was called in. When he heard what had happened, he was furious, ropeable, a maniac in the making. He threatened to sue the school and the families of the girls involved. He wanted them all expelled for defamation of character considering the aftereffects of what this might do to Skye's mentality. Skye figured he had been watching too many law movies.

The rest of the school year was horrible, she mainly kept to herself and didn't talk to her friends anymore, as most of them stood there quietly while these other girls were tormenting her. Her dad had told her stories about her mum, and how beautifully she felt about life, and how sometimes her happiness was a choice as it came down to her individual view, not the situation itself. It was then that she decided she would only be around people that would bring light into her life, and she would be the kind of person that brings light into other people's lives, she would surround herself with positive thoughts to help her through rough situations, and help them slide off her like water off a duck's back … and, she would only be friends with guys, because, fuck girls.

It was her sense of caution that kept her from getting close to Gypsy. Her need for self-preservation and the mistrust she had in the female species. It had grown over the years and she sat there wondering if maybe it was all in her head, maybe she should just stop thinking all females were evil and give it a go; she was her sister after all.

Later on, that day, there was a bang at the front of the house. *What the hell was that? Are we being robbed?* Surely not.

Skye put her book down and jumped up from her bed, she wandered into Manny's room and saw him sitting at his computer with headphones on.

"Manny." She said walking over to him. "MANNY!" She said louder. Manny pulled off his headphones, "Did you hear that bang?" She asked him.

"What bang?"

Clearly not.

"There was a bang out the front of the house. Want to come? I'm going to check it out."

"Coolio." He said and put his headphones back on. Not a care in the world, that kid.

"Great, thanks." Skye left his room and wandered towards the front door slowly, then a strange sound came from the same direction as the bang, it was a…a groan. A weird, gurgled groan. With caution Skye turned the door handle and rubbernecked her head out the opening in the big wooden door. Is that…? *Motherfucker, it's Cam.*

"Manny!" she shouted, "it's Cameron!" Manny still had his headphones on and obviously didn't hear her as there was no response. She looked down and saw that he must have been completely out of his mind drunk. He had spew on the front of his shirt and what looked like piss on his pants. *Fucking hell*, she thought, *what a mess.*

Skye scrunched up her face in disgust, was this the man she once loved? What had happened to him? Then she thought about it – Gypsy kicked him out, he has nowhere to go. A little laugh escaped her mouth and into the colossal situation that had taken up temporary residency on her doorstep.

Cam - all covered in piss and whatever he ate last - looked up at her through bloodshot eyes and squeaked

"Hey Skye. Can I come in?"

Brad could feel shots of electricity jolting through his skin, making him queasy and ill in the belly. He was nervous and full of anxiety. He needed to get out of here, he could feel the onslaught of the law invading his every move. Was he being paranoid? Or was this gut instinct? He didn't know. But he knew wherever he found himself, it sure as hell wasn't going to be in a jail cell; it was going to be in front of a beautiful still lake, in the early hours of the morning while everyone else was asleep, before the boats started up their engines and the sun was still making a painting of the water with colourful reflections that looked like heaven. Tiny fish would jump out to steal the bugs from above them and they would break the water's glass top that mirrored the sky, by sending ripples throughout the world. His feet would dip into the water that wouldn't be cold, but almost warm enough to swim in and cleanse his soul like a baptism. He would stare out to the crystal-clear water and watch it glitter with the rising of the sun and he would breath the salty air into his lungs, letting each breath relax his entire being. This is where he wanted to be, this is what he wanted to do, and this is what will save his soul.

He was fiercely packing the essentials; tarp, billy, swag, firelighters, fishing rod, canned food, bottled water, cooking gear, and a picture of Skye. He threw everything into the back of his car and made a big sign that said 'CLOSED' in red letters to put on the front of his workshop. A voice came from behind him and broke his concentration.

"Brad, what's happening, man? Are you closing up shop?"

Brad turned around to see one of his loyal customers standing at his shed door. "Hey, Mark, how are you going, Mate?"

"Yeah, good, good. You off somewhere?" Mark looked around at Brad's camp gear in the car that was backed up to the doors of the shed.

"Um, yeah, Mate, just thought I'd go on a little fishing expedition. Haven't been in a while, ya know?"

"I didn't know you fished. You should have told me, I go out with the boys most weekends, I could have brought you along. Where are you going?"

This guy is getting too nosey for my liking.

"Ha, a good fisherman never reveals his secret spots, Mark" Brad tapped his nose.

"Haha, true that Brad, true that." Mark laughed. "Well I was going to see if you could make me some new storage shelves for the wife. You know what they're like, ha-ha, they always have too many clothes, and then complain that they have nothing to wear… so they buy more and more and take over every closet in the freakin house!" He laughed and slapped Brad on the arm "Am I right or am I right?!" He laughed more, then became overwhelmed with an obvious discomfort as he remembered Brad had been a widower for as long as he had known him. "Shit, sorry Brad, I…"

"Don't worry about it." Brad slapped Mark's arm. "Sounds like fun." He joked.

"So, how long are you going to be gone for? Just the weekend?"

Brad didn't really know how to answer that question as he didn't know himself.

"No plans, Mark. How about I give you a call when I get back?" As nice as he was, Brad found Mark quite annoying in his busy-body ways and wished he would just fuck off so that he could keep packing his gear. He didn't want to forget anything and needed to focus.

"Sounds good, I'll talk to you then. Have fun, and don't go catching all the fish!" He called out as he walked away back down the driveway.

Thank Christ for that.

Brad turned back to his shed and walked over to a hidden compartment behind his tool cabinet. He opened the compartment and pulled out a handgun and two boxes of bullets. His gun wasn't registered, and he didn't have it locked in a safe gun box, so if he got caught with it, he would be in a world of trouble. Just as he turned around his heart stopped, and he swung back around and threw the gun and bullets in the draw behind him as quick as he could. It was the police, walking casually up his driveway. They were looking at each other as they spoke so they probably didn't see him. Brad had just dodged one big fucking bullet. But why were they here? *Oh fuck.*

"Bradley Mains?"

"Yes, that's me."

"We were knocking on your front door, but the man that just left said you were out the back. Going somewhere?" One of the officer's gestured towards his car.

Fucking Mark.

"Yes, Officer…" Brad looked at his badge "…Sawyer, just a little fishing, get out of the hustle and bustle for a while." Brad's heart was thumping out of his chest so hard he could swear they would be able to see it pounding under his shirt.

"Where are you going fishing?" The other officer questioned.

Brad was growing more and more nervous by the second. Luckily his voice wasn't shaking…yet. "Uh, not really sure yet. I was going to go south and find a nice lake, set up camp, I've heard there's some good spots down that way" He lied. He was going east. "Can I help you officers with something?"

"We hope so, Mr Mains"

"Just Brad is fine." He corrected him.

"Ok, Brad" Officer Sawyer said, "We are looking for some information regarding two men that went missing from High Tide a couple of weeks ago, Thomas McGill and David McGill." They looked at Brad quizzically "We have some information that suggests the two brothers were on their way to Kanville and may have been visiting you whilst here?"

That bitch! She actually sent the cops? She's dead...

"I'm, sorry, what? Who gave you that information?" He put on his best look of confusion.

"We are not at liberty to give out such information, Brad." The officers kept their gaze straight at Brad's face, not budging for a second, catching every breath he made and everywhere his eyes went. Brad stood as still as a statue, cool as a cucumber, and tried not to let his body language give him away. Every ounce of him was trying to control his breathing.

"Well, I'm sorry to disappoint, fellas, but I don't know those two men, I did see it in the paper though. Whatever information you were given regarding a connection between me and them is incorrect. Sorry I can't help." He shrugged his shoulders and grabbed his water jug to put in the car.

"Well, Brad, this is an ongoing investigation, and we may need to speak to you again, so for now we need you to stay in town, and please give us a call if you happen to remember anything that may help with our enquiries." Officer Sawyer handed him a card with a mobile number and email address.

"Hold on, am I a suspect? Or am I under arrest?" Brad asked.

"No, you're not under arrest. But due to the allegations regarding your connection with the two men, we may have a few more questions to ask you concerning their disappearance."

"But I already told you, I don't know them."

"Ok, Mr Mains, ok." The officers put out their hands and concluded their conversation with a handshake before walking back down his driveway. He knew it wasn't the last time he would see them. But now he knew his fears were real, his gut was right, and he had a choice to make. Would he run? Or would he stay? Running would make him seem so obviously guilty. *Fuck it.*

He would run.

Brad threw the water jug into his car and fetched his gun from the draw. He was extremely lucky the police hadn't seen him before, or he would have been screwed. He put the gun and the two boxes of bullets under the driver seat in his car, for hiding, and for quick access – *I just never know when I might need it,* he thought. He paused for a second and thought what an incredibly bad idea this was. Then that thought faded.

He ran to his house and bolted shut all the windows and doors, set his security alarm, and turned off all the power points – why? Who knows, it was always something he was taught to do. He ran back to his backyard and shut the shed, attaching his 'CLOSED' sign and securing it shut with a massive padlock. He jumped into his car and rolled

down his driveway with his heart in his throat, and his balls
in his belly.

CHAPTER 15

"What are you doing here Cam?" Skye questioned with her hands on her hips. She wanted to scream and yell and kick him off her porch, but the sight of him was so miserable she couldn't bring herself to add to his obvious agony.

"Can I come in? Please?"

"No, you can't." Skye slammed the door and turned to heel-toe it with her blood boiling. As quick as she slammed the door her phone buzzed – it was Gypsy. "Argh!" she yelled and threw her phone down the hallway floor letting it slide like a bowling ball down the aisle, ready to hit ten pins, or the wall on at the other end in her case. She grabbed chunks of her hair and walked back into Manny's room ripping the headphones off his head.

"Go and deal with him, please."

"What? Who?" Manny was disarmed and not prepared for the crazy lady in front of him.

"Cam!" She squealed. "He's at the front door."

"You're kidding me?" Manny said, getting up from his seat. "What's he doing here?"

"I don't know, I can't deal with this shit right now." Skye pointed a finger in Manny's face and threatened "You are on my side, Mann, MY side, not his."

"Yeah, I know, I got it, chill out, Dude."

"Don't tell me to chill out, Mann, Cam is on our doorstep."

Manny walked out of his room as if walking towards a carnivorous wild animal; he proceeded with caution.

"Hurry up." Skye shooed him on with two hands while leaning against the door frame of Manny's room. Manny looked back at her and waved his arm – he wanted to say 'chill out' again but knew better than to tempt her anger.

Manny opened the door, walked out, and closed it behind him. He looked down to a ragged looking drunk on his front porch. He smelled the booze and the pee. In that moment, if only for a second, Manny felt sorry for Cam. He shook his head at Cam who looked back up at him with bloodshot eyes and a sorry look in his face.

"You right now, you are the reason I prefer weed." Manny said moving over to sit on the wooden chair that rests surrounded by Skye's pot plants. The cushions thrown on it are old and worn, but they give it that comfy charm.

"You-gunna pick-o-me now?" Cam said, clearly still drunk by the slurring of his words, moulded together to make one big – almost unrecognisable - noise.

"I told you to stop." Manny said, "I told you to stop your bullshit and be a good man to Skye and look at you now." He scoffed and threw his eyebrows up to show his disgust.

"Where-she-go?"

"She's not coming outside, bro. She doesn't want to see you; you can't blame her for that."

Cam's head was nodding up and down, but Manny knew this was because he was drunk, not because he agreed.

"Why'd you keep doing it?" Manny questioned. "You had the coolest girl a guy could ask for. She's beautiful, and sweet and caring, she's funny and chilled out. Dude, she looked after you even after all the crap you put her through over the years. She treated you like you could do no wrong, like you were a king, and I'm telling you now, you never deserved her. She gave you her gorgeous heart, and you may as well have grabbed a pair of scissors and cut it up in front of her. You never deserved her. You fucked it up." Manny's voice was growing louder the more he spoke; it intensified the more he acknowledged what he felt within.

"She's the kind of girl the rest of us can only dream of – a best friend, a lover, a partner for life. She is the only girl I have ever been friends with that I actually want to be around all the time, the only girl that makes me laugh and feel that there is the possibility of love. She makes me believe in happiness and God, and I'm a fucking atheist! Why do you think I sleep with all these other girls? Maybe I'm trying to fill a gap that can't be filled. Maybe I'm trying to put someone into the gap that she should be in…in my soul, you know?" The words were flowing from his mouth like a wild river. It was almost like he was talking only to himself. But then Manny remembered who he was talking to and realised that he had gone too far…he had dug too far inside his subconscious and found feelings that he thought he had supressed for so long they had vanished and were gone forever.

Cam was staring at Manny intensely. It's almost like hearing the words that Manny spoke and reading between the very obvious lines, he had sobered up enough to speak actual words.

"Mann… do you…are you…Bro, are you in love with Skye?" He started trying to get up, but his arms struggled to hold his own body weight, "'Coz it sounds like you're in love with Skye."

"What?" Manny laughed "That's stupid, I'm only saying that she deserves better than you, that doesn't mean I think she deserves me." But Manny knew that he may have shown a little more insight into his true feelings than he meant to.

"If I could get up right now, I'd punch you in the face." Cam said.

"Yeah? Well lucky for you, you can't. I think you should go." Manny said.

"What's that supposed to mean? 'Lucky for me'?" Cam had an anger in his voice and his words – although still slightly slurred – were falling out of his mouth with a little bit of foam, like a mangy dog.

"It means, if you were able to get up, and you actually tried to hit me, I would knock you down before you could say 'twat-waffle'. Yeah, I may be all peace and love and all that shit, but you know I could drop you like a bag of potatoes. And it also means that I think you should go before you cause any more harm to my best friend, who is probably in the house losing her mind right now. You've done ya dash, Cam, you've had your day, and honestly, *BRO*, I grew more and more embarrassed to call you my mate. So, when it comes to sides…" He paused for effect "…it ain't yours I'm barracking for."

"I want to talk to Skye." Cam said.

"Not happening. Pick your shit up and get the hell off our front porch."

"This is my house too!" Cam seethed through dirty teeth.

"As of the last moment you walked out this front door, no it isn't. You gave up your right to be in this house, and neither of us want you here. I will gather your shit and put it out on the front lawn for you, you're free to come and get it, but that is as close as you get to this house. Now, go find somewhere to sober up, and for the love of god, find a shower, Dude, you fucking stink."

Cam held on to the railings of the porch steps and used what looked like all of his might to pull himself up into a standing position. Apart from knowing he got kicked out of Gypsy's house a couple of days ago, Manny and Skye had absolutely no idea where he had been since then. Maybe at the blue haired girl's house? Either way, Manny knew that neither him, nor Skye, would welcome him here anymore.

"I'll be back," Cam said, "for my shit, and to talk to Skye, whether she wants to or not."

"And that right there is one of the reasons you don't deserve her. You don't give a shit what she wants; it's all about you. For the sake of the next poor girl you make fall in love with you, I really hope you get your priorities straight and treat her right, because a relationship is…"

"A relationship?" Cam cut him off "You're schooling me on relationships? Manny, let me ask you this: what was the last relationship you had? Because it hasn't been since I've known you. You don't know shit about relationships. And if you think for one second that Skye is gunna crumble for your pathetic bullshit, think again. She is too good for you, you're just a stoner." His words were intended to cut like a knife, but instead rolled straight over Manny as if never spoken.

"If you're trying to insult me, don't waste your breath. Since you have left and she has realised her worth, she has bloomed. She is a fucking angel, and you…" Manny pointed his finger, "you suppressed her down into darkness for so many years. But since you have gone, she is shining, Dude, and she is brighter than the fucking sun." Manny was almost sweating as he felt the burn of his protection surround him like a force field, "So, come back tomorrow, I will have your shit ready to go on the front lawn, and do not dare step one foot in this house, or I will call the cops, and if that doesn't bother you, then I will make damn sure I'm sitting waiting with a cricket bat ready to swing."

Cam stared at him, swaying a little from the alcohol in his system. "Meh." He threw his hands in the air, "To hell with her, you can keep the stupid bitch." And with that he spat on the ground and turned on his heel, leaving behind his dignity, his anger, and his naive hope of reconciliation with Skye.

"Is he gone?" Skye asked as Manny walked back into the house. She was sitting at the kitchen table with an untouched cup of green tea. It was going cold; she had forgotten it was even in front of her.

"He's gone. He'll be back tomorrow for his stuff, though."

"I won't be here. I'm working, which is kind of perfect. I really don't want to see him, Mann."

"I know." Manny said, reaching across the table for her hand. He could feel the spark of electricity and thought back to the other day when they had got stoned together. Did she feel the same? He was too scared to admit his feelings because he didn't want to destroy what they shared. He didn't want to delve into this thing he had felt for her and find out that her feelings were just that of a woman in the midst of heartache. He was not prepared to be her rebound guy. In fact, he had done so well hiding his feelings over the years that she was with Cam that he brought himself to believe that he felt nothing, until recently when they had all come flooding back.

Skye on the other hand knew exactly how she felt. She had fallen, and she had fallen hard. She could feel the electricity and she soaked it into her skin like vitamin E, ready to soothe her from the outside in. She knew she couldn't quite explain what existed there, or why it had hit her so hard, but she knew her need was there, she could feel her need in every move he made and every word he breathed. Every time he smiled at her, or spoke, or picked the pickle out of his burger. From the morning till the night, from the lustful to the embarrassing, she was there, pining, wanting, loving and holding her breath for Manny in a way she never had before. She didn't believe feelings like this existed in the real world and thought it an impossible reality. How could someone actually feel this way for someone, so deeply? But then she would consider the fact that she had been best friends with Manny for too many years to count on two hands. He was always right there in front of her. And as strong as the feelings were; she was frightened.

Skye sucked it up and decided it was better to bottle it up than wreck her friendship with Manny. She couldn't possibly believe that Manny would like her the same way she adored him. She watched him day after day bring home women that were nothing like her…

Skye pulled her hand away.

"What?" She laughed looking at Manny who was staring into her eyes with a look of desperation. "You got your thinking cap on there, or what? You've got quite an intense stare. Don't tell me he got to you, I told you to be on my side…"

"How long have you known me?" Manny questioned. "Of course, I'm on your side, and I told him that. I don't give a damn about that piece of crap, Skye, I only care about you." Skye's heart burst into pieces.

"Naaw, bestie." Skye joked and gave him a sideways smile.

"Don't you know it." Manny winked.

Neither of them had the courage to be honest and mention what they were truly thinking.

The next day, Skye went to work and imagined what was happening at home. She knew that Cam was going to her house – the house they once shared – to get his belongings. She was intensely grateful that she had to be at work and didn't need to come up with an excuse to not see him. She assumed he wouldn't be drunk again and would probably put in more of an effort to try and talk to her, but not one ounce of her has the energy to fight him, she just wanted him gone and out of her life.

Skye looked around at the office. It was uncanny that her office looked just as bad as the piles of rubbish laying outside in the waste depot.

I mean, really, I could just open the window and throw it all out. Who's going to notice?

She looked at the clock and watched as the second hand seemed to go forward twice, then back once. The smell that came in through the window was terrible; she wondered how she had put up with this job for as long as she had. The mounds of rubbish and waste were being pushed and moved and buried in the dirt by the men in the big machines. At least they got to wear breathing masks. When Skye had asked to be trained to drive the machinery instead of sitting in the office all day, it was like something people only got to witness on Broadway; like a choreographed play practiced and perfected in a chauvinistic man-cave, probably with a 'NO GIRLS ALOWED' sign on the front door; each of the men looked at each other and in perfect unison started to laugh their heads off and point their dirty fingers at the stupid girl wanting to do a 'man's job'. She stood dumbstruck with a look of utter shock, politely told them all to get fucked, scoffed and left the room. She could hear them joking about her nonsense request as she walked out the door, and to this day they still crack jokes about it. She had thought to mention their discrimination to the supervisor, but her plans were deflated, and now she preferred her dirty little office. Safe to say she doesn't bother turning up to any staff parties.

Staring out the window watching the men in their macho machines, she heard a noise coming from the UHF; it was Barry.

"Skye, you there?"

Skye reached for the UHF and pushed the button to talk

"What?"

"Skye, you gotta call the cops, call them right now." Barry sounded a little stressed.

"Why, what happened?"

"Just do it! We found something."

"Righto." Skye said, always left in the dark. She put down the UHF and stumbled for the phone, not sure what she was telling the police, but just doing her job like the good little girl she was.

Being a small town, she rung straight through to the Kanville Police Station. The phone rang only once before someone picked up.

"Kanville Police." The voice on the other end said.

"Hi, this is Skye Mains, I'm calling from the Kanville Waste Depot, the boys have found something in one of the junk piles and told me to get you guys down here as soon as you can."

"No worries Skye, we can have a car there shortly. Do you know what he found?"

"No, sorry." Skye said.

"A bit more information would be helpful. Ok, just tell him not to touch whatever it is just yet, and we will be there shortly."

"Will do. Thanks" Skye hung up the phone and radioed back to Barry, "Barry, what did you find?"

"Did you call the cops?"

"I did, what is it?" Skye pushed.

"Well, looks like a body, smells like a body, I think it's a body."

"Shit. Don't touch it, he said not to touch it."

"Why the hell would I touch it?" Barry said, but Skye had already thrown the UHF and left the office to walk down towards Barry's truck. Barry was standing at the edge of one of the piles with his hands on his hips looking down at the rubbish when he noticed Skye walking towards him. He was a dirty looking guy with a scruffy beard and a beer belly he could use as a dinner table. His high-vis uniform gripped to his gut and threatened each button that held his shirt together.

"Where is it?" Skye asked as she got closer to him, the office clothes she decided to wear today were not quite the right attire for such a landscape.

"Here." Barry pointed to the edge of the mound. And there it was, half a body was sticking out of the rubbish pile like a statue carved into a mountain.

"Holy cow." Skye put her hand over her mouth, it wasn't just the shock of seeing the dead body, but the smell was putrid. In all her years of working in the waste depot she never once smelled a smell like this. The rotting corpse that was feeding the flies wafted up her nose and made her sick. She turned away and vomited to her right, while Barry watched her from her left. Skye had never seen a dead body before, not even at funerals. Her mother had a closed casket as her dad felt she was too young to see her mother like that, and some images can't be washed away with time, so they stick in your mind and haunt you in the night. But this, she felt, was entirely different. If she had got to see her mother one last time laying peacefully in her casket, she would not have smelled this smell, and felt the kind of fear she did right now. What happened to this poor person? What pain did they endure?

"Sucks to be him." Barry said, and laughed. He actually laughed. He looked at Skye to include her in his hilarious joke, but Skye just stared at him, disgusted.

"That was someone's person." She said "He might have had children, or a brother or sister, he would have had parents! He was somebody." Skye couldn't believe someone could be so cold as to joke about this guy lying dead in front of her, thrown away like garbage and left to rot. In that moment she looked at Barry and wanted to slap him for being so disrespectful.

"Not anymore." Barry said.

Then a voice from behind him said, "Not anymore, what?" It was Officer Sawyer.

"Hello, you must be Skye?" He said and put his hand out for Skye to shake, "My name is Officer Sawyer, and this is…?"

"Name's Barry." Barry said, shaking Officer Sawyer's hand. He pointed to the body sticking out of the mound "I found this old mate in the junk down here."

Officer Sawyer radioed back to his partner in the car.

"You better come down here Mick, we have a body in the waste. It could be one of the missing men." Sawyer turned back to Skye and Barry with both arms moving in a wave-like motion "Please move back guys, this is officially a crime scene."

"You think this happened here?" Skye questioned.

"Look, we don't know, but for now there is a dead body, and we need to tape this area off. We will need to close the depot down until the body has been removed and the site has been searched. Skye, do you have the number for the manager of the depot?"

"Yes, sure, I will go and get it." Skye was incredibly calm, but she could still feel her heart thumping inside her chest. She raced up to the office and found the piece of paper stuck to the notice board that held the number of her boss, tearing it off she ran back down to Sawyer who was now accompanied by a younger officer who looked like he had only just left high school. She handed him the note with the phone number and noticed the wrinkles on his face; some were obvious smile lines that somehow made her feel safe, and some were the marks of stress – his forehead like the dunes of the Sahara Desert and his eyes, sagging like bags of fluid from too many late nights.

Sawyer took the number and told them to wait at his car – he had some questions. From the way he said it Skye felt that he was accusing either her or Barry of whatever happened to this guy. Her safe feeling had gone.

CHAPTER 16

The next few weeks tended to go by slowly. Gypsy was busy driving Haz to his drama classes and sitting around the house waiting for Skye to message her back – she hadn't. She hadn't heard from Brad either, so she assumed he had a good camping trip and would be back by now, but was he going to call her? Maybe see if she wanted to meet up for a coffee? She had sent him messages, and not unlike Skye's uncommunicative manner, he hadn't responded either.

She had seen on the news that a body was found in the Kanville tip and a second body was found the next day. It turned out that the two men that were found were the same two men that had gone missing from High Tide weeks earlier. The news brought a little fear into Gypsy as she had always felt that Kanville was as safe as High Tide. Both beachy towns that oozed the chilled-out vibe, she never really thought something like that would happen, so it was a little daunting thinking of going back to Kanville.

"What if it's a serial killer?" she had asked Haz while they were watching the news.

"What would he want with you?" Haz laughed. But Gypsy was too paranoid to brush the thought aside.

So here Gypsy sat, on the edge of her bed, with Haz at her door, and a few agonizing weeks since she had seen Brad or Skye.

"Stuff this." Gypsy said to Haz. "I'm just going to go back to Kanville and talk to her face to face."

Gypsy was sick of sitting around wishing she could talk to her sister who already hated her - not that it was Gypsy's fault, "She needs to get the hell over it." Gypsy complained.

"Just try her again. Don't message, actually call her." Haz said.

"Argh, I don't know what to do. I'm heading out with Marcy tonight; I'll see what she thinks."

"Good plan." Haz said nodding his head. He wasn't much of a talker and didn't really seem to care about the whole thing. He has his own problems, and Gypsy didn't want to continue talking about it since he made it quite obvious that he was sick of listening to it all. Gypsy would wonder what the use of him was. She did everything for that poor fool, but when she needed a friend, he went MIA. Luckily, she had Marcy, and Marcy was as honest as a snowstorm on a winter's day.

"Bitch-face!" Marcy yelled when she walked into Gypsy's home like it was her own. "How you been, Chicken?" They hugged and Marcy slapped her on the arse. Good old predictable Marcy. "You ready for the pub?"

"Yeah, just let me grab my shoes."

"You're wearing them?" Marcy looked at Gypsy's ripped sneakers with two different coloured laces.

"Yeah, why? I'm not trying to impress anyone." She laughed tying up her laces, "Let's go. See ya Haz, don't wait up!" She called out to the quiet house, not actually sure where Haz was, but he was bound to have heard her.

Marcy pulled a small bottle of scotch from her bag.

"For the walk?"

"You know, I'm starting to wonder if you are the reason, I have a drinking problem…give me some of that." She said and snatched the bottle from Marcy, drinking down the burning liquid into her belly, making it feel warm and tingly.

"Slow down there, cowboy!" Marcy yelped and grabbed the bottle back.

"How was your wine tour with Nicki?"

"Um, Mate, have you ever been to heaven? 'Coz I swear that's where we were. I'm talking about a magical place, far beyond the city," - her hands articulating in emphasis - "where the hills roll and the wine flows freely. I would finish my Pinot and be poured a Shiraz, then try a Sauvignon Blanc and finish with…well, with whatever the hell I wanted! It was majestic, Gyps, we ate food that was made by Greek Gods or something and swallowed each mouthful down with the complementing wine. It was, like a I said, heaven."

"Wow, glad I got an invite." Gypsy said flippantly.

"Meh, you wouldn't have liked it." Marcy joked and put her arm around Gypsy as they walked.

"We stayed in these little tents out at the edge of the vineyards. It was like glamping. You know? Like, glamourous camping. There were fairy lights all set up throughout the aisles and around each tent, and the tents had real beds! And electricity!"

"What about the toilet? Or shower?" Gypsy asked.

"Yeah, well they had these portable ones set up for each tent, so I only had to share with Nicki, but they weren't too bad, like they weren't stingy or anything."

"Sounds like you guys had fun."

"We did, we did, Gyps." Marcy smiled. "Oh shit! I totally forgot to ask you about this whole sister thing. So, what's the deal?"

Gypsy thought back to their phone conversation. She had mentioned everything that had happened, but just not about her plan to go to Kanville to see Skye who was neglecting to reply to Gypsy's messages.

"It's a twisted world, Marc."

"Yeah, so you kicked out this Cam guy…then what happened?"

"Cam… what a tosser. So, I have been messaging Skye, because, you know, I want to talk, but she's not replying. I'm kind of thinking about going for a drive back to Kanville, then I can just drop in and she won't have a choice. I mean, I'm a freaking awesome person! Who wouldn't want to know me?" With two raised eyebrows and shrugging her shoulders, she was serious, but let it come across as a joke. She had to love herself enough to let Skye get to know her…the real her.

They had reached the pub and entered through the door to the sounds of high-volume Aussie rock music. It seemed that most of High Tide had come to the pub tonight, and she could only just hear Marcy say;

"I think you should go." While nodding her head. "I will come with you if you want. Now, what do you want to drink?"

"Scotch and coke." Gypsy said and looked around in search of a seat.

None. Fantastic.

"I'm gunna look out back" She said and walked out to the beer garden. She managed to find a seat in the corner surrounded by some pot-plants and hanging lanterns. The walls of the beer garden were painted in graffiti by some local artist, and the lanterns gave them a realistic touch as the light swung around them from above. The beer garden was nicer than being inside amongst the craziness of one hundred people trying to talk over each other and the music. The night was sweet and there wasn't a mosquito in sight, but the atmosphere was enough to make her itchy all over; for some reason, she just wasn't feeling like herself. Usually she would take any opportunity to hang at the pub, drink and tell stories with strangers, dance with a cute guy and laugh at drunken shenanigans. But tonight, she had lost her pizazz. She wasn't feeling energetic and enthused, and she put this down to having too much on her mind. Plus, the smell of the smokers was making her sick.

"Scotch and coke for the lady." Marcy handed her a glass and sat down, scoping out the area. "A bit packed tonight." Marcy said, "I am so picking up a random guy and making him my bitch." She laughed. Gypsy laughed back.

"You're so wrong, Marc." They clinked their glasses to that and skulled down their drinks.

"Another?"

"Why not." Gypsy said.

"I'll be right back." Marcy walked back inside to get more drinks. Gypsy was left alone with her thoughts. Surrounded by one hundred strangers, she felt lonelier than ever. She just wanted to know what to do. If she left Skye alone, they may never make up. But if she turned up on her doorstep, she might hate her even more. Gypsy wondered if Skye even gave a shit that she had a sister.

She concluded it was a hard *NO*.

Suddenly she heard a male voice from in front of her. Her gaze was ripped from the wooden tabletop and thrown in the direction of a drunken guy standing at her table.

"Hey, baby, you want a dance?" He drooled a little while he spoke, and half of his drink was spilt down his shirt.

"No thanks" Gypsy said, hoping he would go away.

"Come on, baby, I'm a good dancer."

Gypsy watched him shake his hips and pour more of his drink down is shirt.

"My name's not 'Baby' and I don't want a dance. Now kindly, fuck off." She smiled a sweet smile.

Ooh he looks angry, her inner goddess giggled. Her inner goddess was a feisty bitch.

"Hey, Jacko, leave the poor girl alone." Some guy yelled from across the way.

"Meh." He turned and walked away mumbling "What a bitch." then stopped at another girl "Hey, baby, you want a dance?"

Gypsy just laughed to herself. She would call him a moron, but she had had so many drunken and embarrassing moments in her life that she had no right to judge others. She had done so many stupid things that she wonders how she hasn't been jailed. – 'But why, Sir, are you arresting me?' she would ask, and the policeman would say 'You are an embarrassment to society and to yourself. We must arrest you to keep you from making a fool of yourself any longer' and she would say 'Fair enough' and then be left to die in a cold cell where she couldn't embarrass herself anymore. *If only*. She thought. But we must live with the mistakes of our past and use them to make proper choices in our future. *Holy cow I sound profound. What is happening to me?*

"Drink up, Chicken, there is a guy in there, and he is eyeballing me hardcore. Mumma's gotta dance."

"Can we just talk, like for a minute?" Gypsy said, giving Marcy puppy dog eyes.

"Oh, ok, only because I love ya." She winked. "You still worried about this Skye thing? Honestly, I think you should just go and see her, what's the worst that could happen? She's not going to hate you for going to her house and showing her that you are putting in effort, that you care about her. Just do it, and like a I said, I will go with you if you want, as support. And if she decides to be cruel, then you've got me for back-up." Marcy put her hands up in a fighting pose and giggled. "Gyps, you are my bitch, and us

196

bitches gotta look out for each other, ok? Now, I love ya, so get up and let's go dance."

Gypsy smiled and shook her head, "Ok, I'm coming, can we just finish our drinks first?"

Marcy grabbed her glass, skulled it down without even tasting it, burped and said "Now?"

"Ha-ha, ok, fine." Gypsy did the same and together they walked back into the crowded pub to dance and laugh the night away. Though Gypsy already knew she would be ditched by the end of the night, since Marcy didn't know how to keep her pants on.

Gypsy woke up feeling fresher than ever. She hadn't drunk too much last night, and what she had drank had left her body in the form of sweat from all of the jumping around and singing in the pub. She had left early and let Marcy stay with a fella that seemed nice enough for her to leave with a guilt-free conscious. Anyway, Marcy was a big girl, she can take care of herself.

She laid in her bed with her eyes still closed but could see through her eyelids the shapes made from the shadows and light coming through the curtains. She could smell bacon cooking and could hear moving around in her kitchen. *Haz must be cooking.* Gypsy dragged herself up and jumped in the shower, thinking all the time that she knew what she was going to do. She was going to Kanville.

"You in there?" Haz called through the bathroom door.

"Yep. I'll be out in a minute."

"I cooked you some bacon."

Confusion. Utter confusion. Haz never cooked breakfast for Gypsy. *Something weird is happening…*

"Umm, ok, thanks, I'll be out in a minute."

"Ok."

Gypsy could hear Haz walk away back towards the kitchen. She stared for a second and then stopped. Why should she question it? He had cooked her breakfast, even if it was out of the ordinary, she should just be grateful. She dried herself off and put on some clean clothes. With peach smelling water dripping from her freshly washed hair, she walked into the kitchen to find Haz sitting at the breakfast bar. Sitting in front of him and next to him were two plates of bacon and eggs, toast and orange juice. There was a little vase of flowers in between the two plates with flowers freshly cut from the garden. She knew they were form her garden because she planted them last spring in an attempt to feel 'earthy'. Marcy had picked on her and said her flowers would die in a matter of weeks, but this only gave Gypsy a reason to keep them alive, to prove her wrong. So here they were, beautiful and yellow, sitting on her breakfast bar soaking up the smell of Haz's cooking.

"Mmm, yum. What did I do to deserve this?" Gypsy said smiling, sitting down next to Haz.

"Not yet, just eat." Haz said handing her a knife and fork.

"So, there is something? Should I be worried?"

"No. Well, maybe…actually, no."

"Oh my god, Haz, you may as well just spit it out." She said putting some perfectly poached egg in her mouth.

"Oh, wow! Haz, why haven't you done this before, Dude? It's amazing"

"Yeah, well, I figured I owe you some eggs."

Remembering back to him throwing her eggs out of the kitchen window when he was upset about his breakup, she chuckled a little, "Yeah, I guess you do."

"So, Gyps…"

"So, Haz…?" She looked at his awkward face and was more consumed in the tasty breakfast than his obvious discomfort.

"I'm moving out." The words came out of his mouth like a lightning bolt.

What the fuck?

Gypsy's face was one of pure shock. She had never lived alone, she had spent years looking after Haz like he was her freakin' child, and now he was moving out?

"Where? Why? With who?" Gypsy questioned in obvious shock, bacon hanging out of her mouth – she had forgotten to chew.

"Um, just, by myself." Haz said. He looked like he was ready for the horror show that would be Gypsy, but he really wasn't deep down. His courage was flailing. "Sorry."

"Sorry? What do you mean, sorry? Haz, if you want to move out, I'm not going to try and stop you, that's your choice. So, what was I? Just a friend to get you through the tough stuff and now you're gonna ditch me? Like everyone else in my life?" *After everything I've done for you, you ungrateful little…*

"That's not fair, Gyps." Haz said, averting his gaze. He picked at his food with a fork and put his other hand in his lap.

"Not fair? What is fair? I thought you were my friend. So, me running around, looking after you and being your support through everything, is that like…I don't know, a nuisance or something? Is me being your friend a nuisance? Is our house a nuisance? What is it? Because I'm finding it hard to believe you want to leave…" Her eyes were welling up with tears and she didn't care. She was hurting, and Haz was the one thing in her life that felt permanent. They had been through so much together; he was like family. "What have a I done wrong?"

"Nothing, you haven't done anything wrong, I just feel it's time for me to find my feet, you know?" He looked at her and at the tears that were now rolling down her face

"Don't be sad, Gyps, this is not a bad thing. I'm at a point where I want to be more independent, I really want to have my own space and start moving forward. I feel like I am bringing you down, and lately…well, you're kind of bringing me down…"

The words hurt like death. "Hold on, so you're saying that it's ok for me to help you all this time, but as soon as something in my life is going to shit, you can't take it?"

"Gypsy, are you serious? All you ever do is drink with your friends. You don't work, you don't clean up…"

"You don't drive! You don't cook!" They both looked down to their breakfast he had cooked. "Ok, you don't usually cook"

"I appreciate everything you have done for me, but I need to be in a better environment. I can't be around all this negative energy all the time. You're either drunk, or hungover, or complaining about your biological dad, or your sister that doesn't want to talk to you, or your parents that never talk to you. How am I supposed to get better when I am living with someone that can't get her own life together?"

"Aah, so I HAVE done something wrong? Geez, Haz, way to kick a girl when she's down."

"Maybe you could get Marcy to move in?"

"Don't try and fix this for me, Haz." She looked back at her food. "Suddenly I'm not hungry." Pushing her plate away, Gypsy got up and walked out of the room. She went straight to her bedroom and packed a bag – a change of clothes, make-up, CDs and her pillow. She grabbed a stash of money she had hiding in her cupboard and threw in a few pairs of shoes. She walked back out to the kitchen and said to Haz "I'm going, not that you care where I am going, but I will be back in a day or two. I am sorry if living with me has been so shit, I really thought we were awesome. And you know, you really should have spoken to me if you had issues with me instead of making me feel fine and then jumping on me like a ninja. A good friend is honest, Haz, I thought we were good friends."

"We are, Gyps…"

"Were." She corrected him and turned on her heel to leave the house.

Gypsy left Haz sitting at the table dwelling in his failed aspirations. She felt a little sorry for him, because she knew that it would have been hard for him to say what he had said, and he tried to be honest with her, then she blew up in his face. But she was hurt. Stabbed in the heart. Feeling lonelier than ever and feeling slightly like a brekky beer.

Gypsy tried to call Skye. It went straight to voice message. Well, I guess that doesn't mean she is trying to avoid me if she doesn't know I've rung. She tried again for good measure. Nothing. She jumped in her car and called Marcy - God, she needed Marcy right now, Marcy had said that she would go with her to Kanville, and after this morning's events with Haz basically telling her she is a drunk, a horrible friend, and he is moving out, she really needed Marcy.

"Hey Marc, how are you feeling?" Gypsy drummed her finger on the steering wheel.

"Gyps, I'm in bed with my future husband, this better be good."

"Oh, umm…" this wasn't a good sign "You still want to come with me to Kanville?"

Please say yes, please say yes…

"Sorry Gyps," Marcy said, as Gypsy cried internally. "Like I said, man of my dreams, asleep next to my naked body. I'm sorry, Hun, you understand right?"

Gypsy breathed in deeply and put a smile on her face – you can always hear a smile through the phone –

"Yeah, no worries, I understand."

"Thanks, Hun. Let me know how you go though."

"Sure, all good, see ya."

"Love ya." Marcy said, but Gypsy had already hung up the phone.

Gypsy sat in her car and cried. She felt the weight of every person who had left her behind, even after they had promised to be there for her. The weight of her problems that no-one was willing to help her hold, and the weight of loneliness and the feeling that no-one would ever truly love her, as a daughter, a sister. or a friend. She was destined to travel the earth alone and never find that one person who would be there with her through thick and thin. That one person who would put her first, above all other things, the way she had always done for everyone she loved. Here she was about to go back to Kanville to try and begin a friendship with her sister, a sister that had no interest in knowing her, but Gypsy was going, damn it, because maybe it was her last real chance at having someone real in her life, someone that made her feel that the world wasn't just this shitty place. Because she knew that everyone else had their own problems, dreams, and fears, that's why she let them put themselves first, while she also put them first… but who was putting Gypsy first?

She started up the car and pulled out onto the street ready for her day to either shine, or crumble.

CHAPTER 17

Skye was lying next to Manny with her arms and legs curled around him like a vine up a tree. Her fingers, like leaves, tickled his chest and played with his skin, creating goose bumps in their wake. He smelt of testosterone and aftershave, and in this moment, he was her sleeping beauty. Her head moved up and down with the rise and fall of his breath, and she wondered what he was dreaming. Up this close she could stare at his features without feeling coy, and she could take in every ounce of him.

The night before had been like any other night. They had some dinner, a couple of wines and watched some boring television. She didn't have to work the next day, so she may have had a little more wine than usual, but that was nothing to worry about. In fact, there was nothing at all to worry about now.

They were sitting next to each other on the couch when Skye had gotten up to get some chocolate from the fridge. The tension had been building over the last couple of weeks, and they could both feel it. It became an unspoken reality that there were feelings between them because the air was thick when they were in the same room. The sparks in the air were causing an electric storm right inside their house, but neither of them mentioned it in fear of…well, in fear of being wrong.

Skye opened the fridge and grabbed her chocolate ready to bring it back to the loungeroom to share with Manny, but when she turned around he was right there, in front of her, and without a word he grabbed her behind the neck, gripping her hair and pulled her towards him, kissing her hard and filling her with passion, like a force of nature. She let it happen and pulled herself closer, kissing him with all of her built-up hunger. They were grabbing at each other fiercely, moving around the kitchen like a lovers' dance. Skye's hands grabbed him all over not knowing where to grab first as she wanted all of him at the same time. Manny kissed her hard and bit her lip, almost breaking the tension with a little laugh, but it only lasted a second and they continued their dance. Skye had been dreaming about this moment for so many weeks that the lust in her centre tingled instantly and ached for attention. She could feel every part of her body starting to get weaker yet stronger at the same time as she consumed more and more of Manny, like shocks of orgasmic energy that took her breath away while it fed her desire. She wasn't sure how they had made it back to her room through their blinding need for one another, but once they did; they made love all through the night, like two souls that had walked the earth for thousands of years in search of each other and had finally reconnected.

Their chemistry was a perfect mix of friendship, love, and lust, pulled together to form two tangled naked bodies that curved with the sheets and moulded into one perfect shape of love.

Skye laid in bed, still stroking his body, while images of the night before filled her head. She could feel that familiar sense of longing creeping back inside her and her heart raced a little faster. She needed him again, and she needed him now.

Suddenly, there was a knock at the door. *No!* Skye flinched, *Go away!* She moved the blankets and got up on top of him in preparation to recreate the night before, when Manny stirred.

A smile swept across his face and Skye's heart melted.

"Good morning, Beautiful." He said.

"Good morning." She smiled back and leaned down to kiss him.

Knock, knock.

"Just ignore it." Skye said, "It's probably the mailman or something."

"Happy to oblige." Manny smiled and kissed her again, thrusting his hips upwards to show her he was serious.

Knock, knock.

Oh, for the love of... "I'll get it." Skye jumped up throwing on some clothes, she leant in for another kiss as Manny grabbed her hand and said, "Make them go away, I've got big plans for you." Skye giggled and left the room, leaving Manny – and her needs – in waiting.

Skye hobbled down to the front door filled with ecstasy, ready to tell someone that, no, she didn't want new blinds, or she didn't want to sponsor a child, or she didn't want to join the fight to save the rainforest…she had bigger things going on. She opened the door and was a little blinded by the light of day.

"Hi Skye" Gypsy said. They both just looked at each other. Gypsy had driven all this way and was now lost for words.

"Oh, it's you. What are you doing here?" Skye asked. Her feeling of euphoria was gone.

"I, umm…"

"He's not here, if you're looking for Cam."

Gypsy was thrown back. Wow, Skye really didn't know her at all, did she?

"I'm not here for him. I told you, I threw him out."

"Right. Ok, so what do you want?" Skye said this pretty nastily, and then felt horrible. She watched Gypsy scratch her head and saw how uncomfortable she was. She thought she should invite her in, but she had Manny in her bed right now, and not a comet falling from space was going to keep her from him.

"I just wanted to talk. I'm sorry I just rocked up at your house, but I have tried to call you and message you. I just didn't know what else to do."

"How did you get my number in the first place? And how did you find out where I live?"

"Brad gave me your number, and he also mentioned you worked at the tip, so I kind of called them and asked where you lived…"

"And they told you?!" Skye was horrified; she could have been anyone, she could have been the serial killer. "Bunch of idiots." Skye mumbled.

"Me?" Gypsy asked.

"The idiots at the tip, obviously." Skye said. "Look, I'm kind of busy at the moment. What time is it?"

Gypsy looked at her phone.

"It's 11:27"

Holy crap, Skye thought, *Is it that late?*

"Ok, fine. Come back in an hour. Bring milk."

Gypsy was starting to regret her decision to come. She thought Skye was a rude bitch.

"Ok, cool, I'll bring milk. Anything else?"

"Just milk." Skye said. "See you in an hour."

Gypsy watched the door close in her face and thought of a saying she heard once that said: 'Nothing worth having comes easy, and if it's easy, it ain't worth having.'

Suitable. She thought.

It was too nice of a day to be driving around, so Gypsy decided to walk in search of a corner store or supermarket where she could get some milk, when in all honesty all she wanted was a beer, or a wine, or a scotch… anything basically to take away her anxiety. But she was going to change. She had just lost her roommate and friend because of her drunken antics that she never even knew were a problem. Until this morning.

She walked down the road for a while and came across a park. It was a big park with a little pond and a playset for the kids. There were trees everywhere and the atmosphere was nice. She looked across the road from the park and recognised the café – it was the café that she had lunch in with Cam. *Arsehole.*

She wandered over to the café wondering where Cam ended up; where he went after she kicked him out. Then she realised she didn't want that piece of dirt in her thoughts. Brushing them away she decided to sit for a minute and watch the birds playing in the trees. Their games were funny if you paid close enough attention. One would chase the others, then the others would chase him, then one bird would squawk, and they would all go flying back into the tree. Gypsy imagined life as a bird, and the freedom that would go with it. Sure, they could fight, but at the end of the day, they would all end up in the same tree, snuggled into the same nest being cared for by their parents, and they would sleep until a new day began, ready to wash away the games of the day before and begin it all again. Gypsy thought she would try to ring Brad since she was in town, but every time she tried, his phone was switched off; either that or he was still in a place with no signal. *He couldn't still be camping, could he? It's been weeks...although he did say he might be gone for a while...*

Gypsy looked at her clock and it had only been twenty minutes since she left. She wandered over to the café to see if they sell milk, because there was no harm in trying. When she got there, she could smell the coffee and breathed it in like it was the breath of life.

"Hi, could I get a cappuccino with two sugars, please? And I'm wondering, do you sell milk, or is there somewhere close by that does?"

"We are a café…we have milk, but we do not sell milk."

"Ok, that's ok… do you know where I can get some? I'm from out of town." Gypsy said. The young waitress looked around to see who was watching and said, "How much do you need?"

"I'm not sure, I was just asked to get some milk. Maybe enough for a few coffees?" Gypsy said, wondering if this chick was nuts or if she was going to sell her some milk.

She then started talking a little bit louder "Ok, so that's one cappuccino, and one large milkshake?"

Gypsy looked at her confused, then the waitress said quieter, "Just four dollars for the cappuccino thanks, Babe." And winked. Gypsy handed over the four dollars and smiled back, not sure what the waitress was up to. She sat and reminisced about the week or so she had with Cam. She looked over at the table that they shared when they first met up for a coffee, thinking about how that whole time Skye was actually watching them from afar. *How horrible that must have been for Skye,* she thought sadly. She looked at her phone and saw it was 11:59. Almost time to go back. The waitress came over to her with a takeaway cappuccino and a takeaway large milkshake. Gypsy eyed the milkshake and looked at the waitress confused. The waitress just winked and walked away. But when Gypsy opened the lid, she noticed it was just a milkshake cup filled with milk. A smile ran across her cheekbones and she looked over to the waitress in admiration; *there are good people on this earth.* Gypsy tipped her pretend hat towards the young waitress and stood up to leave, but as she did, she heard the radio that was playing in the background make an announcement:

"And now we are going live to the policeman on the scene, Officer Sawyer, we believe you have taken into custody the man responsible for the killings of the missing men – Thomas and David McGill?"

"Hi Sharon, yes, after a long investigation we had found irrefutable evidence leading to the man responsible for the killings of the two missing brothers. It has been a long couple of weeks trying to locate the man, who is local to the Kanville area; he was found camping out in swamp land about 450 kilometres east of High Tide. Unfortunately, the perpetrator did expose a weapon and responded to police officer's requests to step down by opening fire. The perpetrator has been shot. Sadly, this is not the outcome we would want, we did respectfully request that the man step forward willingly but that was not the case, and we do need to look out for the safety of our officers."

"So, Officer Sawyer, please explain, it sounds like the man has been shot and injured?"

"Look, regretfully Sharon, this did result in the death of Bradley Mains, as he was unwilling to cooperate with police, and did open fire. It is not the outcome we would prefer, but in a case like this we had no other choice."

"So, the families of Thomas and David McGill may be able to rest easy knowing justice has been served, but really, should Bradley Mains not have received a fair trial?"

Gypsy was gobsmacked. Speechless. Lifeless.

"Pretty hardcore, hey?" the young waitress was by Gypsy's side again. "I mean he was from our own town. It's lucky they killed him; he could have done anything, hurt anyone." Then she inhaled quickly like she just realised something and twisted to the other waitress "Sally! Do you think that's the man that stole my wallet? Oh my god..." Sally piped up and said, "You're so lucky, he could have killed you too." Then they hugged, almost weeping.

Gypsy, in robot mode, stood ever so slowly, gripping her large cup of milk and leaving her cappuccino on the table. She turned and walked out of the café with her gaze in front of her, not moving one eye muscle. She walked in a straight line across the road, not looking for cars first. She was lucky she didn't get hit – not that she cared at this point. She walked across the park, past the swings, past the pond, past the birds flying freely in the trees waiting for dinner time. She crossed over to Skye's street and to her front door. When she got there, she looked down and noticed that she had been gripping the milkshake cup so tightly she had bent and squeezed all of the milk out of it and over her hands. There was only a drop left. How could she not even notice that running down her hands? Gypsy knocked on the door, but this time she didn't wait for it to open, she walked straight in. She didn't really notice her surroundings as she was in search of only one thing – Skye. She walked straight down a hall she had never been in before, not noticing shoes in the walkway that she almost tripped on, or underwear on the floor from a night of pleasure she knew nothing about. The hallway led her straight into a kitchen out the back. She walked in and stared at a fridge in front of her.

"Are you…Gypsy?" A voice said beside her.

She turned to her right and saw a handsome looking guy standing at a kitchen table with his arms on the shoulders of her sister.

The radio was on.

"Skye?" Gypsy said. "Did you hear?"

CHAPTER 18

She walked closer to the two of them and sat down at the seat next to Skye. Skye didn't respond to Gypsy, but Manny nodded his head.

"I…I'm so sorry." Gypsy said slowly moving her hand over the table to rest on top of Skye's hand, who was shaking slightly and staring at the radio. The radio wasn't making any noise anymore, and Gypsy realised Manny must have turned it off. She wasn't sure what to say, or what to do. She didn't even know how she should feel right now; did she have the right to feel as shocked as she did? Was she allowed to feel pain from this? Or should she bottle up her own pain and let Skye feel it all? She had only met him in person once, does that give her a right to be sad? Does that give her a right to feel some of the pain that Skye was feeling? Gypsy has suffered a loss also, and she had waited years to find him only to have him ripped out from underneath her like a cloth on a dinner table; and here she stood, like a wine glass wobbling in the aftermath, waiting to fall. *Steady, Gyps.*

Suddenly, Skye spoke up, "Do you believe what they said? That he…that he killed those two men?" She was still staring at the muted radio, and Manny was still rubbing her shoulders from behind. Skye was in shock for so many reasons that she couldn't even comprehend properly what had happened. Her mind flashed of images of her dad when she was younger – pushing her on swings, teaching her to ride a bike, helping her up through the hard times, and cheering her on in her accomplishments; he was her best friend. She loved him so much that she never even imagined a life without the support of her dad, as he had always been her rock, her confidant, and the only constant in her life. What was she going to do without her dad? It was unbearable to think of such a place where he didn't exist. She numbered off the images and words in her head, trying, grasping for any reasoning to the absurd ramblings of the voices on the radio.

She continued, "One: my dad was killed in a *shootout* with police. How ridiculous is that? That doesn't even seem real, they're obviously insane, I mean, they're insane, right? And wouldn't they talk to ME before blurting it out on the fucking radio? I'm his family, his ONLY family since Mum died, and no one thought to speak to me? Two: they say they have enough evidence that my dad was the man that killed those two men that went missing? I don't fucking believe it! My dad couldn't hurt a fly, and anyway, they hadn't even spoken to him, how would they know? He didn't do it. He couldn't have…you don't believe it do you, Mann?" By this stage she was hysterically laughing and yelling and crying all at the same time as if a symphony of instrumental emotions were flowing through her, not one more profound than the next. Her head was shaking as if confused, and her words were trying their best to make sense of it all, "I saw one of the bodies. There is no way my dad could do that to someone. NO fucking way! When the cops questioned me, I had no idea." She started crying heavily, "I had no idea…"

"Oh, Skye, shhh, come here." Manny leaned down and kissed her on the forehead while hugging her tightly.

"And now he's dead!" She cried the words out with such force it was heartbreaking for Gypsy to watch. Manny picked her up and carried her away into her bedroom and shut the door. All Gypsy could do was sit quietly and wait, left with her thoughts and the painful new awareness that Skye's mother was also dead.

Gypsy sighed. *I thought today was going to be a good day.*

It had been an hour and a half since Manny took Skye away. An hour and a half of Gypsy sitting at a strange kitchen table, with strange surroundings in a strange house. If she left then it would probably seem like she didn't care, but if she stayed, she might be overstaying her unspoken welcome. Every now and then she could hear Skye cry out in pain; they were the painful cries of an orphan. A girl who had now lost her mum and her dad. It was hurtful to hear, not understanding fully what she was going through, but being able to imagine it enough to feel some of the agony deep inside. Gypsy started feeling like she needed to talk to her parents. She stood up from the kitchen seat and walked over to the cupboards opening and closing them in search of, what?

"What are you after?" Manny said quietly as he walked into the kitchen.

Gypsy startled and jumped around, "Sorry, I was just looking for something to …" Gypsy searched for the words. She wanted to say 'drink', but she didn't want to say 'drink' because that would be embarrassing. In such a time like this most people would not be thinking of a drink as most people drink in times of celebration, but in Gypsy's case, she drank to numb pain. She drank when she felt uncomfortable or wanted to subside the anxiety swirling through her body.

Manny pulled a joint out of his front pocket.

"I always have one of these ready to go. Do you smoke?"

"Not in years. You don't have any… scotch, do you?" She could feel her face blush. But when the realisation hit that she was in the presence of someone else who was also finding the need to escape reality just a little, she didn't feel as bad asking.

"Sorry, no scotch. There might be a beer in the back of the fridge."

"Thanks" Gypsy looked in the fridge and found the beer. Cracking it open, she spoke, "So, how is she?"

"Asleep." Manny said.

"Probably for the best."

"Yeah."

"Do you believe it?" Gypsy asked.

"As hard as it is to believe, shit does happen, and I guess he was shooting the cops back for some reason, right?" Manny puffed away at his joint, and Gypsy could see his body slowly relax with each inhale.

"Well, I only just really met him, so I guess it's not as hard for me to believe, but it's still pretty crazy. Here I was thinking I had found my dad and gained a sister..." She could feel sadness creeping up on her.

"You still gained a sister." Manny said, almost like he was trying to convince her to stick with it; keep persisting. "It's horrible that Brad's dead, he was a really great guy, and a great dad to Skye. And it's gonna take a while for Skye to come to terms with the shitty circumstances in how he died, and why he died, and what he did...but, keep trying. Don't push too hard right now, but don't run away, I think she will need a sister more than ever now, and whether she knows it right now or not, I can feel already that she will love you."

Gypsy looked down and had a swig of her beer. It was going down too nice, she needed more. Then she remembered what Haz had said to her that morning, and it made her feel guilty for wanting one at all.

"You don't even know me," she half-laughed, "I don't even think I should be here right now. I'm...to be honest, feeling really uncomfortable, like why would she want some chick in her house that she doesn't know, while she's going through this shit? And I don't even feel like I have a right to cry...sure I didn't know him, but he was my flesh and blood. He was my dad too."

"I get that, but you do have a right to be sad too." Manny said. "Just hang around. Stay, please. Skye truly has the biggest heart, and in my mind, I wouldn't worry about the Cam shit, that wasn't your fault. She will learn to love you not only because you are here for her, and you are trying, but you are her flesh and blood too. She's not the type of girl to throw away a perfectly good sister opportunity, even if lately, she has tried." He said. Gypsy didn't feel convinced. "She's just hurt."

"So, what am I supposed to do? Just sit around here waiting for her to not hate me anymore?"

"I think considering her dad just died, she doesn't have room to care about anything else. Anyway, she is completely over Cam, trust me." Manny had something in his eyes that made Gypsy believe him.

"Ok…well, I'm not much of a cook, I'm more of a local at a place called Frank's back home. But I could go and get some dinner for everyone tonight, if you want?"

"That would be good, thanks." Manny smiled. "Do you want some cash?" He reached for his pocket, but Gypsy stopped him.

"It's ok, my parents kind of gave me a credit card…it's money to live on until I get 'back on my feet', they like to say, but I like to think of it as 'take this card and forget that we are absent parents' money, you know?"

Gypsy laughed, hiding her inner torment, and kicking herself for joking about her parents when Skye had lost both of hers.

"Right." Manny nodded, "I kind of wish I had parents like that, haha."

"No, you don't, trust me." Gypsy said.

"Ok, well, there is a pizza place about a ten-minute walk away, or we could get Chinese? It's up to you." Manny finished his joint and stubbed it out, reaching for a little tin out of his other pocket he started to roll another one. "So, I don't think Skye will mind if I sleep in her bed and keep her company tonight, I know she won't want to be alone. But I'll tidy up in my room and make you a fresh bed for the night, save you from sleeping on the couch. It's up to you though, if you're comfortable with that?"

When Manny smiled, she could see what Skye saw in him; it was a warm comforting smile that made her feel at ease. "I was going to crash at a hotel, but I mean, yeah, sure. As long as she won't mind?"

"I think she'd like for you to stay, and she'd prefer me closer more so than distant. She will need the shelter of my arms."

The shelter of your arms? Who are you?

"Ok, cool. Well, it's only just after 2pm, so I might make a coffee…do you have any coffee?"

"Yeah man," Manny smiled getting up off his seat, "I'll make you one. Milk and sugar?"

"Yeah sure." Gypsy smiled. "Oh shit…I kind of lost the milk."

"So just sugar, then?"

"Yeah, cheers. So, tell me more about Skye." Gypsy said, fishing for info on her sister. "She mentioned that her mum died?"

"Wow, going straight for the hard stuff, hey? You are a scotch drinker." Manny said with one eyebrow raised. He

220

placed a cup of coffee in front of Gypsy and she breathed in the smell.

"I wonder what would have happened if I had gone camping with Brad? Was that even what he was doing?" Gypsy went into deep thought about the conversation she had had with him when he had requested her to go with him. "They said they found him in swamp land. Who camps in swamp land?"

"Maybe he was in hiding. Who knows?" Manny shrugged. "How's your coffee?"

"Good, thanks." She took a sip. It was horrible. "So, has Skye always lived around here?"

"She was born in High Tide, but when her mum died when she was five, she moved to Kanville with her dad. He started his carpentry shop out the back of his house in the shed, and Skye and I met at primary school. She turned into one of those cool kids, you know, the ones that hang out with the popular girls and stuff in high school." He shook his head with a little laugh escaping the side of his mouth, "But we never stopped being friends. Ever since we knew each other, it was like she was only ever her true self when she was around me, not with those skanky girls. She was always a bit of a tomboy." he said whimsically, "I guess you get that growing up without a mum. In high school she ended up having a big fallout with all of her girlfriends and started spending all of her time with me instead. We've been inseparable ever since."

Gypsy sat and listened intently, soaking in his words wondering if this was the closest she would ever get to her sister.

"When Cam came along, she really loved him. They became this mad-tight couple so quickly that once he started cheating on her I just wanted him dead. I didn't want him anywhere near her. I nearly choked him one day and told him he had to tell her, or I would put him in the hospital. I said I wouldn't tell her, that was his business to do it…but I never should have given him that option. I guess I didn't want to be the one to hurt her, and it killed me every single day." Manny looked at her and back at his coffee. He scratched his head like he was deciding whether to speak his next words. "I really love her, Gypsy."

Gypsy's heart melted a little at the pure honesty of his statement. She could see how true his love was from the intensity in his eyes, and she knew Manny would never hurt Skye the way Cam had.

"I still can't believe what a scumbag that guy is." Gypsy said. "He seemed pretty convincing to me." She elaborated, "He convinced me he was a decent guy. I guess I'm just gullible."

"Don't beat yourself up about it, Dude, he was a pathological liar."

"Yeah, well I wish I had known that when I let him stay at my house, and in my bed." The thought made her cringe. "I wonder where he went…actually, on second thoughts, I don't give a shit. He could be living in the land of the cheaters for all I care." Gypsy looked thoughtfully out the window, with a smile, "It's a magical place where cheaters go; they live in tiny little huts all alone and people come into their houses to feed them yummy food, then they take the food away and say 'Gotcha!' and then they laugh, and laugh as they walk away. Plus! There's no beer, and he has no penis, so he can't have sex ever again. Mwahahaha." Gypsy laughed evilly and tapped her fingers together.

"Well...cheers to that." Manny chuckled, and they clinked their coffee mugs, while in the back of his head was the image of the bedroom down the hall, where the girl he loved was asleep, dreaming tortured dreams about the loss of her father.

Manny and Gypsy had ordered Chinese food to be delivered and spent the night watching movies. Manny had checked on Skye a few times, but she hadn't stirred. She was drained from emotion and the tears she had cried earlier that day had almost dried her up to the point of dehydration. She wasn't getting up. Manny changed all the sheets on his bed and tidied up his room for Gypsy to sleep in, which she questioned a number of times to make sure it was still ok; this was just her anxious mind making her feel uncomfortable. She laid in the bed and stared at the pictures on the walls of Manny when he was younger skating with his friends, a photo of him, Skye and Cam at what looked like a concert, and posters of rock bands. There was a computer desk with junk all over it and a little lamp in the shape of a hot air balloon that seemed a bit childish to Gypsy.

It was a large room that smelled like sandalwood and male's deodorant, and there was a warm essence of cosiness about it. There was a lounge chair in the corner that he had cleaned all of the clothes off, but a big green fluffy cushion remained, giving it that soft charm of a place to sit quietly and read…or in Manny's case, smoke weed. Gypsy found a book on the bedside table that read 'How to be Happy, in an Unhappy World'. *Interesting,* she thought.

It felt weird to her that she was going to sleep in Skye's house without really talking to Skye about it. But she figured she would see what tomorrow brings. "Hopefully tomorrow is a better day", she sighed, speaking only to herself.

CHAPTER 19

"Good morning." Manny said to Gypsy as she stumbled into the kitchen like a zombie with her head of brown hair going every direction and covering her half-asleep face. Manny had given her one of Skye's old t-shirts to borrow for the night, and he took one look at her, laughed and said, "Good morning, Sunshine."

"Morning," Gypsy groaned, "Coffee?"

"Kettle just boiled."

"Is she up yet?" Gypsy pulled the hair out of her face and looked around. Her mascara had run down her cheeks and added to the zombie look.

"Not yet." Manny said getting her a cup out of the dishwasher and handing it to her. It had a frowny face and had the words 'I'm not a morning person' on it. *Fitting*.

"This one's cool." Manny said, "When you put the hot water in it, the face changes to a happy one and the words say 'Good morning'"

Gypsy just stared at him. "Cool." She said sarcastically. She needed her coffee, she'll laugh later.

"You're not really a morning person, are you?" He poked. Manny was so easy to get along with and didn't get offended very often. It was tough getting on his bad side, because he didn't really have one…except when it came to Cam.

Gypsy made her coffee and walked out the kitchen door into the backyard. The morning was fresh, and the dew was still present on the tips of the blades of grass. They tended to shimmer in the light like a green carpet of diamonds welcoming her to sit and relax. There was a big willow tree to the right that reminded her of Olly. *Ahh, hello friend.*

She sat underneath the willow tree on the wet grass and let the cool air chill her lungs and body. It was a Saturday and she could hear children playing in their backyards over the fences, giggling and bouncing on trampolines. The morning sun would warm each yard and create an inviting space for each house; a place where children could play while their mothers hung out washing, where Gypsy could sit and let her bones wake up slowly with each breath, and a place where sisters could weep.

Gypsy saw the back door open and a figure appear. It wasn't Manny; it was Skye. Gypsy stood up slowly as Skye walked towards her, not a word spoken by either girl. Skye wrapped her arms around Gypsy and hugged her tight. As they embraced, Skye began to cry. Within a second, they were crying together. The tears flowed in unison down one another's cheeks; Skye's blonde hair mashing with Gypsy's brown like a tangled painting by an insane artist. Skye cried for her father, and Gypsy cried for

Brad and her sister. Though their stories were different, the point of focus was the same.

Skye was glad Gypsy had come. She was glad that Gypsy had the balls to ignore her attempt to make her feel unwanted. And right now, she welcomed her with open arms. As they hugged, the sounds of the neighbourhood vanished, and their hearts started pumping in harmony; not a step out of beat. For Gypsy it felt almost like everything had melted away and she was exactly where she was supposed to be, where she should have been her whole life. Gypsy had never experienced this before; a feeling of pure simplicity, and of belonging. They could both feel the sisterhood connection as if they had known each other their whole lives. Gypsy had thought in that moment: *this must be what normal sisters have.* She had spent her whole life never knowing the importance of sisterhood.

They stood there for a couple of minutes embraced in a hug of loss and a hug of emotion. Like it was a completely normal hug they had had many times before. Eventually, Gypsy moved away and wiped a tear on her cheek.

"Hi." She said and laughed a little at the weird moment.

"Nice shirt." Skye said eyeing her own shirt on Gypsy. "So, you stayed, I see." She didn't laugh but let out a little sigh of relief and wiped her tears away with her sleeve, tears that had flowed a lot stronger than Gypsy's.

"Sorry, I hope that was ok?"

"Yeah, totally. I wasn't really in a state to care yesterday anyway."

Gypsy put a hand on Skye's shoulder, a sign of comfort.

"So, what happens now? Do you want me to go bat-shit-crazy at the radio station for releasing the news without talking to you first? Because I will." Gypsy had a very serious look in her eyes, and Skye could sense the crazy in them.

"I haven't told Manny yet – he's in the shower – but the cops came to the house last night while you guys were asleep." Skye said looking away, remembering the night before. She looked back at Gypsy who was standing there a little shocked, like she couldn't believe she slept through that; she should have been there for her. "I woke up at around 1am and heard the knock on the door. They told me what happened, and to be honest I think I was still in shock. I told them thanks but because of their incompetence I had already heard the news on the radio, for which they apologised profusely and said that supposedly one of the officers was supposed to come here last week and question me about where my dad had gone, but they never did. They never came and spoke to me, they never questioned me apart from when the bodies were found at the tip, and I had no idea my dad was even a suspect! I told them how disrespectful the whole thing was, and then told them to get the hell off my front porch."

"Shit…"

"Yeah, shit, alright. Then I went back to bed, curled up to Manny and stared at the wall for the rest of the night."

"I don't really know what to say, Skye. Is there anything I can do?"

"Nope. Not unless you can bring my dad back. You know what I want? I want to go to the pub and get so smashed that I forget yesterday even happened. But if I do go, I know that everyone will be staring at me and will want to put their two cents in. I probably won't ever be able to leave the house."

"It'll blow over." Gypsy said, trying to be positive, but she knew how absurd she sounded. She really didn't know what the right thing to say was. "You can always come back to High Tide with me?"

Skye thought longingly about getting away and escaping this mess. "Or you could just stay here?" Skye said.

What? Gypsy thought.

"Umm…are you sure?"

"I never had a sister." Skye said putting her hand on Gypsy's arm, "Honestly, this past month or so has been crazy. Things that I couldn't even imagine happening, have happened. Good things, bad things, horrible things..." Her tears started rolling out again at the thought of her dad. "It's seriously been like a rollercoaster." She wiped them away and continued, "Besides, Manny already thinks you're awesome, and think of all the stuff we can catch up on!" She said, trying her hardest to be positive. "Plus, I guess I have a funeral to plan. It might be nice if I could have a sister to help?" Skye hid her pain so well that she almost convinced *herself* she was going to be ok. Her puppy-dog eyes were fluttering, and Gypsy couldn't say no. But how long would she stay for? She wasn't sure. Maybe just until Skye was feeling better and the funeral had been done? She only had one change of clothes with her. *Ahh, but I do have a credit card.*

"Ok, sure, I would love to stay and help," she smiled, "I don't have anything waiting for me at home anyway..."

"Good, thanks Gyps." Skye half-smiled with her puffy red eyes and made it seem like everything was going to be fine, but Gypsy knew deep down, this was going to take a while.

Skye said she was going to have a shower and get out of her tear covered clothes and left Gypsy to finish her cold coffee. Suddenly Gypsy thought about Haz. She picked up her phone and dialled his number.

"Haz, hey, it's Gyps."

"Hey" She could almost hear him scratching his head through the phone.

"Look...are we alright?" She gritted her teeth; she didn't want to lose Haz even though he had hurt her so bad.

"I guess so. When are you coming back? I needed to get to drama class this morning but couldn't get a lift."

"Wha...? Haz, you said you were moving out. You said that you wanted to be by yourself and look after yourself. You said it was a *drain* living with me." Gypsy was confused.

"I know I said that, I'm sorry, are you coming home?"

"Haz, I'm staying up here for a while. You may as well stay in the house for another couple of weeks...if you want to, that is."

"But... I can't get to drama class." Haz said with a shaky voice.

My lord, he's like a child.

"You will be fine, get the bus, or get one of the other people in your class to give you a lift. Better yet, get your licence! Get your own car! For fuck sake, Haz, I have bigger problems to deal with right now." Gypsy was getting frustrated. *The nerve of him!* "Listen, I will be gone for a while, you are welcome to stay as long as you want, but if you only want to live in my house so that I can drive you around everywhere then I think it's probably best if you do what you said you were going to do and just leave. I didn't want you to go, Haz, but your starting to make me realise that maybe I am the one better off without *you* as my friend." She felt horrible. That felt horrible. She was a horrible person. "Hello?"

Radio silence. Haz had hung up the phone. Gypsy put her phone back in her pocket and scoffed. She didn't have enough brain space for everything that was going on. Between Brad, Haz and everything else…she was a wreck. At least things worked out between her and Skye, even if it did take the death of their dad. Gypsy felt so guilty for seeing the silver lining.

Skye, Manny and Gypsy were sitting on the grass in the park. Brad's funeral had been small as not many people turned up except his closest friends, Mrs Cray from the corner store, and the stray cat from the ally. Skye believed that some people felt strange being at the funeral of someone that supposedly killed two other guys. He never had a trial, so no-one ever got to find out if he was definitely guilty or if he was in fact an innocent man suspected of a terrible crime.

"He shouldn't have shot at the cops." Skye said. "He should have just gone with them and let them question him, and I'm sure everything would have been fine, they would have seen that he was innocent."

Gypsy wanted to mention all the evidence they had found and reported on the six o'clock news in the days following the shooting. But now wasn't the time. *Let her grieve*. Manny sat toking on a joint which he passed around the circle to share.

Skye held it up and said, "I think Dad would have appreciated this." As she inhaled the smoke, letting it relax her tense body.

"Since we're all dressed so nice, what do you think we go out somewhere nice for dinner?" Manny said. "No point in wasting such nice clothes."

"They weren't wasted, they were worn in respect of my dad, and my dad's life that was taken away by those fuckers." Skye said a little aggressively towards Manny.

"I didn't mean to disrespect…"

"No, I'm sorry. I know you didn't." Skye said. She was taking her pain out on Manny and he didn't deserve that. He'd been nothing but amazing to her; his support through everything was something she will admire and appreciate forever. Plus, she was pretty sure she had fallen completely, and utterly head over heels in love with him.

"Guys, I might leave you to it." Gypsy piped up, "I'm feeling sick as crap. Kind of like I might throw-up."

"Oh, Mate, you alright?" Manny asked.

"Yeah, not sure. Might have been something I ate. I guess with the planning of the funeral I hadn't paid much attention, but it's kind of been happening on and off for a couple of days." Gypsy grabbed her belly and pushed a face of discomfort.

The weed had started taking its effect on Skye who had more than enough reason to escape her current emotions. A second ago she would have been more than happy to go home and wallow in her sorrows, but now she was looking through the world in a different light. "Gyps," she giggled, "do you think if we changed clothes people would think I was you?" Her eyes were red and squinted.

"I don't think that will work, Buddy." Gypsy laughed. "What about our hair colour? What about the fact that we look completely different?" she laughed.

"Actually…" Manny interrupted, "You guys do have some similarities." Both girls looked at him like he was nuts. "No, seriously, you both have your dad's eyes, and face shape, his smile…"

"Hold on, no, not true." Skye said, "I have my mum's smile." She drew lines in the shape of a smile on both sides of her face. Her teeth were white, and her lip gloss shimmered from the sun through the trees. "My dad always said I had my mum's smile. He said apart from the yellow dress, it was one of the main things that made him nostalgic about my mother. He said it was the most beautiful smile in the world."

Manny looked at her and knew that even though she had buried her dad today and would love to reminisce and feel close to him, he wasn't going to destroy her connection to her mother, and Brad had always told her he loved seeing her wear her mother's smile. Who was he to wreck that?

"You're totally right, you guys do have different smiles, I must be super stoned. But the rest, the rest is the same, it's kind of uncanny." His eyes darted from Gypsy to Skye and back again. As they were all sitting under one of the big trees in the park the shadows danced on their faces like masks at a masquerade ball. They both rested to their left leaning on the same arm and did the same face twitch when a fly went by. He could see the resemblance in a way that it was now impossible to un-see it.

"Skye" Gypsy said, "You said you didn't want to go out, you kind of wanted to avoid the pitchforks of the town's people." She said this facetiously, hoping to make a joke of it.

"I know, but that was before the funeral. Honestly, I'm not too fazed right now."

"Before the joint you mean. It's 'coz you're stoned." Manny said grabbing her around the neck and giving her a noogie.

"Oh my god!" Skye squealed and squirmed away from him, "My hair!"

Manny and Gypsy just laughed as she tried with all her effort to flatten her perfectly straightened blonde hair back down. But she couldn't keep a straight face.

"Dude, you suck" She drew the words out and tried to keep a frown on her face but couldn't suppress the smile. She joined in the laughter with Manny and Gypsy who had begun again.

"Oh my god… Manny?" A voice came from behind the girls. "How are you?" She sounded perky and young. She was standing right above Skye. "Oh, Skye! How are you?"

234

Skye looked up at her trying to place the face. She had nothing. "Remember? Joanne? I was at your house the night of the fire." The girl smiled like she had said 'the night of the fair' or 'the night of the parade'.

"Oh, that's right," *The bitch.* Skye cringed. "How are y…"

"Manny, it's good to see you, you didn't call me." She interrupted Skye, then shifted on her feet.

"Ouch!!" Skye cried.

"Oh, I'm sorry, did I step on your finger?" The girl said it more as a statement than a question.

"Um, Joanne, this is Gypsy, Skye's sister, and of course you remember Skye, whose finger you just stood on…"

"Yeah, sorry. So, Manny, you want to hang out tonight? I'm free after eleven, I've got this gig down at The Tavern, and I was thinking…"

Skye and Gypsy looked at each other and it was like they were talking telepathically. Before Joanne could finish her sentence, Skye leaned over the grass and kissed Manny on the lips. She didn't release him for a good ten seconds. When she finished, she looked up at Joanne and said;

"Joanne, he's gonna be a little busy tonight." She smiled a devilish smile and Joanne's mouth looked like it was going to drop to the ground and lick up the insects in the grass.

Manny just sat there, supremely proud of his possessive girlfriend, and Gypsy, not one to prolong the silence spoke in stereo sound, "He's taken, so don't bother. And if the next words that come out of your mouth aren't an apology for my sister's fingers you might have broken, then the next words out of MY mouth are gonna be 'run mother fucker', 'coz I ain't scared of a bitch fight!" Gypsy started getting up off the ground in her beautiful black dress she had lent off Skye for the funeral. She was ready, she was a sister now, and she was gonna protect her family, god dang it!

Joanne scoffed and walked away with the fear of Gypsy in her rear-view vision.

"What?" Gypsy said shrugging her shoulders at Skye and Manny. "Family's sacred."

"I love you." Manny said to Skye.

"I love you, too." Skye replied.

And they kissed, while Gypsy looked whimsically at the park around her thinking she never wanted to be anywhere else but here.

CHAPTER 20

Gypsy laid in bed and was feeling even worse today than she did the day before. Her belly felt like she had a stomach bug, and she felt weak, oh so weak. She hadn't drunk anything last night due to the funeral and getting a little stoned, but she felt like she had a hangover.

Marcy had tried to ring her a few times and left voice messages. Apparently, she had gone to Gypsy's house looking for her and Haz had told her about Gypsy staying in Kanville for a while. Marcy was not happy. *No, Marcy, not now*, Gypsy had thought. She felt so sick she didn't even have the energy to ring her best friend back.

Her bed was warm, and she had no intention of moving. Manny had a surprising number of pillows for a dude. And all Gypsy had planned for the day was to snuggle in and let the pillows control her life.

Oh shit.

Gypsy felt her body go cold and the water start to swell in her mouth. This was not unfamiliar for her to understand what this meant, but as she wasn't hungover, it was utterly confusing.

"Get out of the bathroom!" She yelled as she ran down the hall, arms flailing and no pants on. Thankfully no one was in there, she raced straight for the toilet. She threw up everything she had eaten in the last year. There could have been apple pie and burgers and salad. Shit, for all she knew there was an entire roast chicken! But by the time she finally finished, and she'd lost 20 kilos, she still felt sick.

Well, that ain't right...

Gypsy got up and washed out her mouth. She looked in the mirror at her face that seemed a little more drawn out than usual. Her skin looked clearer and her eyes looked bigger, but why were her cheek bones sticking out? Was she losing weight? She had so much going on lately that maybe she hadn't been eating properly. But if she wasn't eating much then how did she get this stomach bug?

"You ok, in there, Gyps?" Skye called from the bathroom door.

"Yeah, Mate, all good." She was not 'all good'.

"You want a coffee?"

"Coffee would be awesome." Gypsy said. She looked around at the fancy soaps and the candles by the bathtub and decided that today she would have a bath; she had nothing else to do anyway.

Gypsy emerged from the bathroom and wandered into the kitchen still feeling a little queasy but hoping a coffee would take away the nausea.

"You sure you're ok?" Skye asked sceptically after hearing the noises from the bathroom.

"I'll be fine, just need my cuppa jo"

"Gypsy... um, pants?" Skye laughed.

"Oh shit!" Gypsy ran back out of the kitchen to retrieve some pants, shaking her head and laughing. *What is wrong with me today?*

"Ok, I'm back...with pants. Where's my coffee?" Manny was busying himself with toast and Skye was giggling at Gypsy's clumsiness. "Thanks." She said.

"Outside?" Skye said. "It's a nice morning, we should go and do something today, like out of the house. Apart from the funeral I haven't been out in ages, and my annual leave is almost up. I better get back in the groove of things." Skye said walking out the back door and into the morning sun.

"Yeah sure. Whatever you want to do." Gypsy agreed.

They sat on the grass and let it cushion them from below like a seat of soft greenery.

"You really need some seats out here." Gypsy said. "Why don't I buy you some chairs today?"

"What, with your parent's credit card?" Skye laughed.

"Yeah, they won't even notice." Gypsy shrugged her shoulders. She took a sip of her beautiful smelling coffee and instantly could feel it coming back up again.   Skye looked at her curiously while Gypsy struggled to decide if she could keep it down, or if she was going back to the bathroom.

"I'm, not gonna make it." She jumped up and ran behind the big willow in the back yard, letting loose the coffee that had just touched the edges of her stomach seconds before.

"What is going on with you today? What did you eat yesterday?" Skye questioned, thinking back to everything they had consumed the day before.

Gypsy stood behind the tree and started to become dramatic. She scrunched up her face and wore the look of pure worry on her forehead.

"I just want a coffee," she cried, "Lord!" She swung her hands to the sky in an overly theatrical way, "What have I done to offend thee?! Why can't I drink my coff-ee? Please heal my freakin bell-y and let me drink my coff-ee!" She started stomping her feet in a circle like she was doing a chant and repeated the words. Her sickness had made her hysterical. Skye started laughing and jumped up to join in. Together they stomped in a circle and chanted the words like a song:

> "What have I done to offend thee?!
> Why can't I drink my coff-ee?
> Please heal my freakin bell-y,
> and let me drink my coff-ee!"

They didn't even need to try. It was as if they knew what each other was thinking, and they moulded as one. Their bodies moved in a perfectly synchronised fashion, like a flock of birds moving in motion with the wind. Manny watched from the kitchen window at the crazy girls in his backyard and laughed a full belly laugh. It was like watching pure happiness. He watched the girls and thanked his own lord that they had found each other, that Skye now had this sister in her life to bring her such joy and happiness, especially in such a terrible time. He looked at Skye with so much love in his heart that he felt it may burst. His pericardium was jam-packed with a kind of love potion that he could bottle and sell to loveless souls, filling the world with the same feeling of nirvana that he felt in her presence. *How did I get so blessed?* He would think to himself. Somehow as everything in Skye's life had tumbled down like an avalanche, the pieces landed perfectly at the bottom as if it were all meant to be. The rocks, once unpredictable, falling and injuring everything in their path, had created a place of beauty in the valley below, a bubble of happiness so secure that not a thing in the world could pop it.

Suddenly Gypsy could hear a sound coming from over the fence and slowed to a stop.

"What is that clicking?" she asked Skye, who had also stopped dancing like an Indian chief around a fire.

"Oh," she lowered her voice, "That's Anne. We used to call her Click Clack. Apparently, she is completely traumatised by one of Cam's side chicks; she threatened to kill her and also tried to burn down her house."

"Holy crap." Gypsy stood staring over the fence in horror, "What a nut job. Has anyone spoken to the police?"

"We didn't, she had a lady come and pick her up a while ago while the house was being fixed, we just stayed out of it. Kind of figured she'd look after it all. But anyway, we just kind of keep an eye on her and make sure she's ok."

"Why does she keep saying click clack?" Gypsy asked.

"Something to do with the sound of the chick's high-heels or something."

"Shit. That's rough. Cam really was a piece of work, wasn't he?"

"You have no idea." Skye said. "Good morning Anne." She called out over the fence. Anne popped her head up and didn't say a word. No 'click', no 'clack', nothing, she just nodded and went back to staring at her garden. Skye felt sorry for her as she never seemed to have any visitors; she looked very lonely. She imagined living an 80-year life, the amount of things that she would have been through; good and bad. And then to be living alone, with it all coming to an end. It was sad.

"We should do something nice for her." Skye said.

"Yeah? Like what?"

"I don't know…just something nice." Just as she said it her phone started to ring, pulling her attention from the lady over the fence. She pulled out her phone from her back pocket and saw it was an unknown number. "Hello?"

"Hello, is this Skye Mains?"

"This is she."

"My name is Herbert Hancock. I knew your father and recently went through the process of helping him update his Will. Firstly, my condolences." He paused for effect. "I would like to see you to discuss his assets and what he had wished for them after his death. Is there some time that would suit you to talk? I can come to you if it's easier?"

His assets? Skye hadn't even thought about her father's belongings. She had been too consumed in the fact that he was gone and her own suffering to even think about any of that.

"Um, sure, you can come to my house if you want. I haven't really been leaving the house." She shuffled her feet looking at the ground.

"Understandably."

The way he said this made Skye dislike him straight away. "What do you mean 'understandably'?"

"Nothing, nothing. I just…would 10:30am be ok?"

"Today? … Um, sure." Skye gave him her address and hung up the phone. Just as she mentioned the strange man to Gypsy, Gypsy's phone started to ring.

"Hello?" Gypsy said.

"Hello, this is Herbert Hancock, am I talking to Gypsy…"

"You were just talking to my sister; Skye." Gypsy cut him off.

"Yes, I was…are you with her?"

"I am."

"Great, this will save me doing two trips." He mumbled.

"What's this about? Brad's Will?"

"Yes. So, Skye and I agreed to meet at 10:30 today at her house. Does this suit you, too?"

"Yeah, sure, whatever."

"Ok, great, I will see you then." And he hung up the phone before saying goodbye.

"Who the hell was that? And why is he ringing *me* about Brad's Will?"

They both just looked at each other. Gypsy felt strange that he had contacted her regarding Bard's Will. They had only really just met. But Skye was now stuck in thoughts of her father's house, and how empty it must be without her father's presence. She hadn't even thought to go around and see if it was still standing.

Gypsy broke the silent thoughts that hung in the air between the two of them. "Ok. So, I guess our arses are sitting on the grass until this afternoon?"

"Guess so. I still don't think I'm ready to leave the house, though. I know I need to, I mean, I'm back to work next week, I know I have to bite the bullet at some stage."

"Ahh, you'll be fine, because we need to get some chairs. And if anyone looks at you sideways, I will just drop-kick them." Gypsy laughed and put her arm around Skye as they walked back in the house.

"What are big sisters for, hey?" Skye said, with images of her father's house plaguing the insides of her mind.

The door knocked twice.

Skye walked down the hall and opened the door to a small balding man with glasses that needed a clean, and visible nose hairs that needed a trim. He smelled like aftershave and incompetence. His suit was two sizes too big and his hand was holding an unfinished donut.

"Oh, hi." He said shoving the rest of the donut in his mouth, leaving glaze on the side of his mouth. He wiped his hand on his pants and stuck it out for a handshake. *Eww*. Skye unwillingly shook his sticky hand.

"Hi, you're Herbert?"

"Yes, and you must be Skye." He said. "Is Gypsy here too?"

"Hi." Gypsy said coming down the hall. Skye tried telepathically to tell her not to shake his hand. It didn't work. Gypsy shook his hand and ushered him to the loungeroom. Walking up the hall she rubbed her hand on her jeans and looked at Skye who mirrored her look of disgust. Gypsy laughed a little and Herbert turned around in his steps.

"Everything ok?"

"Yes." Skye said, "I'm just going to use the bathroom quickly." And she dashed off to wash her hands. Gypsy was not so quick thinking.

"Take a seat, Herb." Gypsy said.

"It's Herbert. Or Mr. Hancock." He eyed her through his dirty glasses. "Shall we get started?"

"Let's wait for Skye." Gypsy said just as Skye walked into the loungeroom.

"Ok, so, you have my father's Will?" Skye said, sitting down on the chair next to the couch.

"I do."

"Were you his lawyer?" Skye questioned.

"No, I just looked after his Will." Herbert scratched his head.

"So Herby…" Gypsy said.

"It's Herbert." He corrected again, straightening his tie now. He looked extremely uncomfortable, almost like a mouse stuck in a corner, checking its surroundings, looking for a way out.

"You seem a little uncomfortable, Herb. Are you alright?" Gypsy said a little devilishly. She laughed inwardly at Herby.

Poor Herby. She thought. *Stuck in a room with the daughters of a killer.*

"Can we just do this?" Skye said impatiently, looking at Gypsy with a 'don't be such a smartarse' face.

"Ok. I don't know if he knew the end was coming or he just had fantastic timing, but he had updated this Will with me only a couple of weeks ago. He wanted to add Gypsy as the part owner of all of his assets, and he has divided the whole lot up evenly."

"What does that mean?" Skye asked. "Like his house and car and tools and…"

"Everything." Herby cut her off. "So, both of you - Gypsy and Skye - are equal owners of the house and everything in the house. His business he requested be liquidated and all assets of the business be sold off, where you both have equal rights to the money made from the sale of all things. He requested that the house itself not be sold, and it was his wish that it stays in the family. Now, as it became a crime scene not long ago, I would suggest keeping the house simply for the fact that it will be tricky to sell with the gruesome history. With that being the case, even if it were to sell, it would most likely sell well below the property value…due to the deaths." He added, like it wasn't obvious enough. "But this really is up to you. He has made requests, but as the house will be transferred into the names of yourselves, it really is up to you what you do with it." The girls both stared at Herby, then at each other.

"So, let me get this right." Skye said, "He divided up everything and has given it to both of us in equal parts? What, like we were his equal daughters?" She knew that was hurtful to say, but she was a little shocked. Gypsy was feeling a burning feeling coming from Skye. She could feel the tension in the air and her throat start to close. She didn't care about the house; she was not prepared to lose the sister she had just gained because of a stupid house.

"Skye's right, this should be hers, I should have nothing to do with this."

"I am only telling you what the Will says."

"No, it's fine, it's obviously what he wanted." Skye said. But Gypsy could tell; it wasn't fine.

"Look, seriously, can I just sign my half over to Skye? I will do that right now. Where's a pen?"

"Legally the house is half yours. If you want to, you can sign over your half or you can sell your half to Skye."

"For money? I'm not doing that!" Gypsy laughed a nervous laugh.

"Just leave it!" Skye said.

"No! I'm not taking your inheritance, it's not right, I don't care what he wanted."

"As the beneficiaries…"

"Shut up, Herb!" They yelled in unison. The girls both sat there with their hearts pumping just a little faster, the air's thickness coming alive and whispering in their ears. Their thoughts, a tangled mess of emotion sweeping circles around the devil on one shoulder and the angel on the other. Skye was staring at the floor, Gypsy was staring at Skye, and Herb was staring at his watch.

"Look, seriously, I will just sell you my half…for like, a dollar." Gypsy said - a serious joke.

"A dollar, hey?" Skye said, a tear trickling down her cheek, followed by a slight exhaled giggle. Herby shifted uncomfortably on his chair and mustered up the courage to speak again.

"It is possible for her to sell you her half for a dollar, it has been done many times before."

Skye looked at Gypsy, who really was Brad's daughter, and thought that maybe she was being selfish. Maybe she was being silly, if that is what he wanted, if he wanted Gypsy to have half of the house, then why shouldn't she have it? But it was Skye's house. The one she grew up in, the one that held all of her memories of her dad. Then she was brought back to reality by a sudden forceful reminder that her dad had killed two people in that house. The evidence that was found by the detectives was clear that it was the crime scene, like Herby had said. Could she really live in it now? Could she really feel safe or happy in there now? It was her home, but it was tainted, and the images would haunt her.

"Look, I can't decide on something like that right now. And you know what, Gyps? Stuff it, it's your house too, he left it to both of us. I haven't been there since he left and I'm not even sure if I can go there, knowing what he did." Skye looked at Gypsy. "It doesn't matter how much I try to deny it; he killed people in that house. They say there's too much evidence to disagree with that fact. I don't want to believe it; I still can't even wrap my head around him doing that. If you knew him like I did, you would understand."

Gypsy wasn't sure if that was another stab at her for not being close enough to Brad to deserve half of the house, but she knew it was important to try to understand Skye's pain. The pain of a girl that has lost her dad in the most unlikely way. The pain of finding out he was not the man she had thought he was. Her life was a lie, and her dad was capable of things that she only saw in horror movies. Skye started to cry and walked out of the loungeroom without saying another word.

"I think you better go." Gypsy said, standing up and walking a confused man to the front door.

"Usually people are quite happy to find out they have been given a house." He said, with one eyebrow raised.

"Usually their dads aren't killed in a shootout with police." Gypsy said with a sarcastic smile.

"Well…you got a house. Congratulations, I guess?" Herby said.

"No, Herb."

"It's Herbert!"

Gypsy shut the door behind him and leaned her back against it. She could hear Manny and Skye talking in Skye's bedroom and thought she would leave them alone. She grabbed her keys and walked out the front door and out to her car. She was going furniture shopping.

The next morning when Gypsy woke up, she felt sick again. This morning she wasn't going to have coffee. She was going to suffer without her caffeine fix. *Oh lord.*

"Morning!" She yelled out the kitchen window to Skye and Manny who were sitting on the new outdoor furniture Gypsy had bought yesterday. It was a nice big, round, wooden table with six chairs around it. She had splashed out and grabbed a pot plant to put in the middle of it too, thinking, hopefully Skye is better at looking after plants then me. Joining them at the table, she sat down and held her belly.

"Still sick?" Skye said.

"Dude, trust me, this will make you feel better." Manny said, handing her his joint.

"God, no." Gypsy said waving him away. "How can you smoke that so early in the day?"

"Dude, how can you *not* smoke early in the day?" He laughed.

"We're not all you, Manny." Skye laughed at him. "But, seriously, Gyps, has this happened before? You know, the ongoing sickness? Maybe it's something in our water?"

"Maybe…maybe I'm allergic to something here in Kanville?" Gypsy said. "What are you guys doing anyway?"

"Just writing a shopping list. You need anything?"

"What have you got on there?" Gypsy grabbed the piece of paper and scrolled down the list. Bread, Milk, Butter, Dishwashing Liquid, Tampons, Toilet Paper… *Tampons.* Gypsy's heart stopped.

"Tampons!" She yelled. "Tampons… Fuck…" She started clawing at her forehead searching for something.

"Calm your tits, they're on the list already…"

"I know…" *Shit, shit, shit.* Gypsy started counting back to the last time she had her period. *Oh, hell no. I couldn't be, could I? No…not possible. I haven't been with anyone… Shit, yes, I have.* Her body went cold as she came to a horrible realisation. *The only person I've been with since…oh crap.*

"Um, I've gotta go." Gypsy jumped up and ran back towards the house.

"Hold on, I'll come with you, we'll do the shop." Manny called out. But Gypsy was already gone.

"Well, that was weird." Manny said.

"Ya reckon?" Said Skye.

"Since we've got the house to ourselves…" Manny said, winking at her. "…You do look awfully sexy in your PJ's."

"Shut up." She said laughing at him. "Hey, let's have a BBQ tonight. We'll invite over some friends and see if Gypsy wants to invite her friends? It would be like an impromptu get together to kind of get to know each other's friends?"

"We don't really have any friends." Manny said.

"Sure, we do. Well, you've got friends. And we could invite Click Clack… sorry, Anne."

"Really? You sure you're up for a BBQ?" Manny was still worried about her wellbeing.

"Yeah, I'm fine. It would be good. Plus, I've got to start back at work in a couple of days, so I really need to get used to being around more people." She said, standing up and giving him a kiss on the forehead. "Add BBQ food to that list, and don't skimp on the beer."

Manny watched her walk inside, and he did as he was told. As long as she was happy, he was happy.

"BBQ it is, then."

Skye went inside and grabbed her phone. She needed to call Gypsy and see where she had gone. She wasn't used to having a sister, but she was still a person, and anyone would have seen that Gypsy looked like she was in trouble.

She looked as though she had been knocked on the head with a lightbulb. *What is so important about tampons?*

The phone rang out and went to Gypsy's voicemail: 'Hi, it's Gypsy. No, I don't have your dog or your booze, but please leave a message!"

Random. Skye thought. Skye figured she will see the missed call and call her back if she needed to. This girl has lived 32 years without Skye, she was perfectly capable of storming out of a house and looking after herself. *Wasn't she?*

Meanwhile, Gypsy was wandering the aisles of a chemist looking for one thing in particular.

"Ooh, I need one of these." She said as she saw the hairbrushes, "and one of these." She said towards the eyelash curlers. "Excuse me, yeah you, do you know where the hair dye is?"

A lady came walking over to her and pointed at the shelf right behind her. "Right here. Do you need a hand with anything else, Miss?" The lady asked. She smelled of overly priced perfume and it made Gypsy gag. Her hair was so blow dried and full of hair spray that she could almost feel the puncture in her eyeball if she was to stand too close. Her pink lipstick was all over her teeth and she wore too much eyeliner, but with all of Gypsy's judgmental opinions aside, she still had a welcoming vibe about her, and that is what she needed right now - a welcoming vibe.

"I forgot why I was here." Gypsy laughed. She looked around the chemist at all its chemist-y things. The nice lady put a hand on her shoulder and said, "Are you ok, Honey?"

It was only then that Gypsy realised how dishevelled she must have looked. She looked a little disturbed and was darting her eyes in a troublesome manner and then stopping, biting her nails, and then looking at the woman. Darting her eyes again in a haze of 'what the *hell* am I doing here?' flooding from every pore.

"Um, I think I need a…a pregnancy test." Gypsy said the words, so unfamiliar to her, she felt it must be a dream. This couldn't really be happening, could it? She secretly pinched her arm. Yep, it was happening, and now her arm hurt.

"Oh, how wonderful! Congratulations." The woman beamed, "Right over here." She walked Gypsy to another shelf and showed her the options. "It all really depends on how much you're willing to spend."

"This one's fine." Gypsy said, grabbing a packet with a happy looking couple on the front. "Actually, I'll take five, just to be sure."

"Ok," the lady smiled, "You must be thrilled. Is this your first?"

"Um, yeah." Gypsy did not share her enthusiasm.

"Oh, what an exciting time this must be for you. I remember my first. My husband and I had dreamed about it for so long that when it happened, we were ecstatic! Simply ecstatic." She clapped her hands into a prayer and looked whimsically at the ceiling, smiling like her cheeks were about to burst, "They're just so precious. So, what does your husband do? Does he know you're here getting the test? Or is this going to be a surprise?"

Please. Shut. Up.

"…Are you hoping for a boy or a girl?"

"Neither." Gypsy said. The animosity she was feeling towards this lady was growing stronger.

"Oh…I see." The lady took a step back and put her hand on her mouth. "I am so sorry, I just assumed…"

"Assume nothing. Can I just pay for these, please?"

"Sure, Honey."

"Thanks." Gypsy couldn't even bring herself to smile anymore.

"Are you sure you want the hair dye? I have heard it's bad for the baby if you're…"

"Oh my god, woman! Just give me my stuff, please, I don't care!"

The lady handed over her bag and said, "Well, you have a nice day." Although her smile was gone.

"Thanks." Gypsy grabbed her bag and walked out of the chemist ready to break down in tears or punch a wall. Either one would have been fine.

CHAPTER 21

"Gypsy's back!" Skye called out to Manny when she saw her car pull up out the front of the house. She had been busy cleaning and Manny was about to leave to get the shopping. He had rung around and rustled up a few mates to come over tonight for the BBQ. Skye had been around to Anne's house next door, but she had declined by shutting the door in her face, with a click clack here and a click clack there. Skye was starting to get the impression that Anne was annoyed with her.

"What have I done?" She had said to Manny, who just shrugged his shoulders and replied;

"It's the thought that counts." But, not to worry, Manny had a couple of mates he played pool with, in the local competition at the pub, and they were always up for a good time.

"Where were you? Are you ok?" Skye questioned Gypsy as she walked in the front door with the answers to her future in a bag by her side.

"I'm ok, sorry about before, I just had to do something."

"Is everything alright? Can I help…or…?"

"No, it's all good. Thanks though." She said with a smile.

"So, we decided to have a spontaneous BBQ tonight. Manny's invited some dudes from his pool comp, and he's about to go down to the shop. Do you want anything?"

Gypsy wasn't sure what her future was going to bring. Was she pregnant? Or not? She couldn't even bring herself to think about it right now.

"Can you grab me a bottle of scotch?" She said, handing over her credit card.

"Sure, is that all?" Skye asked. But she could see something was different in Gypsy's eyes. She could see a kind of torment or forced smile. Her mouth turned up, but her eyes drooped. *What is wrong, sister girl?* She thought.

"Are you sure you're ok?"

"Seriously," Gypsy smiled and slapped her on the arm, "I'm fine. I'll be better with some scotch in my hands though." She laughed.

"Ok, ok, cool." Skye said and walked back to the kitchen handing Manny the credit card. "And a bottle of scotch for my awesome sister, please."

"Ok, sweet. I'll be back soon." Manny said, and left.

Gypsy walked into Manny's room – which had become her room – and put the bag on the desk. She pulled out the hair dye, the eyelash curler and the hairbrush. Her eyes stared into the bag at the contents that remained – 5 boxes of pregnancy tests - and she shoved the bag under her pillow. Out of sight, out of mind.

"Oh! I forgot to say," Skye came bursting into the bedroom, "You should call your friends and invite them too."

Gypsy thought about it. "I guess so."

"High Tide's only like an hour away, isn't it? I can make them a bed and they can crash here tonight? It would be good to meet your friends."

Gypsy figured she could call Marcy and Nicki, but not Haz. She was not in the right zone to be trying to make amends with Haz.

"Yeah, ok, thanks Skye, I'll give them a call and see what they're up to." She smiled and a little hint of home came washing over her. She could feel the High Tide air washing through her hair and smell the jasmine in the breeze. She missed home, oh how she missed home. But she was so happy here too. She thought about having Marcy and Nicki here and how it would make everything perfect. Her life, in one house, even if that house wasn't in High Tide. She picked up her phone and dialled Marcy's number.

"Bitch-face!" Marcy yelled in the phone. "What the hell are you doing? I thought I'd never speak to you again!"

"Hey Marc." Gypsy said, "I'm sorry I haven't got back to you, it's just been a bit hectic here."

"I miss you!" Marcy almost cried the words.

"Well, if you miss me, do you want to come for a cruise up to Kanville today? We're having a BBQ and I want you to come up. You can sleep in my bed, or on the couch, or whatever. Skye really wants to meet you, and I miss you."

"Dude, you haven't returned any of my calls! I saw what happened on the news…" Her tone become high pitched, "I was so worried about you!"

"Yeah, sorry. It's been pretty crazy." Gypsy said.

"So, are you coming, or what?"

"Ok, fine, but only because I love ya." Marcy paused. "How are you going since…you know… your dad?"

"Yeah, we're getting there. Slowly but surely, Marc."

"Ok, well I'm coming up to squeeze you so tight, and you can tell me all about it."

"Awesome. Can't wait to see you, Marc. Hey, do you want to see if Nicki wants to come too?"

"Why don't you ring her? Yeah, bugger it, I'll give her a call now." Marcy was sounding happier, "ROAD TRIP!" She yelled and hung up the phone.

Gypsy was left sitting on the edge of her bed, phone in hand and her stomach in her throat. She was excited to see Marcy but anguished over the bag that laid under her pillow. She wasn't ready to know. She wasn't ready for her life to change. And she certainly wasn't ready for a baby.

She figured that maybe, just maybe, if she ignores it long enough it will go away. It will all just float away like the sea spray after a wave. The wave will crash in a mighty roll and the spray that floats into the ocean air will dissipate into nothing. She could dispute that the very thought of it just going away was ridiculous, but for now, it was her only hope. She had a BBQ to enjoy, damn it! And she was going to have fun! Baby? What baby? She laughed and walked out of the room, away from the pillow of answers and away from the anxiety that hung over her head like an axe.

"Marcy's coming, and maybe Nicki too." Gypsy said. Skye was sitting at the kitchen table with her feet up on a chair, stirring the mixture for a cob loaf dip.

"Try this." She handed a spoon to Gypsy.

"Wow, that's amazing." She said.

"It was my mum's recipe. Dad kept this old recipe book of Mum's." She pointed to an old scrap book on the table. "Whenever she found a recipe that she loved, or even if she made it up herself, she would write it down in this book." She stopped stirring and looked thoughtful. "My mum died when I was five, but I still remember her making this cob loaf. She loved cooking and dancing in the kitchen with Dad. I remember this one time, the loaf burned in the oven because they were too busy laughing and dancing. They never left me out, though. They would always tell me to join them for the 'Dinner Dance'. That's what Mum would call it. I can't even imagine what my life would have been like if she hadn't died. If I had been able to have more years filled with dinner dances, laughing, and sunshine." Skye thought about the yellow dress. "What are your parents like?"

"Not like that." Gypsy laughed. "We used to go to the beach on a Sunday and play all day on the sand. It stopped as I got older. It was the only real time we spent together. To be honest, I'm not even sure why they adopted me." Gypsy scoffed. "They give me money, but not their time.

They were always so busy that I never really knew them. I think I knew my nanny more than I knew them."

"You had a nanny?"

"Yeah…"

"So, you really were one of those rich kids?"

"Rich in money, but not in love." Gypsy said. "Maybe that's why I drink so much?" They both laughed.

"You don't even drink that much." Skye said, "Well, I'm not sure what you're usually like, but you've hardly drank since you've been here."

Gypsy thought about it. The nights – and days – in High Tide were filled with booze and hangovers. She really hadn't drunk much at all since being here at Skye's house. *Well, that is strange…* she thought.

"True." She looked at Skye with a jumbled smile. "Maybe I'm happier here?" They both laughed.

"Maybe you should just stay here forever?" Skye said. "And if you get sick of me, there's always Dad's house."

Gypsy sat across from Skye at the table. She wasn't stirring the mixture anymore; she was looking intently into Gypsy's eyes and wore the smile of a clown.

"You're serious, aren't you?" Gypsy said.

"Totally serious. It will be great!"

"Haha, I guess I could think about it." Gypsy laughed.

"No, don't think, just do." Skye said. It was decided. And she returned to mixing her cob loaf mix.

But Skye didn't know that Gypsy may not just be Gypsy soon. Gypsy may be a duo. A dynamic duo that consisted of one alcoholic and one tiny person that screamed all the time.

We could fight crime, Gypsy thought.

Manny returned with the shopping and two of his mates.

"Gypsy this is Sean and Tom."

"How are you going?" Sean stuck out his hand.

"Hey." Tom waved and smiled.

"Guys, Gypsy is Skye's sister. She's staying with us for a little while, from High Tide."

"Sister?" Sean questioned. "I didn't know you had a sister, Skye."

"Neither did we." Gypsy laughed.

The boys put the beer in the fridge and cracked a can each.

"Got your scotch, Gyps." Manny said handing her the bottle and her credit card.

"Thanks, Mann."

"On the hard stuff?" Sean laughed. He seemed to Gypsy like more of a talker, whereas Tom was a bit more reserved. Sean had a nice smile full of white teeth and looked like he actually dressed up for the occasion. He seemed sweet. Tom had a scruffy beard and wore a blue singlet and stubbies. He had a tan line around where a wedding ring used to be, and his eyes looked sleepy.

"Do you want a hand?" Tom asked Skye, who shook her head, thanked him anyway, and told the boys to go sit out the back and relax.

"We actually have some furniture to sit on now, thanks to Gypsy." She beamed a smile in Gypsy's direction. The boys went outside and sat down, leaving the girls to the food.

"So, Tom…" Skye said flicking her head towards the back yard, "He has been separated from his wife for a couple of months. He seems a bit scruffy, but he's one of the nicest guys you'll ever meet. You know, one of those guys that's always there to give you a hand?" Gypsy nodded, looking out the window. Skye continued, "It's been really hard on him with his wife leaving. She left him for another man, and I honestly don't think he's slept since. Manny goes to see him every now and then just to make sure he's ok, but you know what guys are like – they don't' really break down and tell you how they're really going, do they?"

"Poor fella. And what about Sean?" Gypsy asked. It was Sean she was curious about.

"He's just a player." Skye laughed. "No, look, he can come across a little sleazy sometimes, but he's really sweet, and funny, and he's just 'all about the love' – his words, not mine." She laughed. "But, they're both really great guys, and good friends to Manny. And Sean really is like the sweetest guy."

Gypsy's phone started to ring – it was Marcy.

"Gypsy! We are on our way!"

"You got Nicki too?"

"Yep, she's driving, and I'm drinking! Haha."

Gypsy laughed, "Awesome, can't wait to see you guys, I will text you the address."

"Sweet. See you soon, ya sexy bitch!" Marcy hung up the phone leaving a ginormous smile on Gypsy's face.

"They're coming." She said to Skye.

"Cool. Maybe one of them might like to drag Tom out of his depressing hole?" She winked at Gypsy who had already jumped up to pour a glass of scotch. She was so excited to see her best bud that she couldn't hold out any longer.

"You're gonna love Marcy, Skye. She's so funny, and a little crazy, but she's an awesome chick."

"Sweet." Skye smiled. "Hey, can I have one of those?"

"A scotch? Sure, man!"

The girls sat at the table and chatted away while they drank scotch and cut up veggies for a salad. Gypsy was anxious with excitement to see Marcy. It had been weeks since she had last seen her, and weeks without Marcy, was weeks too long. Nicki was one of her closest friends, but not in the way that Marcy was. Nicki was more Marcy's friend who along the way became Gypsy's friend also.

Manny came in to grab some more beer for the boys and roll a joint. His hair was messy from the wind and his face wore a smile that never seemed to fade. Gypsy looked at him and thought he looked really happy to have some of his guy friends around. She had been at Skye's for a couple of weeks now, and this was the first time she had seen him enjoying the company of someone other than Skye. His love for Skye would overpower the atmosphere in any room they accompanied, but Gypsy knew sometimes it was just good for guys to hang out with some other guys. Gypsy got along with Manny so well, she could already feel that brotherly bond. She watched him as he bent down to kiss Skye on the forehead. Skye would close her eyes as if soaking in his kiss like it was a universe of stars made just for her, and he would make it last just long enough for her to feel the love penetrating her skin.

Skye knew this was love. She knew that every breath she made now, she made it for him. She wasn't giving up any part of herself to be with him, and she wasn't having to change her ways, she was just able to be, and be loved as she loved him. It was the perfect relationship, and it made her wonder how she handled being so depressed with Cam all those years. She wondered why she put up with it and thought that maybe she didn't feel like she deserved real love, like she was broken in some way and could only be with someone else who was also broken. But being in Manny's presence and in his heart, she found a place where she could be unconditionally happy, unconditionally loved, and give herself to someone who was deserving.

"You guys are so cute." Gypsy said jovially.

"Gyps," Manny said, smiling of course, "You have no idea how much I love this girl." He looked back down to Skye and cupped her chin. Skye smiled and whispered, "I love you, too."

"Ok, stop, you're gonna make me gag." Gypsy joked. "Have you got the BBQ fired up?"

"Yep, almost ready. Did Skye tell you to bring some friends?"

"Yeah, man, they're on their way!" Gypsy was getting a little tipsy. The hour was almost up, and she could feel Marcy around the corner. Suddenly, she heard a car horn toot. "They're here!" Gypsy jumped up from her seat and ran down the hall to the front door, swinging it open and bouncing down the front steps. "Marcy!!" she screamed, running towards the car.

Nicki jumped out of the driver's seat and walked towards her.

"How are you going, Darling?"

Nicki and Gypsy hugged, and Gypsy replied,

"Nicki, it's been forever, Mate, how are you?"

"Good, Darling, good. I brought wine." She smiled, grabbing a box from the back of the car with six wine bottles in it. Marcy staggered out of the car with a can of rum in her hands and threw it on the front lawn, throwing her arms in the air waiting for Gypsy to run into them.

"How's my favourite bitch going?!" She hugged Gypsy and slapped her on the arse. "I bet you missed that, didn't you?" She said, doing it again.

"Oh, it's so good to see you guys, I can't believe you came!" Gypsy said.

"Are you serious?" Marcy said with a sarcastic look on her face, "Gypsy, Honey, how the fuck could we NOT come and see you? You ring, we come." They laughed and hugged again.

"So, Nicki, Marcy told me last time I saw her that you guys went on a rad little wine tour thing where you got to stay in huts in the vineyards, or something?"

"Gypsy, it was exquisite. The food, the wine…the men." She winked. "I will be doing it again in about a month if you would like to join me? I have this friend Natasha, who advertises for the company that runs the wine tours and she is giving me major discounts on all the 5-star tours." Nicki said this in a very sophisticated manner. "I can totally hook you up, girlfriend." She said.

"Now, where am I putting this wine?"

"Oh, shit, sorry, follow me inside." Gypsy said. Somehow being around Nicki made her feel younger, or almost 'bogan-esque'. They were from complete opposite ends of the spectrum.

Gypsy walked inside the house with a feeling of pride. She was thrilled about her sister getting to meet her friends, but she was more excited for her friends to meet her sister. She was filled with happiness and she wasn't afraid to show it.

Skye watched the three of them walk into her kitchen and got a little jittery. The nerves were taking over, but they were good nerves.

"Marcy, Nicki, this is Skye...my sister!" She beamed. "Skye, these are my two best friends, Nicki and Marcy." Marcy shook her hand, and Nicki gave her a kiss on each cheek.

"Welcome." Skye said. "Just make yourselves at home. There's beer in the fridge and the boys have just started cooking the meat."

"Boys?" Nicki said looking at Gypsy who just said, "Yes, there are guys here. Girls, keep ya pants on." They laughed and walked out the back to meet them.

"Hey guys," Skye said, "This is..." She'd forgotten already.

"Nicki." Nicki said putting out her hand.

"Tom." Tom said.

"And I'm Sean." He smiled.

"Right, sorry, and this is Marcy." Skye said. Sean was drooling at the sight of them, Tom had already sat back down.

Marcy waved, "Sup, fellas?" She said, pulling up a seat next to Tom. "Mind if I sit here?"

Nicki pulled up a seat next to Sean and Skye sat on Manny's lap so that Gypsy had a seat. Gypsy looked around at the people that surrounded her and smiled.

"This was a good idea." she said to Skye, who was resting her head on Manny's chest. "I think we should do shots."

"Shots?" Sean said, "Fuck yes!" he laughed. "I brought some tequila if anyone's up for it?"

Everyone nodded in agreement, and the shots were poured. The barbeque turned more into a party as the night went on, and the music was played loud. Skye brought out the cob loaf dip and the salad, which got devoured with the steak, but the sausages sat burning on the barbeque alongside the rissoles. By 10pm Nicki was sitting close to Sean, giggling and flirting like they were in their own little world, while Manny and Skye danced to the sounds coming from the speaker that was shoved out the kitchen window. Fairy lights lined the outside deck area and there were solar lights throughout the garden, bringing to life the colours of spring flowers and fireflies. Marcy was dancing to her own beat around a fire Manny had lit earlier on, and Tom had gone home. Gypsy sat in the chair she had only recently bought for Skye's backyard and watched the scene of happy people – flirting, dancing, and living. She had had quite a few drinks and looked down to her alcohol filled gut, feeling slightly bad.

It's now or never.

Gypsy picked herself up and went inside, careful not to interrupt the happy people and their happy vibes. She walked to the dreaded pillow and picked it up.

"Hello." She said to the bag of answers. "Fancy seeing you here. Do you come here often?" Gypsy pulled out one of the pregnancy tests. "Now don't freak out, but do you mind if I piss on you?"

She picked up the rest of the bag and walked straight to the bathroom before she could change her mind. Looking around at the candles and soaps, the smell of cleanliness and the pink fluffy mat on the floor, she knew these things were the last things that would join her before she became a mother. *Maybe I'm not.* She thought. *Maybe I'm just late due to the complete fuckery that has been this last month.* "Yeah. Complete fuckery." She said, staring into the mirror. She peeled open the packet and sat on the loo, concentrating hard, careful to make sure she covered the area.

Ok. No turning back now. She placed the stick on the sink and held her breath. *I don't want this, I don't want this, I don't want…*

"Shit, sorry Gyps." Marcy said as she erupted into the bathroom. "Holy fuck! What is that!"

Gypsy was still sitting on the toilet but reached for the pregnancy test before Marcy could get her grubby claws on it. "It's nothing."

"Bullshit it's nothing, give me a look!"

"No!"

"Gyps, what the hell? Why are you taking a pregnancy test? You can't have a baby!"

"I know!" Gypsy said. She could feel the tension inside her entire body. She imagined the tears welling up behind her eyes, having a meeting of the tear-duct managers, trying to decide when the right time to attack is. NOW! NOW! They shouted. And. She. Bawled. Her eyes were like fountains pouring out litres of water all at once.

"I. need. Olly!!" she cried. "I need to sit in my tree, I need to talk to my tree, and I need to NOT be pregnant." Her tears wouldn't stop, and Marcy sat in front of her on the toilet floor, holding her legs and grabbing toilet paper to dry her face.

"It's ok, it's going to be fine." She said.

"No, it won't. I can't have a baby!" she cried. "And if there is a baby inside this fucking belly, then you know whose it is?"

Marcy just looked at her, unaware of all the random men she may have slept with.

"Cam's! You know, Cam, the one that cheated on Skye with me?"

"Holy shit." Marcy said. "That might cause a bit of a stir…"

"Ya think?! I don't know what to do. If it is Cam's, is that gonna make Skye hate me again?"

"I can't answer that, chick." Marcy felt useless. "Hold on, someone's coming."

They both stopped talking and watched the door. Gypsy held the test behind her just in case someone came into the bathroom. Suddenly the door swung open.

CHAPTER 22

Skye was dancing with Manny, in a little bubble of happiness. She looked at him and couldn't believe she was the one that got to touch him and kiss him whenever she wanted. He was her breath of fresh air on a dusty day, her sunshine in a storm. He had a manly smell that didn't need any outside influence. It was testosterone and pheromones that enticed her senses and drew her to him. The heat from the fire that they danced around brought an unnecessary flame into an already burning spirit. Their hearts warming each other with an uncontrollable love she had never felt with Cam – or anyone. How is such a connection possible? How could this have been right in front of her for years and she never knew it even existed? She knew that her doubts in the beginning of it just being a rebound from Cam were incorrect. This was no rebound. This was an insatiable love that filled her with a thirst she could not quench. The more she had of him, the more she needed him, and she was entrenched in this need from head to toe. In the dark of night, dancing by the fire, the stars were like glitter sprinkling down upon their heads, blessing them from above. The sounds of giggling were coming from the table where Nicki and Sean were whispering sweet nothings into the night air, and it took Skye's attention away from Manny for just a moment. She looked around and realised that Gypsy and Marcy were gone.

"Hey, did you see the other two go?" Manny looked around and then back at Skye, giving her a kiss on the lips.

"I only see you." He said. Skye smiled and her body felt that warm glow once again. "I better go and see what they're up to."

"They'll be fine, probably just catching up." Manny said.

"Still, I shouldn't ignore them." She said. "I'll be back."

"I miss you already." He said as she walked towards the house. Skye just laughed and waved him away.

Skye walked down towards Manny's old room – currently Gypsy's – no one was in there. She walked back up the hall and saw the bathroom door open a little bit so figured no one was in there either. She swung open the door and saw Marcy squatting in front of a teary Gypsy.

"Oh, there you guys are…Gypsy, are you ok? What's the matter?" She sat down in front of her alongside Marcy. "What's going on?"

"Nothing I just…"

Marcy looked at her trying to think of a lie she could tell. Why was she sitting in the bathroom crying? *Think Marcy, think…*

"Frank's is closing down." Marcy lied.

"Frank's?" Skye questioned.

"Yeah, it's like her favourite takeaway shop back home. Frank is this guy…"

"No, Marc." Gypsy looked at her and shook her head. As much as she didn't want to destroy this new-found sisterhood she had gained with Skye, Gypsy didn't want to lie to her. She thought losing her by telling the truth was better than losing her by lying. She didn't want to lose her at all… *Maybe I don't have to tell her whose baby it is? Holy fuck! I haven't even checked… dumbass.*

Gypsy pulled the pregnancy test from behind her back slowly and Skye inhaled in shock.

"Gypsy! Are you pregnant?"

"I don't know."

"Turn it over, Dude." Marcy coaxed.

Gypsy turned over the test to reveal the little window that held the answers to her future.

It was positive.

Marcy put her hand over her mouth to hide the shock horror on her face, and Skye exploded in excitement.

"Gypsy! Oh my god, you're pregnant! You're gonna have a baby!!" She threw herself forward and hugged her tightly, nearly knocking over Marcy on the way. She held her firmly feeling the fear sprouting from Gypsy's soul.

"Hey, it's ok, this is a good thing, isn't it? You're having a baby." She beamed.

"Just what I always wanted – single parents unite." Gypsy fist-pumped the air in a sarcastic thrust. She looked over to the half empty glass of scotch on the bathroom sink and poured it down the sink.

"Oh, Gyps," Marcy said. "Mate, you're not going to be able to drink…" she started to laugh, and Gypsy kicked her.

"Shut up, I know that. Nine months of hell!" She said.

"You'll be fine." Skye said, "Now I really think you should stay with me. Oh, it will be great! We can go to classes together, and I will totally look after you." She beamed like the sun. Skye was more excited about the baby than Gypsy was. "You'll come around, Gyps, you'll see, this is a blessing!" She hugged her again.

"Easy for you to say. You're not the one who's gonna get fat and have to push the thing out of your vajayjay." She started to cry again.

"So, is this like, hormones?" Marcy asked Skye. "Is that why she keeps crying?"

"I think it's that fact that she just found out she's pregnant." Skye said to Marcy. "Look, it's getting late, I think it might be time for everyone to go to bed, so you can wake up fresh in the morning and maybe see this in a new light. What do you think?" Skye said. She was very nurturing.

"No, Gyps, this could be your last night as a free woman before you get all preggo and fat. Let's dance!"

Marcy jumped up and reached for her hands. But Gypsy was feeling too emotional for any of that. She couldn't hide her fear. And listening to the both of them talking to her and advising her – one to sleep and the other to dance – she figured, if she was going to have this baby, it could either be born with the influence of Marcy in High Tide, all alcohol fuelled and would probably turn out to be a gangbanger that swears every second word, or it could have the influence of Skye, all sunshine and clean happiness, and it would probably grow up to be a sunflower farmer, or the prime minister, or something. She looked at both girls and slowly stood up from the toilet seat.

"I'm going to bed. Sorry Marc, I will dance with you another time, thank you so much for coming up, but I really need to go to bed." She looked to Skye and said,

"Say good night to everyone else for me, please."

"All good, Gyps, I will make them some beds in the lounge room. You just go to bed, ok? We'll talk in the morning." Skye hugged her good night and said, "Love you."

"You too. Night Marc."

"Yeah, love ya bitch." Marc winked and hugging her goodnight.

"There's something I have to tell you." Gypsy said, with her heart throbbing in her throat. Marcy and Nicki had gone for a morning walk to cure their hangovers, and Manny was busying himself on his internet shop.

"What? Have you decided to stay? Please say yes." Skye sipped her coffee and watched the sky turn dark with rain clouds.

Gypsy had been up all night staring at the ceiling and googling what it would be like to be a mother. The pain of childbirth, and the sacrifices, but also the good parts, like having a tiny human that you apparently learn to love, or some such thing. *It might be alright*. She had concluded. I could still have my life; I would just have a little baby to cuddle and keep me company. "I don't want you to hate me, or this baby." She said with caution.

"Why would I?" Skye laughed. "I am over the moon about this! Manny is excited too. I can't believe I'm going to be an auntie." The rain clouds were getting closer and it started to spit just slightly on the outdoor table.

"We should go inside." Gypsy said.

"No, tell me first, it's ok, are you staying?"

Gypsy bit her lip and then let the words rush out of her, like ripping off a band-aid.

"The baby is Cam's." Gypsy held her breath.

Skye sat motionless at the table. Her hands gripped the coffee cup tightly, and her mouth slightly ajar. She could feel a cold rush of emotion run deep throughout her body that not even Manny could warm. She looked at Gypsy and started weighing up in her mind the evolution of the last two months – was Gypsy more important than her past relationship with Cam? Hell yes, she was. Did she love Gypsy enough to not see Cam each time she looked at her growing belly? She wasn't sure.

She was so excited about this baby, but it would also be a permeant reminder of what Cam did to her. She started shaking the thoughts off in her mind – she was with Manny, she loved Manny, and every inch of her being was glad that Cam had gone, or she wouldn't be in the position she was now, she would still be in an unhappy relationship with an arsehole. Skye was completely over Cam, and she knew she was…but this…this was a little hard to swallow.

"Right." She said. "Ok..." Lost for words, she looked down to her coffee cup as the rain started to fall. "Let's go inside."

Gypsy was unaware of the thoughts that suffocated Skye's mind. She couldn't read her face like a book, and she couldn't tell what she was thinking. They jumped up and ran inside to the shelter of the house. Gypsy looked to Skye for answers, but Skye was a blank canvas of nothingness.

"I think I might just head back home today." Gypsy said.

"No, don't do that."

"I think I should."

"Look, Gyps. I'm not really sure how to take this. To be honest, it's a little strange; I kind of want you to go so I can process this, but I also want you to stay."

"You want me to go…" This wounded Gypsy right in the middle of her beating heart.

"But I also want you to stay…" Skye said, trying to reassure her, but at the same time trying to re-assure herself.

"No, it's fine, you want me to go. I am going." Gypsy went down to Manny's room where she had been sleeping the last couple of weeks. She packed up her things and pulled the earphones off Manny's head. "See ya, Mann. Thanks for letting me stay."

"You going? Where are you going?" He said looking shocked.

"Home."

"Why?"

"Ask Skye." She said.

She looked over to the little table in the hallway that held a bowl filled with keys. One of those keys was for Brad's house. Should I? She walked to the bowl and grabbed her car keys and considered the little blue key that Herby had given them the other day. Picking it up she turned around to see if Skye was standing in the hall – if she wanted to stop her from going – but she wasn't. Skye was in the kitchen waiting for the front door to shut.

CHAPTER 23

"It's been over two months." Manny said, looking at Skye who was growing more depressed than ever. He was struggling to make her smile lately, and she barely had the energy to eat the food he cooked her. He had tried to get her to smoke with him just to cheer her up for a little while, but all she wanted to do was snuggle him. She just needed to be near him, like he made her feel like somehow, deep within, she was still alive and safe. She had been going to work and coming home like a broken record. She had stopped brushing her beautiful long blonde hair, and instead just threw it into a messy bun every day, letting the dreadlocks grow where they may.

"Do you want me to go down to High Tide and find her?" He asked. "I will get in the car right now and drive down there."

"No, don't. She hates me."

"I highly doubt she hates you."

"She said to me… specifically told me, that she didn't want me to hate her or the baby. And look how I made her feel, exactly that!"

"Did you try to call her again?"

"Last night. She never answers the phone. I don't know what to do."

Manny put the safety of his arms around Skye and rubbed her shoulder.

"I hate seeing you like this, Skye. I just want to help you somehow."

"It was a shock when she said it was Cam's baby, but I honestly don't care! I have no feelings towards him whatsoever."

"I know. But you're perfectly right to have been shocked. I was shocked."

"What do I do? I need my sister back." Skye started to cry. She couldn't take it anymore. She picked up her phone and dialled Gypsy's number.

No answer.

Gypsy had joined a group. It was a mothers group for pregnant mothers who were having their first babies. She didn't fit in at all, and while the other mothers wore their perfectly ironed pink blouses with cardigans hanging over their shoulders, Gypsy wore her ripped jeans and a band t-shirt. She was in this alone, and she was going to prove to the world that she was strong enough to do this. Most of the other mothers would bring along a spouse so that they could simulate the birth and learn the breathing techniques – Gypsy had no spouse. She missed Manny and Skye so much, and it broke her heart to ignore the phone calls from Skye on a weekly basis, but she didn't want to be the thorn in Skye's happy little life. She didn't want to bring discontent into Skye's world and destroy the happy bubble that her and Manny had by bearing a child that reminded them of the past.

She had been living in Brad's house and had cleaned it from top to bottom. She slept in the spare room and had been filling it with all the baby stuff that the internet had told her she needed.

Her parents contacted her a couple of weeks into her stay at Brad's, and she had told them the whole story about finding Brad and about her sister. They didn't get as upset as she thought they would, and actually congratulated her on finding a sister out there in the world, even though Brad turned out to be a sad and shocking story.

"He was such a nice young boy." They had said of Brad in his teens when he gave Gypsy up. She then told them that she was staying in Brad's old house and she was pregnant. They were over the moon with excitement and begged her to go back home so she would be closer to them, but when she declined saying she belonged in Kanville, they regretfully agreed to sell the house she had shared with Haz in High Tide and supported her in her choices. When the house sold – only weeks later to an old couple that fell in love with it - they gave all of the money made on the sale of the property to her – 'for the baby' – they had said.

Marcy had stopped calling her, and Gypsy put this down to her not being the best of drinking buddies anymore. She had called Marcy one evening to talk, but when she mentioned her concerns it just caused a huge argument between the two of them and they haven't spoken since. So, Gypsy, alone in a big wooden house, with a garden she had managed to maintain and a stray cat that she fed from time to time, was getting fatter. She decided that it was time to pick up the phone. Afterall, if Skye was the one trying to contact her, then she must actually want to see her, right? But all she could do was hold her phone and stare at it. Her fingers were refusing to dial, no matter how much she tried.

"Fuck it." Skye said to Manny. "Let's do it. Let's go to High Tide."

"Do you know where she lives?" Manny asked.

"No, but I remember Marcy mentioning something about her favourite place called 'Frank's'. I say we just go there and ask around. I can't take this anymore."

"Ok, sweet, let's go." Manny was excited for the sadness to end, and for the love of his life to get back to her happy self. Plus, he missed Gypsy too. "We're coming to get ya, Sis!" Manny laughed. And walked out the front door. Skye grabbed her car keys from the bowl in the hallway. It was filled with so much crap, it was the 'crap bowl'…the bowl that you just threw your crap in when you walked in the door because there wasn't anywhere else to put it. She looked at her keys, and she looked at the bowl. Her memory went back to the day of Herbert Hancock and when he left the little blue key to her dad's house on the bench. After he had left, Skye had grabbed the key and thrown it in the bowl at the front door while continuing to reassure Gypsy that the house was hers too. Back in the current moment, she looked down into the bowl and started moving things around. *Where is that key?* Realisation hit her like a brick to the head.

"Manny!" She yelled out the front door, "I know where she is!" Skye ran towards the car and told Manny to drive to her dad's house.

"You think?" he said, "Why would she be there?"

"The key's gone. I haven't touched it." Her heart was racing, and she was filled with every emotion under the sun; excitement, joy, worry, nervousness. "Just drive!"

They drove in silence towards Brad's old house. Luckily Kanville was small, so it wasn't too far away, or Skye's head might explode with anticipation. She sat forward in her seat while Manny obeyed the stop signs and danced on her anxiousness.

"Hurry up." She said. The nervous smile getting bigger and more intense on her face. "Just here, just park here." She said, opening up the car door before it had even stopped completely. Manny watched her struggle and get tangled in the seat belt as she tried to jump out of the car. He got a little chuckle at seeing her so excited for the first time in months and it was nice to see the old Skye.

She jumped out of the car and ran towards the house with her shaking hands swinging and her brain buzzing with expectation. She ran up the steps of the front porch just as the door opened and a bigger bellied Gypsy came running out and threw herself at Skye. They hugged so tightly that they could hardly breathe; the tears flowing from their faces were unstoppable. Everything that had happened in the months they had been apart just washed away like a message in the sand, taken by a rising tide.

Skye couldn't believe she had Gypsy back, that she had found her, and she was so close this whole time, and Gypsy almost drowned in the flood of emotion – in an instant her loneliness faded away and she felt wanted, cared for, and loved. She had forgotten what it was even like to be around another person, let alone her sister, whom she had ached for.

"I missed you so much! Don't ever do that to me again!" Skye said, still producing tears from her reddened face.

"I'm sorry I didn't talk to you, and I'm sorry that I disappeared." Gypsy cried. "I'm getting so fat." She covered her face and sobbed. She was wearing a blue flowery half-length dress and with the sun shining on her brown hair, she looked beautiful. "None of my jeans fit me, I've had to buy dresses and…" she wept the words "…maternity pants."

"Oh, Honey." Skye said soothingly but with a heartfelt smile, "I think you look really nice. You do!" She hugged her again and turned around to Manny – still sitting in the car – who was waiting for his signal that it was ok to come out. Skye waved her hand at him indicating it was safe to leave the vehicle, and he wandered up the front porch.

"Hey Gyps, I missed ya, Mate." He said giving her a hug. "Wow, look at your belly." He chuffed, "The little peanut's growing."

"Sure is." Gypsy said smiling and wiping away the last of her tears. "Come in guys."

They walked into the house and Skye looked around at the flashes of her childhood, and the flashes of her dad. So many memories held in the big wooden house, it seemed impossible that it could contain such a life. How could so many memories and moments be squeezed in between these four walls? An entire life lived that now just floated away in the dust. She looked at the loungeroom and remembered the things they said about her dad on the news. Suddenly the coldest of cold chills ran down her spine, like a crack across a frozen lake.

"How do you live here?" She turned to Gypsy.

"What do you mean? Oh, with the whole 'Death House' thing?" Gypsy shrugged and looked around the room.

"That was a bit frivolous. But yeah. Doesn't it feel haunted?"

"No." Gypsy looked thoughtful, "I mean sometimes at night I think about it and get a little scared. The shadows freak me out a little bit... Oh, there was this one night where the lights were flickering on and off, and the back door – which I had already shut and locked, mind you – slammed shut. Oh, and this other time when I woke up through the night, I could have sworn there was a black figure standing in the corner of my room, just staring at me." Skye and Manny stood there with their mouths gaping and eyes of horror. "It totally freaked me out, but what are ya gonna do about it, you know?" She asked rhetorically, looking around the room. "Cuppa?" Gypsy started walking back into the kitchen. It was a nice, big, open kitchen with plenty of space. Skye missed this kitchen. But what Gypsy had just said...

"Gypsy, are you serious? That's fucking scary."

"Hey, no swearing around the jellybean." She said pointing to her belly.

"Sorry. How are you so blasé about this? I couldn't sleep a wink in this house." She looked at Manny as if to say, 'how is she not scared as fuck?!'

"Skye's right, Gyps, that's like, really full on." They both stood there nodding their heads at her.

"It's not like that all the time. Anyway. It's kind of nice being in this house. I feel like I've been able to learn a bit more about Brad. You know we both like meerkats? I don't know what it is about those furry little freaks, but they just look so cute, ya know?" She said.

"It's true." Skye said, "I used to get him any form of meerkat trinket I could find each year on his birthday."

Manny was looking around the house in a state of fear. He didn't want to break up their reunion, but he could feel the threat of ghosts creeping around his neck and up the side of his face. He could almost feel the chill.

"Gypsy," Manny started, "I think you should come back and live with us."

"True." Skye said, "We miss you, and I want to help look after you. What about when you're too fat to tie your shoes, or can't bend down to pick something up? Plus, I can make you lots of healthy food and take you to appointments?" Gypsy looked at her, and every ounce of her wanted to say yes.

"I don't want to be a hassle, though. Honestly, this last couple of months in this house, have sucked balls. I couldn't drink due to the alien in my gut, Marcy stopped talking to me, I have been in mothers groups where I have felt like an outcast, I learned how to cook because I figured the baby wouldn't like pizza...but the thing is, I have done it. I have managed to do all of this, by myself. I feel stronger than I have in years, and I feel like I might actually be a grown up." She laughed. "Did you see how I said, 'no swearing'? I'm adulting like a freakin' boss!"

"You can adult and still live with us, though." Skye said.

"I know I can." Gypsy smiled. "But you guys might want to start your own family one day. I wouldn't want to get in the way." Skye and Manny just looked at each other.

"We, ah, haven't really talked about that yet." Manny said nervously. But seeing the look on Skye's face he added, "But it's totally something that will happen...one day. Right, Skye?"

"Chill out, Mann, we're not there yet." Skye and Gypsy laughed at the relief that washed over Manny's face. "Still, I think you should come back with us. I want to be able to see you, but I just can't do it here, Gyps. It's too creepy...and sad." Gypsy understood exactly where Skye was coming from. She assumed she would feel the same if this was her family home that she grew up in with her loving father...who ended up murdering people...in this house.

"Fine." Gypsy gave in, "I will come back. But we should really sell this house...it's scary as fuck."

"Gypsy!" Skye laughed.

"Oh, yeah. Broke my own rule." Gypsy laughed.

Skye and Gypsy were on their way to the real estate. The house had sold to some ghost hunters who felt it was the perfect base for their exploration into the unknown, and the profit made from the sale was pooled together with the money Gypsy had received from her parents for the High Tide property. All together they had enough to buy a nice big house: big enough for Gypsy and her baby, as well as Skye and Manny and their future children. Gypsy was eight and a half months pregnant now and could hardly move.

"I'm like a hippo." She said as she waddled from the car to the real estate. "Like a big, fat, hippo."

"You're fine." Skye giggled at the sight of her. "You're keeping me entertained, anyway."

"Thanks. Glad I can be here for your entertainment." Gypsy said giving her a sideways grin.

"My feet hurt, and I'm so hungry." She moaned.

"You just had breakfast." Skye said.

"That was, like, half an hour ago. Anyway, this lady in the shops the other day told me about dipping corn chips into ice-cream, and apparently it's effing amazeballs."

"You do realise you're about to have a child, don't you?"

"Yeah…and your point is?"

"So, maybe we should work on your vocabulary?" Skye looped her arm around Gypsy's, who looked confused. "Amazeballs is not really correct grammar."

"Correct grammar? Who are you?" Gypsy laughed.

"Yeah, you're right. Amazeballs it is. I like it."

"You just like it because it has the word 'balls' in it." She laughed. "Speaking of which, is Manny meeting us here?"

"Yep. Thank Christ he got that job with Tom. I don't think he would have been able to get his share of the loan from selling random things like toothbrushes online." Skye said sceptically.

"Not that we really needed him to chuck in with the money from two houses under our belts." Gypsy said.

"Yeah, but it's his house too, and he didn't want us to be paying for it all or he said it wouldn't feel like his house."

"He's a good guy." Gypsy said. "Give me a look at that ring again."

Skye showed her the sparkling ring on her finger. Manny had proposed to her a week earlier. He had taken her away for the weekend to a little cabin by the beach a couple of hours away. He had organised with the managers of the site to fill the cabin with flowers, wine and candles, comfy cushions and throw rugs. They had prearranged a platter of food, and of course champagne in the event she said yes - 'Well, if she says 'no' then you can slap a turkey on my head and make me dance a jig, because she will say yes.' He had said. - And when they got to the cabin and she opened her eyes inside the tiny little cabin that sat in a slice of heaven, she was breathless.

"This is the cutest little hut I have ever seen! Oh my god, I never want to leave!" She jumped on the bed, then ran to the fruit platter and ate a strawberry. "Wine!" Skye said and grabbed the red one first. "Oh, Manny, it's so beautiful. Come here." She grabbed him and kissed him, trying to take off his clothes.

"No, wait." He said. He couldn't wait much longer. He was going to take her down to the beach at sunset, but he was too excited and felt that the cabin was too beautiful to waste. He leaned down on one knee in front of her and grabbed her hand. Skye's other hand went straight to her mouth, covering it so it couldn't destroy this moment. Her heart was beating hard and her belly filled with butterflies.

"Skye, beautiful Skye. We have known each other for so long, I can't remember a time when you weren't in my life. The love you have brought into my life is a love that has never faded, never once faulted, and I have never doubted it, not for one second. When you are by my side, I can do anything, *WE* can do anything. You are an inspiration, and the most beautiful person I have ever known. You make me the happiest man in the world, and I want to share every waking moment by your side, looking after you, making you laugh, and making you happy. I want to sleep every night with you in my arms, and I will never let you go unless you ask me too. I want us to grow old together and go deaf together. I want to feed you soup and help you put on your slippers when you can't, and when your teeth fall out of your head…" Manny shuffled on his knee.

What? Skye giggled inwardly.

"…Look, all I'm trying to say is… Skye Mains, will you do me the honour of making me the happiest man alive, by becoming my wife?" Skye's eyes were welling up with joyful tears.

"Yes! Manny, yes." She bent down to Manny and kissed him while he pulled out the ring. He slipped it onto her finger, and she was blinded by its beauty.

"Oh my god, Mann, it's so beautiful." Skye gazed at it and wiped her eyes. It was the happiest day of Skye's life.

So now, Gypsy and Skye were entering the real estate agent, Skye's rock hanging from her finger, and Gypsy's belly hanging from her body.

They had picked out a five-bedroom house with two main bedrooms that contained their own ensuites, and three more bedrooms with a third bathroom for the rest of the house. There was a playroom for kids, and a large open kitchen that reminded Skye of the one she grew up with. The loungeroom was a massive sitting room that had an open fireplace and windows from the floor to the very high ceiling. The doors were covered in led-light glass that painted pictures on the wall of colour and shapes. The floors were stone in parts, and hardwood in other parts, the bedrooms and playroom were carpeted with a light grey plush. The large bifold doors opened from the kitchen and loungeroom into an outdoor sitting and BBQ area that was enclosed from the top with a ceiling and lights – naturally, the girls were going to cover this in fairy lights once they moved in. The gardens, oh, the gardens, were spectacular. The previous owners were garden enthusiasts who had spent thousands of dollars on plants and trees and designed the entire three-acre block into a masterpiece of colour and beauty. In the centre of the garden, through paths that surrounded massive oak trees filled with lanterns, was a large white arch that had fallen victim to the vines that curved and grasped around it – they were blossoming an array of purple and white flowers as a thank you for the hospitality. A perfectly blue swimming pool enticed them from the side of the house with a little path made of cobblestones that pointed the way. The whole house lit up at night with outdoor lights, and then there was Gypsy's favourite part – an old willow tree sat majestically in the middle of the front lawn, spanning easily 15 metres wide. It looked wise and seemed like it could tell her stories of times many moons ago. She had noticed her tree and decided then on the spot that this would be their house.

The realtor's voice broke Gypsy away from her daydreams about the house. "So, the papers are all signed and here are your keys. On behalf of all of us here at Kanville Realty, we would like to congratulate you on the purchase of your new property, and hope it brings you many years of enjoyment. Please think of us again if you are ever in the market to sell." She smiled a bleached white smile and Gypsy and Skye jumped for joy, elated with their new purchase while Manny shook the lady's hand and thanked her for all of her effort in the purchase.

"We couldn't be happier." He beamed.

"Well, time to get packing!" Skye said.

They waved goodbye to the lady and walked out with their new set of keys. Some people thought they were crazy to buy the house together – "Wouldn't you want your privacy with Skye?" Tom had asked – But they all knew it was the right decision. They knew that they were a big happy family, and they would prefer it this way. Why do they need to be like everyone else and live in separate houses? Family is too precious.

"I'll meet you guys at home?" Manny said as he walked back to his car.

"Or…at the hospital?" Skye said. "Gyps, either you just pissed your pants, or your water just broke." Gypsy looked down at the ground.

"Damn it. I was hoping I just pissed myself. Skye, what do I do?!" Gypsy was terrified and the fear was painted all over her face.

"It's ok, it's gonna be fine. Come on, we'll get you in the car and go straight to the hospital."

"I think I got too excited about the house." She said, trying to joke, but the humour wasn't coming across as enthusiastically as she had expected.

"Like when you got too excited about the milkshake I made you and you *actually* pissed your pants?" Skye laughed.

"Hey, shut up, that's the baby's fault. Stupid bladder in the wrong stupid place."

"I told you to do those pelvic floor exercises I was reading about. They're supposed to strengthen the muscles in your bajingo."

"Yeah, right, you're the expert now." Gypsy laughed at her. "I think you've read more of those baby books than me."

"Well, guess who's going to be the best auntie in the world…it's me, I'm going to be the best auntie in the world." She teased. "And, I'm going to ring Sean right now and let him know."

"No! Don't ring Sean. Seriously, it's only been a couple of dates, I don't want him there while I'm pushing a watermelon out of my body!"

"Sorry, sorry, I won't then." Skye held her hands up off the steering wheel. "I still think you guys are gorgeous together though." She winked at Gypsy.

"He's pretty sweet to me." Gypsy smiled whimsically out the car window.

"I wouldn't let him near you if I didn't think he was going to be good to you."

"I know. Though, you did call him a player once."

"I did, but I also said it was a joke, and that he was one of…"

"The sweetest guys, blah blah." Gypsy laughed.

"Ok, I'll stop. We're here." Skye pulled into the car park at the Kanville Hospital. "It's time."

CHAPTER 24

"Well, shit Dude, this is alright." Gypsy said as she climbed on to the queen-sized hospital bed. Skye had already made herself at home on the lounge by the window.

"Are these free?" She said grabbing a little packet of biscuits from a bowl on the table and pouring a glass of water.

"They are meant for the mother-to-be." A grumpy old nurse said.

"That's cool, mi casa es su casa. Dig in Dude." Gypsy said to Skye. The nurse scoffed and walked out of the room with an "I'll be back" thrown over her shoulder.

"Did you see her name?" Skye laughed, "Nurse Humbug." And Gypsy cracked up laughing while Skye nearly choked on her biscuit.

"I can't believe all of the regular birthing rooms were taken and I got to have one of the private ones." Gypsy said with delight, looking around at her private bathroom and big screen television.

"Imagine being in one of those little ones with a tiny bed and your legs in stirrups?"

"I think that's only in the movies." Skye laughed.

"No, don't think so. Hey! A yoga ball…is that for me?"

"It's supposed to help during labour. You can sit on it or bend over it…" Skye got up and started demonstrating the different positions on the ball. "Look," she laughed,

"I'm more flexible than I realised! Hey Gyps, I'm having a baby too…" She grabbed the ball and held it on the front of her tummy.

"Dude, you're an idiot." Gypsy chuckled, shaking her head. "I probably should have read those books, though." Gypsy said, smiling, but there was a nervousness in her voice. She didn't know if it was better to know what's about to happen, or if it was better to just wing it. She figured if she didn't know too much, then she couldn't spend months obsessing over how frightened she was.

"You'll be fine. Here have a bikky." Skye shoved a bikky towards her, but she pushed it away, grabbing her side and putting her head down in pain. "Another one?" Skye asked.

"How many more contractions do I have to go through before this baby comes out?" Gypsy asked, not really wanting to know the answer.

"Well, when they checked you out in the other room, they said you were only three centimetres dilated, and I don't really know what that means…so, it could take forever, or it could go quickly. I don't know." Skye shrugged. "But I did read that you need to get to ten centimetres before that baby starts coming out. And your contractions will get a little bit more painful." Gypsy tried to imagine what ten centimetres would look like by holding her hands apart in the air.

"Holy shit…that's massive! They want me to do that?" Gypsy was a picture of worry, her eyes like saucepans and visible sweat starting to bubble on her forehead.

"Your body will do it naturally, Gyps. How did you miss all of this in your mother's classes?"

"I kept zoning out. I was thinking about food, mainly. And wondering about names…what do you think about Scarlet for a girl, or Jack for a boy?" Nurse Humbug came back into the room to see how she was going.

"How are we all going in here?" She walked to the side of the bed in a very monotonous manner. "Over here we have a little pain relief if your contractions are getting too strong. Just suck on this pipe and it will take the edge off."

"What is it?" Gypsy asked.

"Nitrous oxide. It's an anxiolytic and an analgesic."

"In human words please." Gypsy said.

"It helps a little with the pain and can also help you to relax. Some women find it useful, others don't. But we can give you some pethidine as well to help round off the edges of the contractions and help with the severity."

"I want that other one I heard of…the epi-something."

"Epidural?"

"Yeah, that thing."

"It's a little too early for that, but once you get to around four or five centimetres, we can administer an epidural. It will essentially make you numb from the pain of labour." Nurse Humbug looked at Gypsy and saw a hint of terror in her eyes. Skye noticed it too.

Gypsy knew this was going to get worse. She knew that no matter how much she tried to avoid it, the pain was going to get more severe and she might start screaming like a banshee. But she didn't want to be numb to everything. She had come so far, she thought enduring the pain of labour was more important than being numb to it completely, like everything else in her life. She had numbed everything painful in her life by drinking and neglecting to face it. She would turn away from the things that hurt her, and she would pretend they weren't there. She thought drinking away her problems was easier than facing them. But she was a new woman, and she was about to be a mother. She had come so far through this pregnancy by standing tall in front of her demons and dealing with the shit each day without the need to numb it – or the *want* to numb it. To her, this was something she had to believe in, she had to do this without pain relief, and she had to feel that she was strong enough. *I am a lioness…come hear me fucking ROAR!* When she finally spoke, she saw them both staring at her, waiting for the response.

"I don't want to be numb. I can do this without the epi-whatever."

"Ok, that's your choice completely." The nurse said. "Your midwife will be back in soon to check your progress, but if you have any trouble, please just press this button and I will be back in no time." She pointed to a little button on a remote, "You have Rhonda Daniels, don't you?" Gypsy nodded. "You're a lucky girl, she is lovely." Nurse Humbug said, then turned and walked back out of the room.

"She doesn't seem too bad." Gypsy said. Then grabbed her belly again. "They're getting closer."

Gypsy and Skye sat and chatted, put on the telly – nothing on – switched off the telly, and ate some sandwiches. Nurse Humbug had told her not to eat too much because it might make her throw it back up later on, but Gypsy didn't care. It had been eight hours and she was hungry and bored, and wanted it all to just hurry up.

"Do you want me to get anything for you?"

"I don't know. Maybe a shot gun to put me out of my misery?"

"No." Skye said.

"Let's get up and walk around. You know, gravity and all that crap." Gypsy climbed off the bed with Skye holding her up. They walked out of the room and into the hallway filled with expectant fathers pacing up and down and midwives darting from room to room. Gypsy could hear a woman in another room down the hall screaming and it sent chills down her spine. She looked at Skye with worry in her eyes, and Skye just rubbed her back and said,

"You'll be fine, don't listen to her."

They rounded a corner near a little gift shop. It was filled with flowers and blue and pink teddy bears. Big balloons stuck out of oversized vases that said, *'Congratulations'* and *'It's a boy*!'. The tiny knitted beanies caught Gypsy's eye. She waddled a little closer just as another contraction started that had her holding on to the railing along the wall. Her belly felt like it was tightening so much it might break her spine.

"I think my insides are falling out." She whimpered to Skye.

"Gypsy." Nurse Humbug came walking down the hall, "The midwife wants to come in and check your dilation, please get back into bed." Gypsy groaned and turned around, waddling ever so slowly up the hallway while the sounds of pain came flooding from every closed door along the path. Skye would not leave Gypsy's side and was at her beck and call for anything she needed. It was hard for Skye to watch Gypsy going through so much pain, but she knew there was a baby at the other end of it, and the pain wouldn't last forever, so her main job was to keep Gypsy's spirits up and help her with whatever she screamed for.

The midwife came into the room, all full of cheer. She was in her late 40's and had an overly dramatic amount of blonde curly hair. Her name was Rhonda Daniels, and she was a very spirited gal.

"Gypsy, how are you feeling, Darling?" She said as she dove on in to checking her vagina like she was opening the newspaper – "Did you see the election's coming up? No? Not to bother… Oh, there's a nice recipe for pumpkin pie…' – "So, Gypsy, you're looking good here."

"Um… thanks?" *As in, 'nice vajayjay', or…?*

"What I mean is, you're about seven centimetres dilated. Your contractions are getting closer together and sticking around for a bit longer, I'm guessing?" She said with a large smile that reflected the light and blinded Gypsy's eyeballs.

Nothing to smile about, Rhonda. I'm in pain.

"Yep. Here's one now…" She breathed, and braced for the tightening, "Kill me now!" She yelled.

"That's it, good girl." Rhonda smiled another lightning white smile. Skye grabbed her hand and squeezed.

"Just breathe, Gyps."

"I AM breathing." She huffed.

"Find a spot on the ceiling and try focusing on it. Imagine it holding the pain for you. Focus all of your pain into that one spot." Rhonda said.

"Here try this." Skye grabbed the hose for the gas and sucked on it.

"That's not for you!" Nurse Humbug shrieked from the corner of the room.

"Bar-Humbug." Skye replied. "Here Gyps."

Gypsy sucked on the pipe and sucked some more. Her voice became deeper and deeper which made her laugh and all of a sudden, her entire body went tingly like pins and needles. Was it from the gas? Or was she having an anxiety attack? Either way it freaked her out and she thought that was enough of the gas. She went back to normal air. The air of a sterilized hospital room where many women before her have brought life into the world. Eventually the tingling subsided, and the pain continued.

"You're doing extremely well, Gypsy, you are strong, and your baby's heartbeat looks strong, just like *her* mother." Rhonda smiled and made Gypsy feel at ease.

Hold on…

"Did you say 'her'?" Suddenly it all felt real. There really was a baby in her, it wasn't imaginary. And it was a girl! Gypsy's heart warmed and she nearly started to cry tears of happiness. She didn't mind if it was a boy or a girl, but like giving it a name, it made the whole thing real. And she was secretly hoping for a girl…

"Yes, Gypsy. It's a girl." She smiled and rubbed Gypsy's hand. Gypsy had told Rhonda that she didn't want to know the sex of the baby until she was in labour. She said it would give her a little boost of enthusiasm during the pushing stage to have the surprise. Of course, Rhonda found this information out months ago after a routine ultrasound, and true to her word, Rhonda Daniels kept it a secret until now.

"Oh! A girl!" Skye said joyfully, "You've got a little Scarlet in there, Gyps."

Gypsy knew she had to get out of this emotional state and focus on the job at hand. She wanted to meet her baby daughter. *Wipe the tears, Gyps, get your shit together and let's get cracking!*

"Ok, Scarlet, let's get this show on the road." Gypsy said with determination, looking down to her belly and holding it like a ball. "How much longer?" She asked Midwife Rhonda.

"Well, you're only at seven centimetres so you've got a while to go. Generally, once you have hit active labour it could be about an hour per centimetre, but every labour is different, and every person is different, so let's just cruise and go with the flow…but not a slow flow!" She said cautiously "… we don't want her heartbeat dropping. It's a good idea to get up and get moving, this can help things along. Skye, why don't you take your sister for a little walk. Just outside your room there is a little garden especially for birthing mothers if you want to wander…or should I say waddle…" she winked at Gypsy, "out there. You're doing great Gypsy, just keep up this nice pace, and you'll get to meet your daughter in no time." She said, jumping up to wash her hands. "I will be back to check on you, but if you have any troubles, please…"

"Press the button, I know." Gypsy said, smiling and falling into another contraction that made her cry and scrunch up in pain.

"PUSH!" Skye said, "You're doing great."

"Fuck this! I'm never doing this again!" Gypsy cried. "FUUUUUCK!" She was sweating and popping veins she never knew existed. And she had clearly given up on her 'no swearing' rule.

"You're doing great." Rhonda said. "Just a couple more pushes…"

"Is my vagina still there? Is it?"

"It's still there." Rhonda said reassuringly.

"Is it a baby or a basketball?!"

"Definitely a baby." Rhonda said.

Skye rubbed Gypsy's back, "You can do this, Gyps, show Scarlet how strong you are."

It felt like one big contraction now. There didn't seem to be any space in between and they fused together into a torturous monster that was crushing Gypsy into a ball and breaking her back. It was eating her for dinner and burning her privates. 'Chomp, chomp, chomp', it said as she struggled to stay conscious. She was running on adrenalin and shock, but she was mother nature right now, she was bringing the storm into the birthing suite, and it was raining supreme power down into her spirit and fighting with the force of one thousand men to push out her human, her creation, her miracle. Her tolerance for pain had risen with each contraction and all she felt now was her strength. Her inability to give up was proving to be a virtuous characteristic, and although she felt powerful and felt the enormous strength inside her, she still wanted to rip the penises off every man she ever saw again. She summoned all the power she had left and focused on one thing – one more push.

"You're nearly there Gyps, the head's out, give us one more big push…"

Gypsy pushed with all her might and felt like she might faint, but she kept going.

"Breathe" Skye said as she sat by her side with a wet cloth on her face, coaxing her along and telling her how strong she was. Then Gypsy felt the strangest of things…something slithered out of her body and within an instant, relief washed over her, and a baby started to cry.

Oh my god, I've done it… it's over…

"Here's your beautiful girl." Rhonda said laying Scarlet onto Gypsy's chest and into her arms, while she proceeded to cut the cord.

"Oh my god. Look at her." Skye said in complete awe. "She is perfect."

"Hey little girl." Gypsy whispered, wiping away some of the mess from her daughter's face, and wiping her own tears. "It's nice to meet you." Scarlet did a little yawn and Gypsy lost control of her emotions. She had happy tears fall from her eyes like a waterfall and a smile that couldn't be wiped away. Her heart was bursting with a kind of love she had never known before and euphoria filled her soul.

"Congratulations, Gypsy, she is absolutely gorgeous." Rhonda smiled. "Do you mind if we take her for a minute, just to clean her up and weigh her?"

"I don't want to let her go." Gypsy said.

"I know, Darling, it's ok, we will be right here." Gypsy reluctantly handed over her baby but held tightly onto the invisible string that kept them spiritually joined. She watched intently while they cleaned baby Scarlet, and Skye sat on the bed beside her accompanying the watch.

"Dude, I totally just had a baby." Gypsy whispered, not moving her gaze.

"I know." Skye replied. "I can't believe you made that tiny little person. She is adorable." Skye wiped a tear from her elated face. She was almost in disbelief at the miracle that had just happened. She was so proud of Gypsy, and unbelievably in love with her new little niece.

"We'll have to come back later." Skye said to Manny as he stood outside the hospital room with a bunch of flowers for Gypsy. Skye had just left the room, leaving Gypsy and baby Scarlet both sleeping peacefully.

"So, a girl?" Manny said. "I'm going to be surrounded by girls." Skye smirked.

"You'll be fine. Here, give me the flowers, I'll sneak back in and put them on the table."

"Skye." Manny grabbed her arm. "She didn't scare you away from having kids, did she?"

"God, no." Skye lied just a little. "She did so well, Mann." Skye was full of pride looking back into the room that held the two most precious females in her life. It was hard for Skye to think back to a year earlier before she knew Gypsy, before she got together with Manny, and before they became such massive parts of her life. She could never have gotten through the death of her dad if it wasn't for Gypsy and Manny being by her side. "Gypsy wants us to be Scarlet's godparents." She looked at Manny.

"Of course, I said yes."

"Well, I feel honoured." Manny said, putting his hand on his heart with a face that was painted with gratitude.

"She doesn't really have anyone else close in her life anymore." Skye said sadly. "Should I ring her friends and let them know?... Oh, shit, what about her parents?!"

"Dude, I would ring her parents." Manny nodded in agreement.

"I'm gonna have to look through her phone to get the number; that feels dishonest. Let's just go and sit in the garden for a little while."

"Can I smoke in the garden?"

"What? Surrounded by mothers in labour and hospital staff?" Skye laughed.

"Yeah, why not?" Manny said frivolously. They walked out to the garden and sat on a log seat near a garden bed. White flowers were sprinkled with buzzing bees and harmony. The bees scurried around collecting their pollen to make delicious honey, and Skye watched them with a feeling of peace as they flew around so freely. One sting would be enough to make her scream, but if she left them alone, they wouldn't feel threatened and would go about their business happily without interruption. She looked at the bees and pondered. "I don't want to ring her friends or parents."

"Why? They should know." Manny said.

"Yeah, but it should be up to her if she wants to do it. I don't think I should interfere, you know?"

"You know her well enough by now to know what she would want. Sometimes interfering is the right thing to do. Imagine if you had a daughter who had a baby and didn't call you to let you know."

"That wouldn't happen." Skye said, waving a hand of dismissal at Manny who was pulling a joint out of the front pocket of his shirt. All of a sudden, a woman on the other side of the garden starting yelling, turning their attention away from the beautiful bees.

"I'm having the baby, Cam! I don't give a shit if you've got ten dollars on a horse and it's about to win, get the fuck down here!" Skye and Manny looked at each other with wide open eyes, their mouths dropping from their faces with a look of stricken disbelief.

"Is that…?" Skye managed.

"Yep." Manny said nodding slowly.

"Holy fuck…"

They stared across the garden towards a birthing mother in worlds of pain. Her bright blue hair blowing and sticking to her face from the sweat and tears, and her voice screaming angrily down the phone.

"You what?! You're leaving me? Are you kidding?! THIS IS YOUR BABY, YOU ARSEHOLE!" She cried.

"Umm…I think I want to go." Manny said getting up from their peaceful little spot in the garden.

"Good idea." Skye said following him back down the concrete path, looking back over her shoulder at the mess that Cam had made. "What a scumbag. If there ever was a bullet to dodge, I think I win the fucking prize for that one."

"That you did, my gorgeous girl." Manny tensely laughed and put his arm over Skye's shoulder. "That you did."

Gypsy woke up to a pain in her breasts. She had slept for two hours before Scarlet woke up in tears, and it felt like she could do with another three days of dreamland. Being woken up was hard, but the tiny little human that woke her up was worth dragging her away from the sleep that she needed, oh so badly.

"Hello, little one." She whispered, leaning out of her bed and towards the tiny cot beside her. *Oh my god, she is so gorgeous, and oh my god my boobs hurt.* Gypsy winced from the tightness in her chest. They felt so hard and full of milk she thought they might explode. She climbed out of the bed just as nurse Humbug gently opened the door.

"Oh, it looks like I'm just in time." She smiled. "How's our little angel doing?"

"Good, I think…I just woke up." Gypsy said. "I think I need to feed her."

"Are you full?" Humbug asked.

Gypsy grabbed her boobs. It was the first time she had grabbed her boobs in public without being drunk…and it felt totally normal.

"Somehow I'm completely comfortable grabbing my boobs in front of you. Is that what being a mother means? Randomly grabbing myself in front of people?" She questioned.

"It's totally normal." The nurse laughed. "Now, let's get little Scarlet some lunch." She said while picking Scarlet up from her cot. She was wrapped up nice and tight in a beautiful blanket that Skye had bought her from the gift shop and she really did look like a little angel.

"Where's my sister?" Gypsy asked.

"She's in the cafeteria," Nurse Humbug leaned down closer, "with a fellow who smells like marijuana." She whispered the words disapprovingly.

"Oh." Gypsy giggled. "Can you let them know I'm awake and would like them to come in, please?"

"Not until this baby is fed." She said sternly.

Gypsy fed baby Scarlet and couldn't take her eyes off her the entire time. She had given her life, and now watched as her body fed her the food she needed for survival. *It was like magic*, she thought. Yesterday she was just a girl, lost in her own little world. Apart from her belly growing bigger, she felt like she only had to look after herself. And now here she was, with a tiny little human that she created, and it needed her to survive. The anxiety she assumed she would feel in this realisation was obsolete, and she was left with a feeling of calm. A feeling that somehow, she had been blessed by a Buddhist monk, or a God, or a white witch without even noticing.

I could stay like this forever, holding you, you precious little thing, with your cute little eyes, and your cute little nose, and tiny little hands that curl into a tiny little ball.

Gypsy was overwhelmed with love, and she wondered how her mother could have given her up. She wondered now more than ever how a mother could look at her newborn baby and give them away. She tried to put herself in her mother's position; 16-years-old and trying to do the best thing for her daughter. Nope. She still couldn't do it. But she can empathise with how tough the decision would have been now that she stared at her own daughter's face. Her tiny vulnerable features that lay in Gypsy's arms. She imagined the life she may have had if she was never adopted, and she quietly thanked her parents for giving her a better chance at life than the dark path they may have unintentionally led her down. Like the overgrown thorny strip of garden in between two roads, she could see both sides, and saw that, like the cars whooshing past, her life could have gone either direction. And she finally realised for the first time that even though things weren't perfect, she was thankful for the road her biological parents put her on, and she wouldn't want it any other way.

Gypsy picked up her phone and dialled her mother's number.

Skye and Manny eventually came back into the room with chocolate and more flowers. Gypsy told them that she had spoken to her mother and father and they were both so busy with work that they wouldn't be able to make it to Kanville for another week, but they send their love and can't wait to meet Skye and the baby. Skye thought that was a bit awkward and assumed her own mother would be more excited about dropping everything to come, but she let it be.

"Have you spoken to Marcy or Haz?" Skye asked, but Gypsy just looked down and then over to Scarlet who was sleeping like a champ. "Apart from a quick catch up, like, two months ago, I haven't spoken to Marcy. And Haz," she continued, "we haven't spoken since Mum and Dad sold the house."

Skye felt so bad for Gypsy. It was like her coming to Kanville had destroyed the other life she had. But she also knew that Marcy and Nicki were in their own little 'child-free' life and didn't have time for Gypsy and her alcohol-free pregnant lifestyle. *Bitches*, she thought.

"Do you want me to call them?" Skye asked. But Gypsy brushed it off and told her 'another day'. Skye was going to tell her about the girl with the blue hair, and Cam's other baby – if it even was his – but she didn't. The girl with the blue hair carried things of the past that brought pain and discomfort, and Gypsy was in a bubble of happiness and positive new futures; she didn't need to know.

"Let's get you out of this stinking hospital and back home." Skye said. "We have a surprise for you."

"What's that?"

"Well…thanks to you taking three years to push out my gorgeous niece," She laughed "Manny has actually…"

"And Tom and Sean…" Manny included.

"…Yes, and Tom and Sean, have managed to move all of our crap from home and we are…" she grabbed Manny's hand and smiled, "officially moved into our new home!"

"What?! Serious? Oh my god, you guys are amazing!" Gypsy said with excitement. "Oh man, get me the fuck out of here…oh, shit I mean…oh crap, I mean…"

"Dude! No swearing." Skye laughed.

"Can. You. Please. Get. Me. The… Hell…out of here?" Gypsy laughed, looking accomplished in her efforts.

Manny and Skye both laughed and harmonised, "Sure thang, chicken wang."

"Oh, my god!" they both laughed and pointed at each other. Gypsy just laughed and said, "I love you guys." Shaking her head. She loved those idiots.

Bags were packed and Rhonda checked in with her one last time. She didn't need stitches after the birth, so there was no need for all the fuss of postnatal care towards Gypsy's lady parts. She thanked all the nurses, but especially Nurse Humbug for all her support and gave Rhonda Daniels a massive hug that nearly made milk come out of places she never would have worried about before.

She looked around at her little room that had housed her for the last one and a half days and sighed. The window to the garden was open and shining sunlight onto the bed she birthed Scarlet in. She would never be back here again, and she would not get to keep this room for sentimental value. But as much as she appreciated this room, she was overjoyed to get home and into her new house. The thought of having to care for her baby without the nurses and her midwife was a little daunting, and she had a little anxiety at the thought of it, but she knew she could do it. If she could make a human being, and push it out of her body, she could do anything.

Skye and Manny connected the baby seat into the car and Gypsy strapped Scarlet's tiny body into the seat. She sat in the back just to make sure Scarlet's head didn't swing with the corners the car turned…and also because she didn't want to leave her side.

I love you so much it hurts. Gypsy thought.

When they got to the new house the driveway was long and peaceful. Surrounded by trees, they drove up the winding entrance that was about 200 metres long. There were beautiful rose bushes and flower beds, a little pond that had an overhanging tree that housed two birdfeeders and a tyre swing hanging from the closest tree to the house. The house was dark, but Manny stopped the car and told the girls to wait there. "I'll be back in a second, just stay there." He said excitedly.

All of a sudden, their surroundings were flooded with light and exposed the secrets of the garden. There were lights that stretched around the perimeter of the property, but also the house, and one over every doorway. A fountain started behind them in the midst of an orchard in the distance and Gypsy could not only hear the water trickle but smell the freshness from her window bringing scents of orange and lavender.

This is perfect, she thought.

"It's beautiful, Manny!" Skye yelled from the front seat of the car, bewildered by the magic of their new beginnings.

Gypsy took a breath and looked at her beautiful baby girl,

"We're home." She smiled.

CHAPTER 25

"Is it weird that I'm scared?" Skye said, one eyebrow raised and a glass of champagne in her hand, holding it steady in anguished shakes.

"Dude, you're fine!" Gypsy said. She was wearing a turquoise gown that made her boobs feel like she was going to milk anyone in front of her. "Just don't stress, because you'll sweat and wreck your makeup."

"What, like you wrecked yours?" Skye laughed at her.

"Hey! It wasn't my fault Sean tried to 'fondle' me right before feed time." Gypsy snapped back with a giggle.

"I'm honestly amazed at how fantastic he has been with Scarlet."

"Amazed?" Gypsy said, looking at Skye perplexed, "But I thought he was the most…"

"…Sweetest guy, yes." Skye laughed.

"Yeah, I kind of pinch myself sometimes." Gypsy smiled. The music started playing.

"Holy shit." Skye looked at Gypsy who was full of smiles and excitement. Skye could feel her heart thumping hard in her throat and she had anticipation in her eyes. "It's time."

"Last time you said that, I had a baby."

"I feel like I'm about to have a baby. Ok, take this."

Gypsy grabbed the champagne glass from Skye and skulled the rest. She walked through the bifold door and out into the garden where fifty people sat in white chairs, lining the path to the vine covered arch where the celebrant stood.

Gypsy walked down the grass path in her turquoise gown as Skye trailed behind her in her white dress. Skye was barefoot and her dress swept along the ground behind her, rustling up the rose petals beneath her and swirling them up into the air like a beautiful dance. The sounds of violin strings waved throughout the gardens and created a playground for the birds, who seemed to whoosh around them and fly with the sweet vibrations. Gypsy reached the end and stood to the left of the celebrant who gave her a quick nod and awaited Skye who walked down the aisle alone. Sean had asked if she wanted him to walk her down, but she refused, saying "My parents will be there. I know their spirits will be there." So, she walked down in the arms of herself, and with every rush of the breeze that played with her hair and chilled her shoulder, she knew she wasn't alone.

Gypsy looked into the crowd at Sean who was holding a sleeping Scarlet and rocking her ever so gently. Beside him Marcy waved and smiled, then blew her a kiss. Marcy had decided it was time to quit drinking, and in her search for a cleaner lifestyle, realised that she had pushed away her one true friend – Gypsy. She was saddened that she had disregarded Gypsy enough to destroy their friendship and realised what a horrible friend she had become. So, after a lot of AA meetings and apology visits to Gypsy, they were back to normal – minus the booze. And Marcy was completely smitten with little Scarlet.

Gypsy's parents sat behind Marcy and Sean, and her mum was telling her dad to put the phone down. *Just once*, Gypsy thought. Her mum looked up at her and waved, and Gypsy smiled back. Her dad put down his phone and looked up to her with a proud smile. He mouthed the word 'beautiful' while gesturing towards her. Gypsy was glad they came, and glad that, despite their busy schedules, they made the effort. *They're ok*, she thought with an inner smile of appreciation and adoration.

Manny stood across from Gypsy and together they watched as Skye walked towards him, flowing like a picture of grace, like glitter in the sun, like a glass-top lake that reflected a cloudless sky. Her blue eyes glowed under the sun and her smile became contagious among the witnesses who beamed as she passed. She wore a piece of yellow thread around her right wrist that had fallen off her mother's favourite dress, and one of her father's leather necklaces wrapped around the other. Just as she got to the end, she stopped and looked up to the sky. She closed her eyes and sent a quick blessing to the heavens; a quick blessing to let them go. A single tear fell from her eye and ran over the peaceful smile on her face, wetting her lip and bringing her back to reality.

"We are gathered here today…" The celebrant started, but Manny and Skye hardly heard a word he said. They stared intently into one another's eyes with a love so pure it blinded them to their surroundings, and all they saw was each other.

"Oh, sorry, what?" Skye said, breaking away from Manny's stare.

"Please repeat after me." The celebrant said. Gypsy watched as Skye and Manny brought fifty people to tears with their wedding vows, expressing the love inside of them as best they could. But how can you truly express a love so deep? Words cannot bring an image to life in the way a heart feels nor emphasise how fierce a feeling is. It can only be felt between the two people involved and shown in a way that is not just physical, mental, or emotional…but spiritual.

"You may now kiss the bride." The celebrant said. And as Manny leaned forward and bent Skye over to arch her back, he kissed her passionately, holding on to her like a silhouette of a ballroom dance. The crowd cheered and stood to their feet, clapping in a united orchestral beat. Manny and Skye waved to their loved ones and blew kisses in the air, letting them settle on the hearts of their family and friends. Skye looked over to Gypsy who was floating on a cloud of joy and beaming in the light. She had found her sister, or more so, Gypsy had found her.

"Gyps." Skye said, walking over to her with Manny in her arms. Gypsy looked at her and the only words that drifted between them were telepathic. Nothing needed to be spoken out loud… they both eyed the same unspoken words.

"I love you."

"Have fun." Gypsy eventually said as she hugged Manny and then Skye. "Love ya, sis."

"We will be thinking of you." Skye's words were trickled down her face in the form of a happy tear.

"Actually…" Manny looked at Skye and grabbed her on the arse, "No, we probably won't be." He shook his head with a cheeky grin, and they all laughed.

"Go dudes, you guys have to go. And don't worry about Scarlet and me; we will be fine." Gypsy smiled giving them one last hug before shooing them away.

Skye and Manny walked back down the aisle and said thank you to the guests. They welcomed everyone back to the house for the reception.

"There will be dancing and food and drinks, but we are being shit and leaving because we need to catch our flight to Paris, so please enjoy the party, and bust some moves. There will be a prize for the best dance moves that get sent to my phone… I'm lookin' at you Grandma," Manny pointed to his 96-year-old Grandma. "So, everyone, just… party on!" Manny said, pumping the rock horns signal in the air.

"We love you all." Skye added.

The DJ was setting up, and the evening was full of fresh beginnings. The stars were starting to come out and Gypsy stood in the twilight of another day done, engulfed in her surroundings and soaking in the love that was in the air.

Sean came up to her and handed her Scarlet who had just woken up, looking for her mum.

"Hey beautiful." He said.

"Hey." Gypsy looked at him contently. She held her three-month-old baby and gave Sean a kiss on the cheek. "I think I might sit out the front for this feed." She said.

"At Olly?" Sean asked.

"Yeah." Gypsy looked down at her precious little daughter and then back at Sean. "I love you." She smiled. Sean gave her a kiss and watched her walk away in her turquoise gown, baby in her arms and peace in her heart. She walked down the driveway past the front of the house and sat on the bench seat under the willow tree that Manny had made especially for her, and she looked to the stars. She thought back to her days of sitting in her other willow tree in High Tide and dreaming of Paris and other adventures. She imagined a whole world that she wanted to explore and become a part of. She would be free in places that were different worlds, different cultures, and different views. But then she stared down at her baby Scarlet, and this was her adventure now. This was her new beginning. This is what she had needed all along. She no longer felt like she didn't belong, like she was searching for meaning. She watched as the car rolled down the driveway that held Manny and Skye on their way to their honeymoon. Skye noticed her sitting at the tree and blew a kiss to her out the window as they rolled past. "We love you, Gypsy!" She yelled cheerfully. Gypsy chuckled and blew them a kiss back. She looked back at her house that was full of life and light and music. So many people dancing and laughing and enjoying themselves, and she could feel her baby breathing in her arms, warming up her soul. Gypsy's heart was like that house: it was full of love. And like a gentle realisation, it hit her in the most peaceful of ways, breaking any doubt or question. She had found her happiness in the world, found where she belonged; the oasis she had searched her whole life for.

It was right here.

THE END